EXIT WOUNDS

SHANNON BAKER

SEVERN RIVER PUBLISHING

EXIT WOUNDS

Severn River Publishing
www.SevernRiverBooks.com

This is a work of fiction. Names, characters, businesses, places, events and incidents are either the products of the author's imagination or used in a fictitious manner. Any resemblance to actual persons, living or dead, or actual events is purely coincidental.

ISBN: 978-1-64875-417-3 (Paperback)

ALSO BY SHANNON BAKER

The Kate Fox Mysteries

Stripped Bare

Dark Signal

Bitter Rain

Easy Mark

Broken Ties

Exit Wounds

Double Back

Bull's Eye

Close Range

Michaela Sanchez Southwest Crime Thrillers

Echoes in the Sand

The Desert's Share

The Nora Abbott Mystery Series

Height of Deception

Skies of Fire

Canyon of Lies

Standalone Thrillers

The Desert Behind Me

To find out more about Shannon Baker and her books, visit

severnriverbooks.com

1

Family is the most important thing. At least, that's what I've always believed. But I was seriously rethinking that philosophy.

Louise, my older sister, had her plump arms elbow-deep into a cauldron of fresh tomatoes as she wielded a paring knife like a ninja, pulling skins loose, coring and cutting. It didn't take a creative mind to imagine blood and guts of a multiple murder.

Not that I was thinking about murder...much. Only because there had to be a less violent way to shut Louise up.

Poupon, the apricot-colored standard poodle who'd been dropped at my house because he'd been an inconvenience for my other sister, Diane, was lying in the doorway to the living room. He pretended not to care about me, but he liked to keep me in his sights. I had to admit I liked having him around, too.

The kitchen smelled of fresh garden produce, the tang of chopped onions, peppers, and tomatoes bubbling on the stove, sending a wave of heat and humidity into the fall morning.

Louise kept pounding away on the same tired subject. "Whatever is up with you and Diane, you need to fix it. She won't come back for homecoming in two weeks, and she's a past homecoming queen, and now that

Ruthie's in charge of the bonfire on Thursday night, if Diane doesn't show up, it will make Ruthie feel like a failure. At this age, girls need to feel successful and empowered."

Ruthie was Louise's oldest daughter and, in my opinion, getting her out from under Louise's magnifying-glass mothering would go a long way in helping her self-esteem.

I kept my head down, chopping my way through a mess of jalapeños. This October ritual of my brothers and sisters putting up massive quantities of salsa had come down to me and Louise this year. Diane, who was hit-or-miss with helping but didn't mind taking a share of the finished product, refused to show up this year. My youngest sister, Susan, was in her junior year at the University of Nebraska (Go Big Red), and since she agreed to return for homecoming, she couldn't be here now. The brothers requested a weekend day for the task, knowing Louise wouldn't go for that since at least one of her five kids would have a weekend event, and there's no way she'd allow salsa-making without her leading the charge.

I tried to appease Louise. "I'll be at the bonfire. And so will you and Susan." The Fox sisters were five for five on homecoming crowns. Three of us showing up for the ceremony represented a quorum. Enough Foxes for anyone's taste. The four brothers split homecoming and prom, but we all had scored some kind of high school royalty. Not saying much when our graduating classes ranged from twenty to thirty students each.

Louise dumped a pile of parboiled tomatoes into the sink of ice water. "You need to tell me what happened between you two. This has gone on long enough."

No. I did *not* need to tell Louise that Diane blamed me for her ex-husband's death, even though it wasn't me who pulled that trigger. And I blamed Diane for putting my—technically our—niece, Carly, in harm's way. I didn't see any road to reconciliation, and I wasn't losing a lot of sleep over it. Okay, full confession, our rift did keep me up most nights.

I dodged. "Did you talk to Mom this morning?"

"She passed through on her way to the basement. She's working on a new piece."

Mom was a sculptor and also created pottery. She spent more time in her walkout studio downstairs than anywhere else, even when she had a houseful of children who could have used a hot meal and some attention. I figured it made us a resourceful lot who were adept at looking out for each other.

I continued to push Louise further away from the subject of our rift. "She's already working on something new?"

Louise was like a hound after a hare. "I know it happened that weekend Vince died. And it has something to do with you breaking up with Josh. You can't keep this bottled up inside."

"I'm a stopperless bottle spilling my feelings all over the place."

She huffed at me. "That's always been your problem. Feelings fester inside you until they get infected. Let in the air, cleanse your heart."

It would take a stronger person than me not to crack up, and I wasn't holding back. "What are you talking about?"

Louise stopped skinning tomatoes and turned my way, dragging all of her chins with her. She seemed surprised to see me. My guess was that her five kids and husband had her on mute most of the time and she wasn't used to anyone paying attention to her prattle. She'd been caught speaking like a self-help manual. She dipped her head and furiously jerked a red skin loose. "I'm saying if you want to talk about Josh or Diane, I'm here."

"I'm good." My knife chopped through a fresh pepper, and I stopped at a noise that didn't sound like Louise. "What?"

Something like a muffled shout made me strain to identify what I thought I heard.

She gave me a confused frown, deepening the creases on her forehead, foreshadowing wrinkles on the horizon. "What?"

We both stopped a beat, then said simultaneously, "I didn't say anything."

Before one of us could yell "jinx," because somehow, you never grow up when you're with a sister, an explosion vibrated the floor.

Not an explosion. A gunshot.

In the house.

Downstairs.

Poupon jumped up and let out one alarmed bark. He plopped on his haunches and turned to me to find out if we should be alarmed, sort of like how I always found the flight attendant when we hit turbulence. I'm sure I didn't relieve his anxiety.

Louise's eyes sprang wide, showing the whites, and her mouth flew open. Maybe she said something, but I was already running for the stairs at the far corner of the kitchen.

The smell hit me, and I instinctively hesitated. I barely registered the oily gunpowder that drifted almost delicately over the more earthy, organic odor. A swell of raw meat, rusty metal, and sewer that nearly triggered my gag reflex.

"Mom!" I heard my scream, surprised I'd opened my mouth.

All of this happened in less than the two seconds it took me to understand that someone in the basement had been shot. Mom was the only one down there.

My whole life she'd battled her demons, often withdrawing from us for days or weeks. Had she found the final solution for what stalked her in the darkness? But not with a gun. Mom hated guns, railed against violence of any kind.

My brain filled with images and thoughts too convoluted to really make sense as my feet took the steps two at a time, all the while fighting the urge to run the other way. I didn't want to see what waited for me at the bottom.

The room looked much the same as it always did. A platform took up a large swath of the room. If Mom worked on a large piece, it would be perched there. Smaller pieces, such as mugs, plates, vases, and even small animals, in various states of completion lined a workbench. Art supplies, knives, spatulas, pots of glaze, paints, and brushes were stuffed onto shelves along with rocks, seedpods, fall grasses, and whatever interesting flotsam she picked up on walks. Her studio always seemed like chaos to me.

A pottery wheel took up one corner. The back wall was a bank of windows with French doors that opened onto a poured concrete patio where the lawn gradually sloped up to a big yard. The doors were flung wide, letting in sunlight and probably fresh air, though the heavy stench of blood and meat draped over everything.

My frantic brain sent surges of panic through my veins. Where was

Mom? What had she done? I fought against the pictures that popped up, scenes we'd studied at the police academy. Not in my family home. Please, God, not my mother.

My eyes finally settled on what was different in Mom's studio.

It was so much worse than I could have imagined.

2

The body was crumpled on the concrete where a thick crimson smudge, almost like a splash of paint from one of Mom's brushes, shone on the floor. The raw and coppery smell, so identifiable and unlike anything else, coiled through my nose and filtered into my head, where vestiges of it would probably linger forever. Jeans, a navy blue T-shirt, worn running shoes. Greasy gray hair so thin scalp showed in places.

None of this made sense.

If Mom wore anything at all in her studio, it would be a silk kimono. She had a head of wild silvery curls, the unruly mop she'd passed down to me, Diane, and Susan. She wouldn't wear shoes unless she was leaving the house, and even then they wouldn't be running shoes.

It felt as if I'd been deposited into someone else's nightmare, with a setting and characters conjured in another person's subconscious.

A peep, like that of a tiny chick, made me remember I had a body and could move. I turned to the sound.

Like a scarecrow, Mom stood next to her pottery wheel as if suspended, a hunk of clay slapped onto the center. It spun with a dull whir. She stared at the spot of blood pooled on the floor. Slowly her gaze traveled across the ground and focused on my feet, then climbed to my face. The faded blue of her eyes seemed even paler than usual, her pupils big and black and somehow unfocused, as if she, too, couldn't quite register what she saw.

"Mom?"

She blinked and looked back at the body heaped on the floor. Mom wore her usual work outfit, which is to say, she was naked. Mom believed in the freedom of nudity, and I'd seen her often without her clothes. It was always a bit of a jolt. A slight figure of pale skin, not an extra pound anywhere, though at seventy, her skin sagged some and stretch marks from birthing nine kids added to the crinkles. All her wiry curls hung freely down her back. Rust lined her voice when she spoke. "I always knew it would happen."

That's when I noticed her right arm hung at a weird angle at her side. A small revolver gripped in her fist.

"Oh my God!" Louise's shriek sucked the air from the room. She stopped halfway up the stairs, her hand slapped onto her mouth and her eyes glistening. Small choking noises worked from her throat.

I kept my focus on the figure trembling in front of me and lowered my voice. "Mom? Are you hurt?" Slow steps brought me to her side. I pulled a swirl of turquoise silk from the back of a wooden chair and draped her kimono around her shoulders.

She stared at the man heaped on the floor, her eyes wide and dry. She'd hit him in the heart and probably stopped it beating immediately, which would account for the surprising lack of gushing blood. I couldn't tell if she knew I was there.

I reached for the gun in her fist. "Let me take this." I spoke with as much gentleness as I could, even though my body vibrated with tension and, internally, I felt more like Louise, paralyzed on the steps, doing her best to keep breathing.

Mom relinquished the gun with a great gush of breath, as if she'd stopped breathing since firing the shot. I set the gun on the sculpting platform.

She allowed me to work her arms through the slick fabric and knot the belt at her waist without seeming to be aware of any motion. I struggled to quiet the spinning in my brain. A dead man on the floor of Mom's studio. Dead. And she'd shot him.

Louise's choking turned into yacking, like a cat right before it.... There it was, Louise puked, and that smell mingled with all the musky, rusty, fetid odor, and I fought to keep from joining in the upchuck fun.

I hollered at Louise, even though she was only a few feet away. "Call 9-1-1."

"What?" she yelled back at me. "I don't...where is...what is?"

"Go. Call. Now." I didn't take my eyes off Mom, but I needed to get Louise out of here. Not that I'd seen enough dead bodies to make me immune, and I wasn't sure that was even possible, but I was a darn sight better at coping with this grisly scene, even without my sheriff training.

Louise stumbled, turned on the steps, and landed with a thud on her butt. She scrambled to her feet and crashed into the kitchen. The ceiling above us creaked as she searched for her phone.

Using a calm voice, I spoke to Mom. She trembled as if a series of earthquakes erupted in her core and rumbled outward to her hands. I put an arm around her shoulders. "Let's sit down." I directed her to a worn stuffed chair in the corner of her studio. The open door let in the warm fall breeze, but it didn't temper the awful smells, and my stomach threatened revolt.

Mom dropped down to the threadbare seat and closed her eyes. She inhaled long and deep, her years of yoga making a cleansing breath like second nature. The smell didn't seem to penetrate her consciousness, and she actually seemed to relax and take on that Zen calm she wore like a cape.

It seemed obvious, but I needed to check to make sure he wasn't alive. I circled the body to avoid the blood that oozed across the concrete. He'd dropped partially on his right side, as if all his bones had dissolved in a single second. His head rested on his cheek, eyes half open, mouth agape. The hole in his chest showed blackened fabric and a spread of blood a couple of inches in diameter. The exit wound visible on his back was several times larger, and that's where most of the blood had come from. Spatter marked the paint-stained cabinet behind him, looking no different than the mess from one of Mom's projects.

He was definitely dead; the glassy eyes and utter stillness left little doubt. But I pressed two fingers on his still-warm neck to feel for a pulse. Nothing.

I hurried back to Mom. "Are you hurt?"

She shook her head, eyes still dry. She didn't seem to be able to speak.

I knelt in front of her and put my face close to hers. "Tell me what happened."

Her throat worked, and she opened and closed her lips, then shook her head.

Louise called from upstairs. "She's sending the state patrol."

The "she" would be Marybeth, the dispatcher in Ogallala.

Louise stayed in the kitchen and hollered down again. "She's calling Ted, too."

At that moment I didn't even mind if Ted, my ex-husband and the sheriff in an adjoining county, arrived. As long as he got here quickly.

Mom studied the body as if memorizing it for a sculpture or even one of her rare paintings. The pottery wheel in the corner spun with a quiet whirring, the plop of wet clay out of kilter in the middle. I skirted the body and flipped it off, letting the wheel slow. A few blobs of dark crimson had landed on the clay and spidered out along the wheel. The whole scene had a surreal feel, as if I operated from behind a camera, taking it in but not able to assign meaning to it.

Most wrong was my mother holding a gun. She hated guns and violence of any kind. The dead man bleeding on the floor couldn't be real. And, dear lord, the smell. I had to get Mom out of here.

"Louise, help me bring Mom upstairs." I stepped toward Mom, who held the body in her gaze.

There was no movement on the stairs.

"Louise?" Without waiting for her to answer, I put a hand on Mom's thin arm. She felt frail, not at all the confident woman who traveled her own trail, never paying attention to what convention dictated a mother, wife, or regular Sandhills woman should do.

Mom moved as if in slow motion, tilting her head to me before she brought her focus to my face. She still didn't say anything and didn't make any attempt to rise.

"Louise. I could use your help here." I tugged on Mom's arm, and she blinked again, letting her head dip so she could see the body on the floor behind me.

A helpless voice drifted from the kitchen. "I can't."

As the middle child in a family of nine kids, I was used to my three older sisters bossing me around. I grew up following orders a lot, doing what I wanted when no one was looking, and dipping so far under the radar I stayed invisible. But I didn't often run into one of my strong-willed sisters not rising to whatever challenge confronted them—again, maybe a reaction to our nearly feral upbringing that made us self-reliant. I wasn't used to Louise not taking charge.

Still, I'd give her a break for balking at all the blood and the stomach-roiling smell. And even more, the billowing cloud of death. And the added weight of my soft-spoken, yoga-practicing, naked-snow-angel-making artist of a mother wielding the lethal weapon.

I cupped Mom's elbow and hoisted her to her feet. At five foot four, Mom was only slightly taller than me, and her vegan diet kept her as thin as a flower petal. But getting her to her feet took some coaxing. I decided to go out the back door and around to the kitchen instead of maneuvering past Louise's mess on the stairs.

The bright sunlight cast the day in a cheery, golden glow, the dying summer giving one last hurrah. Deep green grass, orange and yellow marigolds, pink and red hollyhocks dancing at the edge of the yard. The perfection of the day added to the surreal feel of the situation.

By the time I helped Mom through the side gate and up the path to the kitchen, Louise stood in the open door, ready to help usher Mom inside to the table, where Louise had a tall glass of water waiting.

As soon as we stepped into the kitchen, Mom stopped, took in the scene, and shook me off. She pulled herself up, straightening her shoulders. Her face, so slack a moment before, gained a certain solidity. "I can't stay here."

I didn't know what I'd expected, but this wasn't it. "Who is that guy? Did you know him?"

She stretched her lips tight, and her eyes flicked around the room without seeing it. "Where is Hank?"

Louise looked as if she'd just stopped crying and might be on the verge of starting again. "He's on his way to Lincoln. His train left this morning."

Mom frowned, and she gnawed on her lips. "I need to call him."

Louise, several inches taller than me and Mom and with a clear weight advantage, took hold of Mom's hand and tugged her toward the table. "I already left a message on his phone to call me immediately."

Dad would have his phone shut off per FTA rules. As an engineer on the BNSF, Dad had trained us all not to count on getting in touch with him while he was working. When he wasn't on the train, he was available for everything from handyman service to talk therapy, though he always kept his opinions to himself.

Louise reverted to her bossy ways. "Sit down. Drink some water." She led Mom to the picnic table against the back wall, big enough to seat a good portion of the Fox clan, including grandkids.

Mom pulled back and focused on the basement door with a look of fear, as if the dead man might rise and walk up the stairs. She whipped her head to me. "Take me someplace. I have to get out of here."

I pulled her chair from the head of the table, and Louise urged her into it.

"You can't leave until the state patrol arrives." I pushed the water closer to her.

She didn't touch it.

Louise looked over her shoulder toward the stairs. "You don't have to go down there." She had the practical tone of a mother dealing with a child who didn't want to play on the jungle gym. "Stay here, and we'll be with you."

I lowered myself to the bench and leaned into Mom. "Did you shoot that guy?"

Mom shifted her gaze to me. "Of course I did."

So steady a moment ago, Louise's face paled and tears filled her eyes. "Why?"

Mom looked irritated. "He was going to kill me."

Louise shook her head as if she couldn't take in Mom's words. I understood that feeling.

I wanted to slap the table to pry the answers from Mom, but I spoke slowly instead. "Do you know him?"

Mom bit her lips again, a frantic glint tinging her eyes. "I need to leave here. Now."

I patted her hand. "You can't. The investigating officer will want to talk to you. It was obviously self-defense, and I'm sure they'll let you go after you tell them what happened."

"What did happen?" Louise spit out exactly what I wanted to know.

Mom shook her head, making the phrase "contents may settle" run through my mind. After a second, a sharper focus seemed to come into her blue eyes as if putting things together. "It was the interview. I knew better than to expose myself, but it's only Nebraska and I thought it would be okay. And then Susan's friend. That big kid with all the hair."

She continued with sentences that felt as if they had no relation to each other, mumbling about privacy and generosity ruining her life. She dropped Susan's name a few times and retreated to her well-tromped ground about media destroying the country by not reporting news The People needed. Mom was big on The People, a group never well defined.

We didn't know much about Mom's raising. What we'd gathered was that she'd hitchhiked across the country in the heydays of the hippie movement. Hearing her talk about power to the people and bringing down "the man" was not new. Seeing her vacant, sad, and lost wasn't fun, but it constituted our normal. On her good days, which were frequent, Mom was serene, if eccentric. I was never sure she had both fists clamped onto the rope of sanity, so this kind of trauma might leave her grasping for traction.

Louise and I made eye contact over Mom's head. Louise had pulled herself together again and gone into full maternal track, a gear Mom didn't possess but one Louise had cultivated in herself. She might not be able to deal with a murder scene or the reality that our mother had killed some-one, but handling a soul in distress fell in her wheelhouse. Her normal form of mothering would call for baked goods and a heartfelt talk, but this was far from normal.

Louise stood up. She picked up Mom's water glass and in a directorial voice said, "Let's go to your room. It's safe and quiet back there. Kate can wait for the cops and deal with this."

Mom quit rambling and considered Louise, then swiveled to me. "I can't leave?"

"Where do you want to go?" This obsession with leaving seemed odd.

She shook her head, the silver hair swaying across the bright turquoise of the kimono. "Somewhere they can't find me."

An arrow of fear shot into me. "Who?"

She clamped her mouth shut and sucked in air through her nose, then let it out slowly. More of that getting-in-touch-with-the-universe stuff she practiced. Mom lived by the *Desiderata*, a poetic anthem about navigating serenely through life, and I was sure she was channeling some kind of "placidness amid the noise and haste."

"Mom." I tried to get her to answer me. "Did you know that man?"

She shook her head.

"Why did you shoot him?" Louise asked, not even close to the state of tranquility Mom had achieved.

It looked like Mom drew a shawl of composure over herself. "He came into the studio. He wanted to hurt me."

It made less than no sense that some man would venture to Hodgekiss, a town of a thousand people in the remote Sandhills of Nebraska, to break into Mom's studio to hurt her. "Why would he come after you?"

Louise seemed to be a few steps ahead of me. "She's a famous artist. Crazed fans come after celebrities."

Mom barely ventured away from the Sandhills. She had no friends here that I knew of. Unlike Dad, who considered you family if you had an ounce of related blood or had married into the clan no matter how many generations removed. In other words, for Dad, family included the whole danged Sandhills. Mom, on the other hand, limited her involvement to her children and grandchildren, although saying *involvement* might be an exaggeration. I couldn't say she was happy living within her own mind, but she seemed to prefer her solo company.

"It's not like sculptors are rock stars." I'd never heard of anyone stalking an artist.

Louise started to herd Mom out of the kitchen. "It's like that movie *Misery*. You wouldn't think there would be lunatic literary fans, either, but Kathy Bates chopped off James Caan's foot."

"That's fiction," I said.

Mom's bare feet slowed. She tilted her head to Louise's face. "Yes. He must have been a fan. He saw my work, and it turned something in him.

You hear about these things. A broken soul whose only release of passion is through killing." The more she spoke, the clearer the idea seemed to her.

It sounded nuts to me. But why else would a stranger show up in a place as remote as Hodgekiss? The beaten path was three days' ride from here. It's not like murderers were lining up to take their shot at Mom. She didn't interact with enough people to have enemies.

Mom stepped in front of Louise and marched through the kitchen door to the hallway. Louise spoke over her shoulder to me. "I'll see if I can get her to rest. You do whatever you need to."

3

I stood close to the French doors to keep the odor from penetrating my skin. It wouldn't do any good, I knew. The phantom fume would linger in my nose for a long time, and any encounter with spoiled meat or wildlife kill would bring it alive again. The fallout from the grisly experiences of law enforcement had a way of scarring a person. And I'd only been at it for slightly less than a year. What baggage would I carry after a long career as sheriff?

Poupon lay in the shade of the lilacs by the back fence, panting and watchful but not offering any words of wisdom.

I planted myself inches outside the doorway, shaded from the afternoon sun by the two-story house of my childhood. Sparrows flitted through the leafy boughs of the lilacs lining the yard, the purple blooms a distant memory and the green leaves living on borrowed time before the first frost. I'd been standing there for nearly a half hour, strangely more and more disturbed by the stillness of the man behind me. His body seemed to give off a chill, and I thought his face showed a little mottling, with purple marring the pallid skin.

Of course, I knew he was dead. And obviously, dead men didn't move. Knowing it was one thing. But being near a corpse while the minutes ticked by slammed the truth home in a way that writhed in my head like an angry snake.

Or maybe the man was haunting me, trying to tell me his name and why he'd shown up in Mom's studio.

Footsteps on the path by the back gate made me turn, surprised I'd been so focused I hadn't heard a vehicle. Ted's dark head peeked around, and when he saw me, he strode my way. At least now, after almost two years post-divorce, his Ben Affleck looks didn't drive a stake into my heart. "I saw the open gate. Figured you'd be in her studio."

I shouldn't feel relief to see him since even the thought of him usually frosted my tomatoes, but having another professional on site gave me comfort. Ted could be a turd in a bucket, especially when he was cheating on his wife (me), but he had a way of coming through in a pinch. "Thanks for getting here so quickly."

He took a step into the doorway and studied the body lying in a heap with bits of flesh and blood splashed across the shelves of art supplies. "Have you checked it out?"

"I confirmed he was dead. Took the gun from Mom and left it on the platform in there. Brought her out and haven't stepped back inside. I didn't want to compromise anything for the investigator."

"You're the sheriff here. You could have started to process the scene."

Sometimes Ted didn't think things through to the end. At least, that might explain him leaving me for Roxy. Or maybe it explained why he married me in the first place instead of Roxy. A case could probably be made for me thinking in circles. "Seems there's a conflict of interest here."

Ted huffed. "If you want to get technical. But this looks pretty clear. An intruder. Marguerite was well within self-defense."

"You picked up all that from Marybeth?"

He pulled a pair of Latex gloves from his pocket and stretched his hands into them. "Louise gave plenty of details, I guess. Marybeth explained all that to me and Trey. I filled in the rest, knowing your mom and that she'd have had to feel a serious threat to shoot anyone."

He looked at the body before moving inside. "I'm surprised she had a gun. Doesn't seem like her, does it?"

Not in the least. "I haven't asked her about it. Thought I'd leave that up to you and the state patrol. Glad Trey's on his way."

Trey Ridnour was a friend. We'd both had inklings of taking things a step further, but I was pretty sure Trey was as happy to stay friends as I was.

"I called Ben. He didn't see any need to come up, so go ahead and take care of that part." Ben Wolford was the coroner, but he lived in Broken Butte, a good hour's drive away. In our rural area, the appointed coroner was likely to be anyone willing to take the job. In our case, Ben Wolford, a lawyer, had agreed to the task about a hundred years ago, and no one saw a reason to change. He often signed off on showing up in person, especially if there was no mystery involved. Since we all knew who'd done the shooting, no sense in getting a geriatric attorney with poor eyesight on the road if he didn't need to.

Ted stepped slowly across the threshold. "So, who is this guy?"

"Don't know. Mom says she's never seen him before. Louise thinks he's a John Hinckley."

Ted stopped and gave me a curious look, his dark eyebrows drawing down over brown eyes. "John Hinckley?"

Ted was smarter than a box of socks, but he wouldn't be first pick for a trivia team. "He shot President Reagan because of his obsession with Jodie Foster."

Ted gave a little puff of annoyance, clearly showing that if he didn't know something, it probably wasn't worth knowing. "Being an artist isn't like being an actress or a rock star."

Did he have to say it like that? "Check for ID."

He curled his lip. "I know how to process a scene. Been sheriff a lot longer than you have."

Maybe, but I'd helped him every one of those years.

I paced the concrete slab outside the door while Ted checked the man's pockets and came up empty. He stayed in the studio, giving everything a good inspection.

When I heard a car pull in, I waited. The gate squeaked fully open this time, and Trey Ridnour stepped into the backyard. Tall and muscular, Trey had a round face and a light complexion that colored at the slightest embarrassment. He had the kind of solid presence that brought the temperature of any scene down a few degrees. He wore his short-sleeve black uniform top and gray trousers but had left his Smokey Bear hat in the car. With a few long strides he was at my side.

I could tell he wanted to put an arm around me or hug me or do any of those protective things heroic guys were prone to do. In fact, that was the main reason we couldn't be more than friends. I wasn't given to being sheltered.

He stopped when he read my face and stood in front of me. He didn't ask the typical law enforcement questions but led with, "Are you okay? How's your mother?"

His concern chipped away at the hard shell holding me all together. I tried to bring the professional me back to the scene. "The threat has been eliminated. By my surprisingly capable mother. She's rattled but unhurt. My sister is with her in the house. Ted's inside securing the scene. Coroner's been called, and he's turned over authority to us."

Slashes of red flamed across his cheeks. "Good. Guess I'll get to work. We'll call an ambulance to transport the body once we get what we need."

The rumble of a pickup coming toward the house at high speed and the sound of tires sliding to a stop on gravel sent me on the run out the back gate.

The white pickup with a logo for Magnuson Research Facility was pulled up amid the dust it had created with its racing approach. The door flew open, and my brother Douglas burst out.

Douglas reminded me of a teddy bear in so many ways. He was taller than most of us Foxes, a little soft around the middle, had a sweep of honey-colored hair, and even if we weren't the huggiest bunch, always gave off a vibe of comfort, as if he cuddled you close. But not today.

He bounded to me. "What's going on? Where's Mom?"

I held a hand up to slow him. "Louise called?"

He acted as though he wanted to barrel through me. "She said Mom shot an intruder."

"Ted and Trey Ridnour are working the scene. If there's any information to be found, they'll find it. Louise took Mom inside. There's nothing you can do here."

He glared at me. "I'll see."

I let him skirt around me heading to the backyard and Mom's studio. "They aren't going to let you close," I yelled at his back.

He ignored me, and I followed him. We stood outside and watched Trey and Ted take pictures and place markers to catalogue where the bullet landed. The studio was in its usual chaotic state with half-completed projects, paint tubes scattered, and canvases with slashes of color stacked here and there. Boxes of clay and mud-splattered tools lay in normal disarray. It looked like a battle could have taken place here, but Mom preferred this tangled mess, and I often wondered if it wasn't a reflection of her mind.

I explained what little I knew and Louise's theory of a misguided fan.

"How do you think he found her?" Douglas asked.

Good question. Mom guarded her privacy almost obsessively. She rarely visited galleries, even when the owners begged her to attend an opening of her work. Her official bio totaled two or three sentences, none giving away so much as the region she lived in or that she had a family. She allowed no pictures of herself in promotion or catalogues. It was part of the Marguerite Myers mystique.

More engines roaring and the sound of vehicles turning in made me grab Douglas's arm and direct him out of the yard. "We need to let them work."

He didn't resist, and we came through the gate to more brothers parking their rigs, their faces full of concern and questions. A quick inventory tallied Robert, my older brother by a year, Michael—Douglas's twin—and Jeremy, my youngest brother. That left only Diane, who lived in Denver, and Susan, in Lincoln.

This count didn't include Robert's wife and two-month-old baby, and Michael's wife, whose kids, thankfully, were in school along with Louise's.

There were nearly enough people in the gravel lot between Mom's house and the neighbor's to form a football squad and enough bursting energy to tackle any foe.

I stood on the broken cement path and posed an inadequate barrier to keep them from creating unnecessary havoc. "They're investigating the studio now. Mom is resting. There's really nothing anyone can do, and we don't need a ton of people here."

Sarah, Robert's wife and my best friend, hung back, the baby resting in her arms. Her eyes held a hint of resignation, and she shook her head at me, clearly telling me to save my breath. She knew the Foxes as well as I did.

Michael, the most aptly named Fox because he was quick, smart, and crafty, wasn't having any of my sass. Much smaller than Douglas, his twin, Michael made up for it with confidence and verve. He stomped toward me with a bead on the kitchen door. "I need to see Mom."

Douglas stood next to me, but he didn't seem inclined to help me with this mob as Michael led the way and the others fell in behind him.

The kitchen door banged open, and Louise filled it, hands on hips, every aspect of her body stern, including her jowls. She might have been a full-on action hero if not for the tomato splatters down the front of her stretched-out T-shirt.

Lauren, my brother Michael's wife, gasped. "Oh my God. Is that Marguerite's blood?"

Michael started to trot toward her.

Louise stood taller. "For Pete's sake. Kate and I are putting up salsa." She flung both hands in the air, and her voice sounded like George C. Scott's version of Patton. "Everyone take a breath. Mom has been through an ordeal. She's dealing with it in her way, and we need to give her some space. Now, I know you're concerned. You can all come in, but you'll sit in the living room and wait until she's ready to be with you."

Louise trying to take command of the Fox brigade wasn't that unusual. But seeing her with this much authority and witnessing the brothers pay attention might be only slightly less shocking than coming on Mom holding a gun.

Michael stopped, and everyone grouped behind him.

"Dad got to the depot in Lincoln a while ago, and Susan picked him up. They're on their way back. The rest of you can come inside if you promise to stay quiet."

Sarah and I exchanged looks that included raised eyebrows, twisted lips, and all the other indicators that said, "Do you believe this?"

Douglas started toward the door.

Louise said, "I'll tell you what I know, which isn't a lot."

I watched as everyone passed me on the sidewalk.

My youngest brother, Jeremy, brought up the rear. The cutest and most charming of us all, he'd always been full of mischief. From the time he was little I'd bailed him out of all manner of trouble, from running off with a combine crew when he was seven to stealing beer off a delivery truck in front of The Long Branch when he was thirteen, to dealing with triage when he broke hearts right and left. Last summer, he'd gotten into a deep pit of trouble from which he'd barely survived. It pained me to see that goofy spark gone from him these days. "How is she, really?"

Jeremy and Mom had a connection deeper than most of us. Part of me envied it, the other part was glad Jeremy had it. "Hard to tell. She seemed weirdly okay."

"Yeah." Whatever that meant, he seemed to think the word was sufficient to sum it all up, and he sauntered into the house.

Not knowing what else to do, I took up my role as chief patio pacer and watched Trey and Ted work.

The state patrol crime scene team arrived along with an ambulance. They took over the preliminary investigation from Trey and Ted. It took a couple of hours to process the scene, and by then twilight had fallen. When the two EMTs wheeled the body out, they didn't seem to notice me standing there.

The young woman at the front of the gurney spoke first. "They said she's a little old lady, like in her late sixties or something. Can you believe she did this?"

The older guy bringing up the rear answered, "Center mass. You wouldn't think a little gun like that could do so much damage or that she'd have the guts to shoot."

"Yeah," she said. "That's so cool it's cold."

4

Mom and Dad's bedroom was at the end of the hallway that ran alongside the kitchen. With a bathroom and another space that wasn't any larger than a closet that had served as a nursery for the babies and toddlers until we grew old enough to join the squadron of kids upstairs, theirs was the only bedroom on the ground floor. Two big bedrooms, more like dorm rooms with a couple of double beds each and a toilet with a sink, made up the second story.

The living room housed an old leather sofa and a couple of recliners along with a rocking chair. My childhood home wasn't large or luxurious.

Lauren, Michael's wife, had taken off at some point. I assumed she'd had to pick up the kids from school and would probably get Louise's little hellions, too. Hopefully, she'd take them someplace besides here.

A cookie tray with a half sandwich on white bread sat on the coffee table in front of the couch. Someone must have mustered something to eat.

The four brothers sat in their usual places, and Sarah stood by the front windows, jiggling the baby. They all looked at me when I walked in. Robert said, "Anything?"

I shook my head. "They took the body away. Trey and Ted are done. They said we can clean it up. They need to talk to Mom, and then they'll get going."

Only two rooms mattered much to Mom. The kitchen, that she'd taken the energy to decorate in a whimsical nod to the traditional '60s housewife, all in red and black and polka dots, complete with a kitty-cat clock with a rhinestone tail ticking off the seconds. And her studio, which housed her soul.

The heart of the Fox family, that thumped with life, activity, and—even if most of us would never admit it—love and acceptance, was the large kitchen.

No sound came from the other side of the bedroom door when I walked down the unlit hallway. I eased open the door to a dark room where Louise sat in a straight-backed chair by the shade-drawn window that looked out at the backyard. In theory, Mom could keep an eye on us kids playing back there. I was sure sometimes she actually did supervise us, but probably with no intention of interfering.

I'd expected to find Mom stretched out on the double bed she shared with Dad when he wasn't gone on the railroad. Instead, she whipped around from the closet where she stood with a handful of bright, flowing dresses. A suitcase sat open on the bed containing a stack of black yoga pants.

"Are you leaving?" I asked.

Louise caught my eye and shook her head as if to tell me talking to Mom was hopeless.

Mom tossed the dresses on the bed and started folding one. Her movements were jerky, and she kept glancing at the window, her eyes haunted and skin around them pinched. "I can't stay here. I'm not safe."

"From what?" I weighed whether her actions were sane or if I needed to haul her to the hospital for sedation.

She inhaled with such deliberation, I knew she was calming herself. "You've never been an overly curious child. That practicality and steadiness is so much like Hank. So, please, simply accept that I know what I know. I need to leave."

What? Not curious? She didn't mean it to sting, but it did. I wanted to argue, pointing out my job as sheriff required curiosity. But right now, taking care of Mom took precedence. "Okay. We'll figure out some place for you as soon as you talk to Trey and Ted."

A spark of fear flashed in her eyes, and she shook her head. "I don't want to talk to them."

Louise stood, letting out a muffled "oof" as she hefted her pounds. "Come on, Mom. You've always liked Ted."

She had? Sure, when we were married, my family welcomed Ted into the fold because we're the-more-the-merrier kind of a family. And, yeah, I'd been irritated since our divorce that my brothers and sisters continued to include Ted, and Roxy, the woman he'd had an affair with. Then married and had a son with.

Mom quieted and stared at the dress half-folded on the bed. Her forehead wrinkled as if she worked a puzzle. Finally, she lifted her chin as if deciding on her best course. "Yes. I should talk to Ted."

Louise and I followed Mom down the short hallway. She paused when she reached the living room. "Oh." Her hand rose to her throat, and her eyes teared up.

There was a general rustle and fumble as all the brothers rose and rushed to her. Lots of bumbling and hugging, some discreetly swiped tears —way too much movement and emotion for this small room.

She hugged them all and clung to Jeremy's hand. "I'm so grateful for you all. You've sustained me from the beginning, and I feel overwhelming gratitude to the universe for the blessing of your souls."

Jeremy kissed her cheek and let her go.

We followed her into the kitchen, where Ted and Trey sat at the picnic table. From years of being a Fox-by-marriage, Ted knew where the glasses were kept and had pulled out iced tea from the fridge. He and Trey sat with sweating tumblers of tea in front of them, ignoring the pot of salsa now cooling on the stove and empty jars and lids lining all the counters. Chopped onions and peppers piled on cutting boards and filled the air with their sharpness.

Trey and Ted jumped to their feet as soon as we entered. Ted hurried from the table to Mom's side. "Are you okay, Marguerite?"

Poupon's toenails clicked on the floor as he wandered from the living room. His stubby tail started to wave, and he sniffed Ted from his thighs to his shoes.

When Ted gave me an alarmed look, I explained, "He smells the baby. Poupon adopted him when you left him with us."

Ted shoved Poupon away and mumbled, "I didn't leave him."

I let it go, not interested in rehashing the incident of a couple of months ago.

Poupon gave Ted an accusing look (or maybe I imagined that) and plopped in the corner of the kitchen behind the picnic table.

Louise strode to the sink. The others crowded by the door. Trey stiffened, as if worried about an invasion.

I lowered my voice. "Maybe wait in the living room? I'll stay here with Mom."

They looked to Mom and she nodded, and with a show of reluctance, they retreated.

Mom granted Ted one of her serene smiles. "Whatever path he was on, I'm sorry he chose to travel into my world. Taking someone's life is not something we're meant to do. But I have a family and home to protect."

By this time Trey had moved to stand behind Ted. His face glowed red, attesting to how flustered he was to meet an idol. He thrust a hand toward Mom. "Marguerite Myers. I've been a fan of your work for years. I'm a UNL grad and just want to say thank you for your kind donation of the statue."

Criminy. How long had he been working on that formal speech? I'd known Trey admired Mom's work, and I felt a little guilty I'd never introduced them before. "Mom, this is Trooper Trey Ridnour. He's conducting the investigation, and Ted's assisting."

Mom's acknowledgment held the same distracted and accepting nod as usual. She managed to bestow acceptance and dismissal at the same time. It's probably the message she handed out to most people she met and why Sandhillers waved her off as "an artist" and mostly left her alone. Although I knew they talked about her and judged her behind our backs.

They settled themselves around the table, and Louise scurried around the counters, starting to set the kitchen to rights. I leaned against the refrigerator and folded my arms to listen to the interview and maybe step in to help Mom if she seemed distraught.

But she didn't show any signs of distress. She acted as if the two law officers at her table were nothing more than family friends, who filtered in and out of the house and who she rarely kept track of. Gone was the near panic of her packing her suitcase. She waited for them to speak.

Ted leaned in, his voice gentle. "In your own words, tell us what happened, starting with the moments before the man appeared."

She gave him an amused expression, a twinkle lighting her eyes. "I'm not one to use someone else's words, now, am I, Ted?"

He said, "I've never known you to." But the look on his face said he'd wanted to reply, "No, ma'am."

Trey laughed as if she'd told a joke.

Mom turned to him as she spoke. "I'd just thrown clay on the wheel. I thought I'd make some coffee mugs for a gallery in Santa Fe."

Trey's round face filled with excited color. "I have one of your mugs. I bought it at a fundraiser for Maudy Dempsey when she got cancer. Then I saw one similar when I went to Santa Fe for a seminar." He beamed. "I got mine at a real bargain."

Mom tilted her chin down as if saying thank you. She grew serious again. "I had the doors open because the morning sun sent out tremendous energy, and I wanted to capture that sense of creation in the clay."

Trey didn't seem thrown by the way Mom always spoke, like a guru imparting the mysteries of the universe.

Louise plopped another box of ripe tomatoes on the counter. "Since everyone is here, we might as well put up the rest of this salsa."

Power might have gone to her head, but at least it would give the clan something to keep them busy.

Mom's eyes sharpened as she seemed to choose her words carefully. "I looked up when a shadow filled the doorway. And the man stepped through, bringing a heavy darkness in the air. I knew immediately he meant me harm."

"We found a knife he'd fallen on," Trey said, confirming Mom's claim that she was in danger.

She closed her eyes briefly, as if feeling a surge of painful emotions. "Yes. He lunged toward me, and I reacted immediately. I fired on instinct."

Louise paused in her busyness and sought my eyes. We both recognized how odd this sounded for a woman who professed a oneness with the world and all creative energy. How could killing someone, even in self-defense, be instinctive for her?

"You had a gun handy?"

Thank you, Ted, for asking what had been bothering me and not sounding as incredulous as I felt.

She nodded. "Oh, yes. I believe in the miracle of life. But, like every moral code and religion in the world, I am not ignorant to the reality of evil. The threat to my life and safety of my family was revealed to me many years ago by a talented tarot reader in Taos. I knew a time was coming when I'd be called upon to choose. My life and that of my children, or the life of a man succumbing to the dark forces."

Again, Louise and I exchanged baffled looks. Mom spoke as if a whole world operated on a plane only she and a select few could see. She'd embarrassed most of us kids by making these kinds of announcements in front of our friends. We'd all come to accept the medley that was Mom. Artist, mother, disturbed spirit, kind advisor. Seer into our souls and distant ghostlike presence. Like Forrest Gump's box of chocolates, we never knew what we'd get. But she was ours.

Trey took that in without a hiccup. "Did he say anything?"

Mom shook her head. "He held up the knife and came at me. That was all. I've never seen him before."

Ted was used to Mom's rambling. "Where did you get the gun?"

She centered on Ted's face and sounded as if it hurt to reveal it. "I bought it at a gun show. It's a Smith and Wesson Airweight. I needed something small enough for me and powerful enough to protect me. I suppose it was the right tool."

"Is it registered?" Ted asked.

She gave him a look of apology. "No. I probably should have done that. But I wanted to believe I'd never need it."

Trey sounded gentle, and high color stained his cheeks. "Can you think of any reason someone would want to hurt you?"

Mom's head moved slowly back and forth, a slow creep of grief clouding her face. "Life is precious."

Here it was, the horror of killing someone was catching up to Mom. I took a step toward her, wondering if it would rip her soul in two. Would I need to pick her up from the floor? I feared the realization would shred her frail psyche.

She brought her gaze to Trey's face and straightened her shoulders. "He had no right to come here. He's an abomination to deliberately set out to destroy my life or those of my family."

Trey offered a tentative smile. "You were protecting your home. He left you no choice."

She relaxed slightly, as if finding solace in his understanding. "I believe I did the right thing. He narrowed the world to a place where both of us could not exist. My time has not come yet."

For the first time, her blue eyes filled with tears, though none of them escaped. "Sometimes the only way to deter aggression is to prepare for war. I'm sorry he didn't understand that."

"Was there any identification on the body?" I interrupted. Ted hadn't found a wallet, but maybe they'd come across something after I'd left.

Trey glanced at me. "Nothing. No vehicle outside and no sign of how he got here. We'll run prints and see if we get a hit."

Again, Mom sucked in a long breath and let it out. "How long will it take to get results?"

Trey focused on her. "It's hard to say. But I'll do my best to get them to prioritize this. With any luck, it will be a matter of days."

She seemed to draw that in and let it steep before she mumbled, "That's not much time."

5

I walked Trey and Ted to their cars. The sky was pulling the blinds down on the day, and the cool breath of fall shoved aside the heat of the sun. In another few weeks the ground would swirl with fallen leaves. Borrowed time. The phrase kept running through my head. "Thanks." What else was there to say?

Trey's radio chattered, and he went to his cruiser and leaned inside the door.

Ted let out a whoosh of air. "This is bizarre, that she had a gun. I mean, your mother, the woo-woo pacifist of the Sandhills, has been packing her whole life. It's like she's always been ready for this one moment. That's enough to make the hair on my neck tingle."

I rubbed at a spot between my eyes. It didn't hurt, but this was the kind of day that made you think you had a headache even if you didn't. "She's always talked about being one with the universe and talking to the trees and grass. She traps spiders when they're in the house and releases them outside. I'm having a hard time reconciling the mother I've always known with a woman ready to take down an intruder."

Ted eyed the house and lowered his voice. "I've always thought your mother had a sixth sense or something. I don't know." He paused and checked to make sure no one lurked nearby to hear him say something ridiculous. "I think maybe she did know this guy was coming for her. Like the tarot person told her."

Maybe there was too much Dad in me to buy into that much mysticism. Or maybe Mom, for all her eccentric ways, was still Mom to me, a flawed human and not an oracle who could tell the future. "I can't quite believe she's got a *Prayer for Owen Meany* kind of thing going on."

"What?" Ted said.

I waved him off. "It's a book. And a movie, I guess, but the book is better."

He gave an irritated sigh. "That's one thing I don't miss about being with you. You always had your nose in a book. Not that Roxy's a whole lot better." What a prince. It wasn't that I was such a big reader, but that he didn't like to read. But the way he said it made me wonder if there were things he *did* miss about me. He could go right on missing them because I'd finally rid myself of any desire for Ted. Trouble was, I definitely hadn't rid myself of *all* desire. I quickly shut down the image of Glenn Baxter that pushed into my head.

Fortunately, Trey rejoined us. "They found an old Civic parked a couple of miles outside of town. No VIN. They ran the plates, and they're stolen and expired, but the stickers are current from Montana. I'm thinking it belongs to our John Doe. They're towing it to Ogallala, and we'll process it there."

"That explains how he got here. But not who he is and why he came after Mom," I said.

Trey studied the house in the gloomy light. "I'm thinking it's a one-off lunatic. But keep an eye on your mother. We don't want anything happening to her."

Ted grinned, all white teeth and dark eyes. "Who knew you were such a fanboy?"

Even in the darkening shadows, Trey's cheeks glowed. "Well, she's a huge talent."

We said our goodbyes again. Like all good Sandhillers, it took a few short conversations before we really meant it and they drove away.

By the time I entered the kitchen, the place was its usual fulcrum of activity. Jeremy chopped onions, Robert jiggled baby Brie, Sarah set empty pint jars into a boiling pot of water to sterilize them, and Louise seemed to be in three places at once.

Mom sat at the kitchen table with a tall glass of iced green tea. She watched the hubbub absently, in the exact way she always did on days she hadn't killed a man in her studio.

I slid onto the bench next to her. "How are you?"

She inhaled deeply and pushed it out her mouth. "I'm letting the vibrancy of this family refill my soul. It's a terrible thing to take a life. Even when it's justified, it steals essence. But balance seeks itself, and the good this gathering generates will even the scales. If I didn't believe that, I'd never have brought these souls into the world."

I didn't have anything to add. Though I'd seen death in my short stint as sheriff, it had never come at my own hand. I'm not sure I'd be as sanguine as Mom seemed to be.

"No plans to take off?" I asked.

She glanced at the basement door. "I'll be fine when Hank gets home. Until then, I'll stay here. With all of you. My strength."

Sometimes I felt as if Mom had birthed us as her living art. She enjoyed watching us grow and change, observing but not interfering. She rarely gave advice but would listen as long as we wanted to talk, at least when she wasn't in the studio. She was never in the middle of the fray but often on the fringes, an amused smile on her face.

Once, she'd told me she loved her home to be filled with her children and grandchildren because they kept the ghosts quiet. My sense was that she was driven to her art but it sucked something from her. Being with her family refilled the emptiness left from her work.

Robert passed by me and plopped Brie into my lap. "If you're going to sit there, at least make yourself useful."

Mom focused on the plump little bundle.

Brie's dark blue eyes hadn't changed yet, and who knew if they would. She stared at me and spastically kicked her legs.

"Here." Mom reached for the baby. "Let me. I want to feel her new essence."

I settled Brie in Mom's arms. We sat in the chaos of the salsa processing for some time, not speaking.

The side door to the kitchen burst open, and Diane filled the threshold, the dark night emphasizing the brilliant emerald of her dress. With three-inch shining black pumps, ropes of chains and beads around her neck, and her hair in its impeccable Diane-do, she appeared to have stepped from the boardroom to the kitchen with one stride. "What the serious fuck is going on?"

A paring knife slipped from Louise's tomato-drenched fingers. "It's lucky Lauren has all the kids at their house. What you do in your home in front of your children is your business, but you have got to quit speaking like a sailor when my kids are around."

On any given day, Diane might engage with Louise and curse her into a thousand knots of frustration, or she might ignore her existence. We all waited a beat to see.

Diane scanned the room, located Mom at the table, and jetted that way, making Robert scuttle a step back to keep from being rammed. She thrust one foot over the bench, straddling the seat, and inserted herself between me and Mom. She leaned over, shoving her butt into me and putting her face next to Mom. "Are you okay? You don't look injured."

Mom lifted Brie to her shoulder and gently patted her little bottom. "It's been a terrible day, but Hank is on his way home. He'll take care of this mess."

I caught Sarah's eye, and we both gave a "What the hell?" forehead crinkle.

Diane lowered herself to the bench I sat on and slid back, pushing me away and canceling my interaction with Mom or the conversation. She'd literally cut me off without saying a word.

I climbed from the table and went over to Louise, who was now filling the hot jars while Robert popped lids and rings on them and twisted them down. Jeremy loaded the jars onto a rack to go back in the boiling water.

The Fox family motto might be "Many hands make light the work." Or "One for all and all for one, except when it's time to pick on someone." I glanced at Diane, and my stomach wrenched. We'd broken the Fox family bond, and the pain was a thousand times worse than when I'd broken my wrist in second grade.

I asked, "Where are Michael and Douglas?" Our family always referred to them in that order. Mom and Dad had named them after the Academy Award winner for best actor the year they were born, as they had named us all, and it felt natural to keep the rhythm.

Louise whipped her head toward Mom, probably to make sure she wouldn't hear and be upset. Her attention back on pouring salsa, she tilted her chin toward the basement. "They're cleaning up."

Diane held Mom's glass up and commanded, "Someone get her more tea."

Jeremy rushed over to take care of it.

Diane turned around and managed to give everyone the stink eye, except me. She passed over me as if I were no more than a bindweed taking up too much air. "Did anyone think to call an attorney?"

I spoke up. "There are no charges. Clearly self-defense."

Diane didn't so much as flick an eye my way. She snatched her phone from the table. I hadn't been aware she'd carried one inside, but then, Diane wouldn't be unavailable. "Because whatever the Barney Fifes around here say, we need to make sure there's no chance anyone will come after Mom."

Louise wasn't happy to give up ground on being in charge. "This isn't Denver. If Ted and Trey Ridnour say there isn't any reason to call a lawyer, I see no reason to waste a fortune. You know they charge by the quarter hour."

Diane let out an exhausted breath. "I'll pay for it. My attorney is on retainer."

I wondered why and what it must be like to need an attorney on call. I didn't even have one, unless you could count Annette Stromsburg, Dad's cousin in Broken Butte, who drew up my divorce papers.

The kitchen seemed to get smaller and smaller. Brie started to fuss, and Mom shifted her to the other shoulder. Robert and Jeremy manned the stove, and the whole salsa operation cluttered the room with bodies. Speaking of bodies, my brothers downstairs scrubbing blood and guts from the concrete floor of the studio made my stomach clench again.

Diane held the phone away from her ear, probably waiting for her attorney to be summoned. "If you're relying on the local law," she spit that out with such vehemence I thought it might leave a stain on the wall, "you're going to expose Mom to any manner of repercussions."

Robert, my favorite sibling and the one closest in age to me, didn't seem to understand Diane was targeting me. "Yeah, probably wouldn't hurt to get a hold of a lawyer."

Diane took the call into the living room, stomping past me with enough force in her heels to perforate the kitchen floor.

Mom patted Brie's bottom and mumbled to her, seeming oblivious to the wrangling.

The clanking of pots and pans and water running while they washed dishes accented Diane's assertive voice. Those in the kitchen spoke as needed to keep the operation progressing under Louise's direction.

Clumping up the basement stairs heralded Michael's and Douglas's entrance. They both looked pale and drawn.

Douglas got a look at the salsa operation and pursed his lips and closed his eyes.

Michael growled at Louise. "Seriously? Do you have any idea what that looks like?"

Without warning, the outside door flew open again, and Dad stepped inside with Susan, our youngest sister, close behind.

Mom's face melted, as if she'd held out to the end and now that Dad was here, she could let go.

Dad wore his khaki Dickies and dirt-streaked T-shirt with a flannel shirt flapping at the cuffs and hem. His graying hair stuck out in a dozen directions, and his peppery scruff showed he hadn't taken the time to shower or change since stepping off the train in Lincoln.

With total focus on Mom, he was at her side in less than a heartbeat. He scooped the baby into one arm and wound the other tight around Mom's shoulders, drawing her close and accepting her head dropped into his chest.

From where I stood across the kitchen, I noticed Mom's trembling. Robert hurried over to take Brie. Sheltering her in his arms, Dad led Mom out of the kitchen, past a glowering Diane, and down the hallway to their room.

Susan slammed the kitchen door and surveyed the room. She'd cut her hair in an asymmetrical style, with a section of her left side shaved to her scalp and the other side full-on dark Fox waves. "Will someone tell me what's going on?"

Jeremy looped an arm around her shoulder and gave her a half-hug that served as an exuberant expression of affection. They dipped their heads together, and Jeremy spoke in a rapid, soft voice. Jeremy and Susan were the youngest by a few years, and they always seemed to have their own language. Since they were toddlers, their heads would tip together and their words stayed between them.

Louise and the crew kept working. Diane punched furiously at her phone. We were all here, a rare occurrence. Only one Fox was missing: our oldest sister, Glenda. She wouldn't be here in person again, but she'd never left us. The familiar feel was like being in the middle of a hurricane, everyone speaking at once, moving, touching, giving and taking, and the constant current of the Us that made our family.

And me, standing back. Out of the flow. Not like Mom, watching my creation and marveling at its workings, but staying back as self-preservation. When I was younger, I kept a stack of comic books under a bed upstairs. Often, the swirl and commotion of the family, their conflicts and curses, joys and pains, felt like more than I could take. I'd crawl under the bed and spend time with Daredevil or Spiderman.

I inched toward the living room. If Diane noticed me slipping past her, she gave no indication. Once in the dark room, I hurried to the front door and eased it open, crossed the closed-in front porch, and stepped into the cool, dark night.

It felt as if I drew in the first full breath since we'd heard the gunshot. I hadn't had a moment to think, and now that I stood in the quiet darkness, with the echoes of the boisterous and concerned family inside, I wasn't sure I wanted to.

Nothing added up. Why Mom had a gun. Why someone would show up and want to hurt her. Why she was terrified and wanted to run.

This wasn't my puzzle to solve. Dad was home. He'd do what, if anything, needed to be done. Trey would identify the body, and we'd figure out if any action needed to be taken from there.

Sure. Good plan. Nothing rested on my shoulders.

Then why did it feel as if I'd fallen into the middle of a whirlpool and the turmoil was only beginning?

6

Not wanting to return to the noisy vortex of my brothers and sisters, and realizing I'd eventually have to go back inside to rescue Poupon from the chaos, I weighed my options, discovered I really only had one, and started my trek through the front yard, down the steep grade to the railroad right-of-way, across the tracks, and up the other side.

From there it was a trot across the highway—even though headlights from a vehicle were plenty far away—and into the glass door of the Long Branch. The vestibule, about the size of a coat closet, opened to the right into the café and to the left into the much noisier bar. This crowd rivaled my family for volume, but at least here, I could ignore them all after a quick hello and maybe relax with a cold beer.

I looked through the glass door into the bar. Two tables had been shoved together in the middle of the room, and a group of ranch hands and younger couples shared a half-dozen pitchers. Since it was close to suppertime, they hadn't been at it long. Maybe they were a crowd that had worked cattle or some other group chore at a nearby ranch. A few day workers sat at the bar, and two middle-aged couples—small business owners on Main Street—shared a four-top toward the windows, the women with wine-glasses and the men with amber liquid in rocks glasses. If I made straight for my favorite stool at the bar with a smile and nod to them, maybe no one would engage me in conversation. I had no idea if the news of the excitement at Fox Central had hit, but I'd be a fool to think no one had noticed the cop cars and ambulance.

I pushed open the door and stepped inside. It was like those sitcoms where everything is over-dramatized for effect. But honest to God, everyone swiveled toward me, and all conversation stalled.

Dad's sister, my aunt Twyla, piloted the operation from behind the bar. At about my height—meaning pretty darned short—with long, thinning hair in a ponytail down her back, she wore a plaid Western shirt with so many washings it hung like tissue paper on her bony shoulders. Twyla preferred Jack Daniel's to solid food, and the sagging skin on her thin face showed her lifestyle gaining on her. She rotated her arm in a come-over-here loop. "Got one of those hoppy sons-of-bitches you like. Looks like you could use it."

Murmurs and whispers fired up as I ignored everyone and made my way to my stool.

Twyla had a sweating beer bottle plopped on the scratched and graffiti-carved wood bar by the time I got there. She lifted her own rocks glass and sipped Jack, then leaned across the bar. "We saw the ambulance. Counted all the cars that pulled up. Saw Hank and Susan on the run inside. No one called and said anything happened to Mom." Twyla and Dad's mother, my Grandma Ardith, lived in the old folks' home in Broken Butte. "That leaves Marguerite. Stroke?"

I tipped the bottle back, relief at the cold on my lips and the spicy feel of the bubbles against my tongue. A tap on my shoulder made me choke on that first welcomed gulp.

Shorty Calley stood with a serious expression on his weathered face. I hadn't spotted him when I'd hurried in. A local rancher, Shorty and Dad had been friends probably before they hit the womb, since Grandma Ardith and Shorty's mother were favorite cousins. "Don't know what's going on, but is there anything we can do?"

The women from the four-top crowded behind Shorty, the two cowboys at the bar held their bottles in front of them while they faced me, and the whole table in the middle stared at me.

From behind the bar, Twyla's crackly voice said, "Vicki Snyder was here earlier and wants to talk to you as soon as you can. Said she's got a day or so before deadline and didn't want to butt into private family time. She said if I saw you to tell you she needs an interview."

I should have expected this. Actually, I was kind of surprised the whole story hadn't leaked out somehow. Or at least enough of it to lead to wild speculation. Might as well rein in the rumor wagon myself.

I nodded at them and took a long pull on the marvelous bitter brew Twyla had provided. "None of the Foxes are hurt." I turned to Twyla. "Mom's fine." Sort of.

I might have seen a split second of disappointment on Twyla's face, but I chose to dismiss it.

I raised my voice to the room. "Someone broke into Mom's studio, and she shot him."

I paused for someone to gasp and most of them to give some version of, "No," "Oh, shit," and "What?"

"We don't know who it was or what he wanted. He had a knife and threatened Mom. It was self-defense, but the man didn't survive. State patrol is involved to find his identity. It's all weird and upsetting for us, so we'd appreciate it if you'd give us some space."

There was a chorus of "Of course." "So sorry." Plenty of nods and a bunch of confused faces. There would be a stampede of texts bursting from these phones as soon as I was out of sight. At least, I hoped it would hold off that long.

As for giving the Foxes privacy? Yeah, I didn't see that happening.

I spun back to face the bar and Twyla's frown. "There's more to this," she said.

"The theory is that a fan with a few loose wires came after her."

Twyla *humphed* and finished the dregs of her Jack. "Pretty flimsy theory. Marguerite isn't a rock star."

That sentence was getting old. The beer wasn't doing much to soothe my nerves. "Unless Mom has enemies, what else could it be?"

Twyla shifted her attention to the cowboys at the end of the bar. She bent over and fetched two bottles of Budweiser from the cooler and shuffled down to them, even though they still had bottles clutched in their fists and they hadn't called to her.

She didn't make eye contact with me when she walked my way and kept going as if she planned on making the rounds to the other tables. Twyla never waited tables if she could help it. She trained most patrons to come to her.

I wasn't about to let her get away with this. "Does Mom have enemies?"

Twyla gave me a defeated look. "You know I've always accepted your mother."

I did not know that. My experience was that Twyla huffed her annoyance, rolled her eyes, and probably gnawed a chunk of Uncle Bud's ear off about Mom's strange ways.

Twyla's gaze flicked from left to right, everywhere but at me. "But not everyone around here thinks she's all that and a bag of chips."

"Specifically?"

Her gaze settled on me, and she slapped her thighs. "Well, hell. Just about everybody. She picks and chooses when she'll honor us with her presence. I don't even think she went to all of your graduations."

She hadn't. But she'd done something special for each of us. She'd given me a beautiful hand-embroidered jacket she'd picked up at a gallery in Santa Fe on one of the few openings she'd attended. Robert scored intricately tooled boots she'd ordered from a craftsman in Mexico. Others were given paintings or sculptures. Louise had never mentioned what Mom had given her, even though we'd all asked. Louise loved gossip more than most of us, but I knew she could darn well keep a secret if she wanted to.

I blew her off. "She's not friends with anyone, so I can't believe someone would want to kill her even if they thought she snubbed them."

Twyla grabbed the bottle of Jack and sloshed three fingers into her glass. She never liked someone disagreeing with her. After a sip, she set the glass down and spoke in a conspiratorial tone. "We don't know who she knew before Hank dragged her home. Could be she gathered a shitload of enemies that only just now found her."

That made me laugh. "She's been here for over forty years. She's never been in touch with anyone from before then. Not even her family."

Twyla thrust a finger at me. "That you know of."

I couldn't believe Mom was hiding a diabolical past. "Mom barely goes so far from home she has to drive. I'd think one of us kids would find a clue if she was hiding a secret life."

Twyla jumped on that. "What about those times she went to her art shows?"

I scoffed. "I can think of two, maybe three times she left home."

Twyla's pointed look preceded an ominous tone. "And always on her own."

"You're reaching here."

Twyla swirled her drink and gave it a fierce scowl she might have wanted to turn on me. "Hank was discharged in '72, and I nearly dropped dead when she climbed off that bus with him in Broken Butte." She calculated in her head, something familiar to her from adding bar tabs on the fly. "That's forty-five years ago. And I'll sing 'Twinkle, Twinkle, Little Star' at Carnegie Hall if she didn't have handfuls of secrets in that hemp bag hanging from her shoulder."

Might as well indulge Twyla. Sometimes watching her get wound up was entertaining. "Did Dad ever say she had secrets?"

Twyla blew a raspberry. "You know Hank. Compared to him, a bank vault is like a sieve. He never spills the goods."

I'd been accused of inheriting that character trait.

Twyla gave a sage nod. "But she had that way about her. Kind of jumpy and always looking over her shoulder."

I didn't argue, but I gave her an annoyed scowl to show I didn't buy it. Then thought about how she'd acted in her bedroom.

My aunt tapped the bar. "No, really. And she never made friends here. Admit it, forty-five years and no women over for coffee or gossip. Never once sat her royal butt in any of these barstools."

I had to give her that. "She's different than most. But you've been around her a lot. She talks to people. Does nice things for people, even if they're random." I pressed that point. "You know, she made a coffee mug for Enoch. He told Josh it fit his hand perfect, and now he won't drink out of anything else."

When Twyla lifted her chin and opened her mouth, I wanted to snatch the words back. "Speaking of Josh. What the damn hell were you thinking, breaking up with that man? He's stable, nice, responsible, and handsome as hell. You're not likely to find a better match around here."

I'd had some form of this harassment for the last two months. Ever since the terrible and wonderful few days in Wyoming. Terrible because Diane's ex-husband had wound up dead. Wonderful because I'd seen my niece Carly again and even hugged her.

And even more wonderful because Baxter and I had shared an incredible night together. Terrible because now he was gone forever.

My beer suddenly became important, and I gulped it, with the unrealistic hope Twyla would drop the subject by the time I set it back on the bar.

She didn't. "Whatever you did to send him packing, you ought to undo it. He was in here last night."

A big part of me wanted to know how he was doing. A part just as big knew I had no right to ask. So, I kept quiet.

Twyla wasn't about to let it go. "He's got no clue why you up and quit him. I told him I think you suffered momentary insanity and you'd come around soon."

My stomach rolled and dumped. "I like Josh. A lot. He's all those things you said." Plus, he'd be a great father, and he'd be loyal and steadfast. "But don't you think he deserves a woman who is head over heels in love with him?" Not someone so lost in longing for a man she'd never have. A man who drilled so deeply into her heart she heard his voice in her dreams.

Twyla waved her hand as if swatting at those images. "You had all that heart and roses and sap running so hot you couldn't keep your hands off each other with Ted. What'd that get you? Eight years with a two-timing bastard who broke your heart." She pulled out her finger again. "I'm telling you, make it good with Josh. He's a keeper."

"Done talking about it."

"Just sayin'."

I let her have that last word and sipped my beer.

Twyla knocked back a slug of Jack. She didn't wince like most humans would. "Marguerite was never my cup of tea. But I think what really gets my goat is that she never tried to fit in."

It seemed appropriate to defend her. "Mom wouldn't knowingly hurt anyone. She's a gentle person."

Twyla's eyebrows shot up. "But she gunned down someone only a few hours ago."

"Self-defense."

Twyla's sniff showed her skepticism. "Come on, Kate. We don't know much about Marguerite except she does as she damned well pleases all the time."

Laughter erupted at the center table, saving me from replying.

Twyla squinted and wrinkled her nose, spying above the heads of her customers to see out the window at our house. "There were so many girls that had their eye on Hank back in the day."

That surprised me. "Dad? I never thought of him as a ladies' man."

Twyla cackled. "He had his pick, that's for sure. He was like that danged little brother of yours."

I scrolled through my three younger brothers. Douglas, quiet and shy, hadn't dated much and was single. Michael had hooked up with Lauren while they were still in high school, and they'd been a solid partnership ever since. Jeremy, the charmer, had dated half of the women in the county, though *dated* might not describe his encounters. That half of the women included married, single, older, and younger. None of those choices seemed to fit my image of Dad. I must have looked confused.

Twyla knocked back the rest of her Jack. "Jeremy. That free-lovin', good-time guy."

Now it was my turn to cast her my skeptical look.

As ever, Twyla didn't soften her delivery. "Before he left for 'Nam, he spent most of his time rodeoing, brawling, and chasing tail."

"Dad?" My beer sweated in my hand, but I didn't lift it.

She snorted in disgust. "And then off he went and left all that piss and vinegar over there. He came back with this hippie and set to having babies. Took up working on the BNSF, and the Hank we knew disappeared."

Sounded like she missed the younger version of her brother. "And you think Mom changed him?"

Twyla spun around and reached for the Jack Daniel's bottle again. "Who knows? He probably saw and did things over there that changed him.

He might have got over all that and got back to normal, but he married her and all that daisies and art and woo-woo karma malarky. Hell, he barely has more than two beers back-to-back. And I'm talking about a guy who could go on a three-day bender and ride a bronc the next day."

"I don't think a person can really change another person. They might be able to support change if someone wants to be different." Of course, I wasn't thinking only about Mom and Dad. My thoughts, as they tended to do these days, drifted to Baxter and what it might have been like with us if I hadn't ruined it. Would we have supported each other's changes? Would it have been good? With a mental slap and *Moonstruck* admonition to "snap out of it," I turned my attention back to Twyla.

Her nose tweaked to the side in distaste. "All's I know is that he never got the chance to be normal again. He brought her home, quit rodeoing, bought that house, and got on with the railroad. And before we knew it, she's shelling out kids one after the other."

Maybe I looked a little offended by the way she referred to me and my brothers and sisters because she patted the bar in front of me. "Not that I don't love all my nieces and nephews to bits. Some more'n others, of course." She raised her chin. "But that's fair. I've been at the other end of more than one of Louise's lectures."

I raised my bottle in agreement, and we both drank.

One of the cowboys down the bar hailed her. She set her glass down with a little more force than necessary and scowled at me before turning to grab two more Buds from the cooler. "Hold your horses. You ain't got to shout."

The glass door opened, and Susan stuck her head in, that shaved side giving me a shock. Susan, named for Susan Sarandon in *Dead Man Walking*, was my parents' ninth child. She could have been pampered and spoiled by a cadre of older siblings willing to cater to a little princess. Instead, she grew up defending her independence and with a determination born from struggling to keep up. She spotted me and strode across the bar, stopping to greet the folks at the middle table.

They asked after Mom, probably more out of curiosity than sympathy. Susan assured them everything was calm and taken care of. She answered a few more questions, mostly by saying no one knew anything, and then made her way to me.

"This isn't going to die down for a long time," she said, hoisting herself onto the barstool next to me.

I turned to face the mirror above the bar and caught her eye. "Mom killed someone. We don't know who he is or why he was here. Doesn't it freak you out a little?"

She glared at me via the mirror. "Of course it freaks me out. You didn't have to drive four hours with Dad, who wouldn't say a word the whole time except to tell me he'd pump and pay for my gas and to hurry up when I went in to pee."

"And you didn't have to see a dead man bleeding all over Mom's studio."

She winced. "Okay. You win."

Twyla appeared in front of us. "What'll you have, short stuff?"

Susan eyed my beer and grimaced. "Not that."

Twyla nodded agreement at the vileness of my beer. "I've got Coors on tap."

Susan held her hand like an imaginary pistol to shoot at Twyla and let her know she'd hit it right. I thought it was a poor choice of gestures, and it must have hit Susan, too, because she quickly dropped her hand onto the bar.

Twyla spun around. The group at the center table scraped their chairs back and, amid loud chatter, shuffled toward the door. The two middle-aged couples had left, but a few other couples and families had entered and settled into seats.

Twyla plopped the wet mug in front of Susan, slopping beer over the side. She scurried down the bar to take someone's order.

After a quick sip, Susan turned to me. "Do you think Louise is right? This guy was some insane fan?"

"Makes as much sense as anything. How anyone would know where she lives is a mystery, though." I heaved myself across the bar and grabbed a plastic tumbler and the soda sprayer. With a half-full glass of tepid seltzer, I slid back to the barstool.

Susan drank and set her mug down. Through the mirror, I watched her face do that pinching thing that told me she was deciding whether to confess something.

I elbowed her. "What?"

She sat a moment longer before inhaling and turning to me. "I might know how someone found her."

7

That stopped me mid-gulp, and the seltzer fizzed before I swallowed. "How?"

She clamped her teeth a second, then gave another inhale. "You know how she donated that sculpture to the university last month?"

It was one of my favorite pieces she'd created. An abstract work about four feet high, it looked like a series of nine birds rising in a circular formation from an inverted dome. It flowed together but carried a sense of energy and hope. It didn't take a lot of analyzing to understand the nine birds represented her children and the dome was her womb. That she donated it to the University of Nebraska (Go Big Red), where eight of her children had attended at least some college, seemed appropriate and generous.

"She didn't allow them to have a ceremony or do any publicity. She was super careful that none of her publicity bios even say she lives in Nebraska. How would anyone link her from that to Hodgekiss?"

Susan's eyes shifted uncomfortably away from me to focus on Twyla slamming drinks onto a serving tray. "She came up to oversee the installation. Remember she was really concerned they would put it in a corner or against a wall, and she said it needed to have three-hundred-sixty-degree viewing?"

I didn't remember that, might not have ever known it, but I nodded so she'd continue.

"Well, so, yeah." She took a long pull on her mug.

"Just tell me," I said.

She slowly placed the mug on the bar. "Sask is taking a film-making class, and for the final they have to do a documentary, like three minutes long or something." Sask was short for Sasquatch, Susan's roommate for the last three years. A towering young man with enough hair for a village, his nickname seemed apt.

She paused.

"Come on," I said.

"Okay, yeah. So, Mom and I went to the gallery, and Sask took some video."

I already knew the answer, but I asked anyway. "And Mom was okay with that?"

The bar crowd grew and got louder. I didn't tune in to their conversations because I didn't want to hear their theories about why my mother, the pacifist most people in Grand County either didn't understand or didn't like, or both, would shoot someone.

Susan's cheeks flamed. "Mom didn't know. He used a zoom lens thing. Honest, I didn't think it would make any difference. I mean, it was only for class, so like, maybe twenty people and the prof would see it."

"But...?"

She tilted her head as if dragging the story from her depths. "Sask did this whole thing about mothers and daughters, and the film made it look like Mom was really nurturing and loving. I mean, he somehow captured Mom actually hugging me and kissing my forehead. Like she's ever done that before."

She had. I'd witnessed it. But Susan had been pissed at Mom for so long she probably blocked out the good.

I raised my eyebrows in a sign of impatience.

She swiped her finger down her wet beer mug and studied it. "Sask's prof was so impressed with the film, he sent it to the local news affiliate in Lincoln. And I guess they liked it so much that it got bumped up."

My stomach clenched. "What do you mean?"

She sat back and let her hands plop into her lap. "You know how at the end of the news at night they have these little feel-good stories?"

"Sure. Ted called it the cat-in-a-tree section, and he usually turned it off." I always liked those little bits of humanity.

"NBC picked it up and aired it."

I stared a minute. "Mom was on national TV without her permission? Why didn't we know about it? We'd have wanted to see it."

"I didn't find out until after it ran. Sask and the prof got around permissions somehow, don't ask me how because I don't know—which is a whole other story and why I haven't talked to Sask for three weeks."

"Does Mom know?" I couldn't imagine how my ultra-private mother would react to being on the news.

Susan bristled. "Of course she does. I told her as soon as I found out. She went ballistic."

I leaned back and studied Susan. "Mom doesn't go ballistic." I'd seen her deliver a soft-spoken burn or even give a quiet reprimand, hardly ever to us kids but sometimes to adults she believed didn't have the proper respect for the environment or compassion for those less fortunate than themselves.

Now the Fox feisty pushed through Susan. She whipped her head back, preparing to set me straight. "See? This is what I've tried to tell you for years. Mom is all peace and serenity to you guys. I mean, that 'Go placidly amid the noise and haste' bullshit. And you all bought it."

I opened my palms to show I had no idea what she was talking about.

She looked into her beer. "Never mind."

I elbowed her again. "What do you mean?"

Twyla reappeared and snatched her Jack. She took a sip and eyed Susan. "She's got a dark side, huh?"

Susan's head snapped up. "You've seen it?"

Twyla wrinkled her nose and sidestepped. "Not to tell about. But there's something in her past she's not proud of."

We knew so little about Mom's early life. I admitted to curiosity. "Why do you say that?"

Twyla leaned across the bar. "Early on, Hank said something to me."

Susan's eyes drilled into Twyla with the concentration of a border collie.

Twyla's voice was so low I could barely hear her above the bar noise. "Not long after he brought her home, we were at a family barbeque. Of course, Marguerite wouldn't honor us with her presence. I asked him why he brought her to the Sandhills if she didn't want to be here. He said she needed him and a quiet place where she could hide."

Susan's lips pursed, as if Twyla had confirmed something.

"Hide from what?" I asked.

Twyla gave her head a firm nod. "That's what I asked. And he said he didn't know if there was anything specific. Just that the world was too much for her."

"Always running away and expecting everyone else around her to pick up the slack." Susan gulped the rest of her beer.

I gave them both a glare I hoped showed reproach. "Not everyone has the ability to process the world. She's probably on the spectrum and doing the best she can."

Susan twisted her mouth. "Your undergrad degree in psychology doesn't make you qualified to diagnose people."

Twyla lifted her glass. "Don't give me that bullshit. She's always been a spoiled princess. Probably came from a protected home with lots of money and got her claws into Hank so he could take care of her."

I wasn't buying it. "It's not like Dad is rich. And when they met, he'd just been discharged from the army and didn't even have a job."

Susan locked eyes with Twyla. "But hiding from something makes sense."

"Right?" Twyla seemed to like having an ally.

I placed both my hands on the bar and pushed back. "You guys are being ridiculous. Mom's been here for over forty years. If she's only been using Dad to hide, why would she have nine kids and a thriving career as an artist? Wouldn't she lay low for a while until the threat went away and then take off?"

Twyla narrowed her eyes. "What if the threat never went away?"

There was no stopping my eye roll. "You can't deny she and Dad love each other. She's devoted to her family. That's not someone biding their time until they can get away."

Susan's face pinched in irritation. "Is she? Devoted, I mean."

"Of course she is," I said.

Twyla let out a huff of disbelief. "Hank's got a loyal nature. He married her, so he's not about to abandon her, no matter what she's like."

Susan whipped her head to me, her face flushed with passion. "Do you want to count the times she let you down? Because if I start, I'll never stop. Maybe she went to all of Glenda's school plays or volleyball games. But by the time I came along...nothing. You stood with me on parents' night my senior year, remember? Dad was working, and Mom, who even knows?"

Her resentment and pain blew at me like a January blizzard. "I'm sorry. I didn't know this bothered you so much."

She shifted away from me and held her mug up to Twyla. "Can I get another?"

Twyla grabbed it. "Sure, honey."

I started, "I believe she does the best she can and—"

Susan slapped the bar. "Don't. She does the best she can for *herself*. We come in a distant second."

Twyla sat a fresh beer in front of Susan, foam overflowing down the side to puddle on the wood bar.

Susan wrapped her fingers in the handle but didn't raise the glass. "I don't want to sound all jealous and needy, but here's the truth: Mom definitely has favorites."

I opened my mouth to protest, and she held up her hand.

"Glenda, of course. Then you and Jeremy." She looked to Twyla for confirmation.

Twyla's eyebrows lifted as if she considered what Susan said. "That's about right."

"I don't—" Guess I wasn't allowed to protest.

"Ask Jeremy if you don't believe me. Louise is always trying to get Mom's attention. Diane checked out early and only blows in and takes up so much space we all notice her. The older boys made their own lives. I swear she doesn't even remember she had me."

I wouldn't let that stand. "She just donated a sculpture to your school and spent a weekend with you in Lincoln."

Susan's laugh was a belt of resentment. "It's a representation of all the kids. So yeah, technically I'm one of them. Probably the littlest."

"You're the youngest, so that would make sense."

She glared at me. "I don't know what it is about you and Jeremy, though."

Twyla studied me. "Nothing special I can figure." She topped it off with a wicked grin to let me know she was teasing. Her attention focused on the crowded tables. "They can't stir their asses to tell me what they want? Expect me to tromp back and forth." She slammed her glass down and stomped off to get their orders.

I finished my beer and looked Susan in the eye, trying to give her a warm hug without the physical embrace because of that not-a-huggy-family thing. "I'm sorry you feel neglected. I know Mom loves you. Loves us all. I'm not saying you don't have reason to be hurt and resentful." I wanted to suggest she see someone, but that seemed pretentious, patronizing, and a few other words.

"She wasn't the same person with me and Jeremy as she was with the rest of you." She hefted the mug and drank.

I didn't answer, but my face must have showed that I thought she was being too sensitive.

"If she was so devoted to us and being on the spectrum is the reason she wouldn't face the public, then why would she have a hidden cell phone?"

It felt as if she'd galloped to a different pasture altogether. "She doesn't have a hidden phone."

"As of last summer, she did."

8

Now she was making me mad. "You're full of it."

She matched my heat. "You don't know everything about Saint Marguerite. And I absolutely know she's got a phone hidden in her studio."

I threw down the challenge. "How do you know?"

There was no shifting her gaze or staring into her beer. She spoke full at me. "I was home for a weekend last summer, and I think Mom flat-out forgot I was there. I was upstairs and heard her talking to someone. All the windows were open, and she was outside of her studio in the backyard. I wouldn't have thought anything about it except she was acting different than I'd ever seen her."

"Different?"

Susan didn't like the interruption and struggled to explain. "I don't know. Like, maybe she was like, lighter. Younger? So, you know how she always seems to act slow and controlled. Like maybe she's weighing her thoughts and reactions? This was like she had no restraints. You had to see it."

I still wasn't buying into this. "Okay. How do you know it's a hidden phone?"

"I was curious about who she'd be talking to. So I went downstairs to be, like, casual and see if I could figure it out. She turned and saw me, and I swear, all the color left her face. I don't think she said goodbye, just dropped the phone into her kimono pocket."

"Did you ask her about it?"

Susan looked disturbed. "I started to, but she grabbed my hand and pulled me upstairs. She got all excited about going to collect cattails and wanting me to go along. She took off to her room to change, and then we went to get the cattails." She swiveled her mug around to leave a trail of foam on the bar. "I'm like Louise, so thankful for any attention. She seemed happy I was with her, and we had fun. She asked about school and my job. I didn't want to ruin it."

My heart cracked for Susan. I hated that she felt a lack of love and attention. I'd always accepted Mom for who she was and figured everyone else would come to terms with Mom's limitations. Maybe I had, but maybe not. I'd made a bad pick in my marriage. I'd rejected Josh, a perfectly wonderful man. Had fallen for someone totally unattainable, but when it seemed like it might work, I'd messed it up.

Susan's story brought me back to the noisy Long Branch. "But I checked her phone later when she left it in the kitchen. There hadn't been a call for about three days. So then I did ask who she was talking to in the backyard, and she said Diane."

"Maybe you got it wrong."

"You're not the only investigator in the family. I called Diane, and she hadn't talked to Mom for a couple of weeks. I tried to find the other phone, looked in her kimono pocket. Nothing. Searched around her studio, but she came downstairs and got me out of there right away."

"I don't know. Sounds like a misunderstanding or something. Maybe you should talk to her about it."

Finished delivering a drink order, Twyla set the tray on the bar and tuned in to our conversation.

Susan opened her mouth in disbelief. "You're making excuses for her. Unbelievable. She gets a bye on everything."

Not what I intended. "No. Wait. I'm sorry." I inhaled. "I need a minute to think about this, okay? I understand your experience with Mom is different than mine. She's not like most people, and I've reconciled myself to that. So, poking around and rethinking it is going to take some time for me."

Twyla snorted and shook her head.

"Reconciled? Or denied there's anything wrong with her?" Susan shot fire at me and gulped her beer. "You all make excuses for her." She waved me off. "Whatever. Use all that Psych 101 to calm me down but go on believing she's this fragile artistic soul. Whatever it takes for you to live in peace."

Twyla's head jerked to the left away from us, then back to me as if gauging a threat.

I looked down the bar. Ah.

Diane stood several feet away, exchanging greetings with the cowboys finishing up their beers. She might be a big-deal financial exec, but she'd grown up in the Sandhills, where everyone knows everyone for generations back. One of the cowboys was a younger brother of Diane's classmate, and the other was the son of Diane's freshman-year boyfriend.

Twyla sauntered down the bar to Diane. "Hey, sweetie. Didn't know you'd made it back."

It wouldn't be coincidence Twyla called her sweetie. Diane hated that term, so naturally, Twyla would ding her with it. Susan and I watched them.

Diane didn't turn to me, and I had to strain to hear. "Someone had to take care of things over there. You know they hadn't even called a lawyer?"

Twyla faked shock. "Can't believe it."

Diane smiled at her. "Amateurs. Anyway, I've got to get back to Denver. Some of us have real jobs."

I swear she'd upped her volume on that last sentence just to dig at me.

She slapped a credit card on the bar. "I need the biggest coffee you've got. To go."

"You got it," Twyla said.

Diane flicked her hand down our way. "And put whatever Susan's having on that."

Susan grinned and shouted down the bar, "Thanks."

Diane gave her a side-eye but didn't smile. She shouted back, "I like your hair. Come see me sometime."

Susan elbowed me. "If you'd be nicer to her, you'd get your drinks paid for, too."

I drained my warm seltzer. "I can buy my own." It wasn't her not buying my drinks that hurt.

Twyla returned with the coffee and the card. She and Diane exchanged a few words, and Diane marched out.

Trying to tell myself I didn't care that Diane hated me didn't make it so.

Susan ran a hand over the shaved spot on the side of her head. She had a satisfied smirk, as if getting a compliment from Diane carried weight. Then she eyed me. "So, what's up with you and Diane, anyway?"

I spun away from her and stood up. "Nothing."

Susan frowned. "Come on. It has to do with Carly, doesn't it?"

"Why?"

She picked up her beer. "I asked Carly, and she told me to stay out of it."

"So, stay out of it." I hated the image that flashed into my mind. Vince lying in a pool of blood on the floor of the Wyoming cabin. Diane's uncharacteristic wails.

She loved him. Who would have thought Diane was capable of that kind of irrational commitment to a man who was so bad?

I shouldn't judge, since I'd married Ted and he'd cheated on me. It took me a while to get over loving him. Now he mostly irritated me, but if I was honest, seeing him dead might do a number on me, too.

But I didn't kill Vince, so Diane shouldn't hold his death against me. Though I'd had a hand in it.

I clenched my teeth to stop that line of thought. Why did I always argue against myself? Diane had no reason to hate me. It wasn't up to me to make amends for something I didn't do. Let her stew in it.

Susan's eyes flashed. She hated being dismissed. Probably from being the youngest and not always included in the rest of the brothers' and sisters' doings. "This family is so full of secrets. Don't tell me. I don't care."

All I wanted to do was check on Mom once more, collect Poupon, and go home to my quiet house on Stryker Lake. Alone. But I didn't want another sister mad at me. "You and Carly hang out much?"

Carly, my niece, had been under my care when she'd run away and been gone for over a year. The daughter of my oldest sister, Glenda, who'd passed away ten years ago, Carly was ballsy and passionate. Glenda had died when Carly was twelve, and then a few years later, Carly's father's small plane had crashed into a hillside, killing him. When her beloved granddad was killed two years ago, the tragedy sent her on the run, determined to prove foul play.

I finally found Carly two months ago at that Wyoming cabin. Those terrible events would take a long time to fade and, in the case of me and Diane, might change our lives forever. But one good thing that came of it was reconnecting with Carly. I'd been successful in persuading her to start college at the University of Nebraska (Go Big Red), mostly because Susan was still there and I thought Carly could use her support. They'd always been close.

Susan shot me disdainful eyes. "You won't tell me about you and Diane, but you want me to tell you all about me and Carly."

I didn't want to play games. "Don't be a brat."

Susan's mouth ticked into a smile. "Yeah. We hang. It's great being together again, but, I gotta tell you, she's not the same Carly."

Dang. "What do you mean?"

She thought about it. "You know how she was always the first one to think of doing something. Usually getting us into trouble or causing chaos. Like when we wrote HHS in gasoline in Vina Carpenter's yard for homecoming?"

Vina Carpenter lived next to the football field and cultivated a vast green expanse to rival any high-end golf course. When those letters turned a dead brown against the green, it might have inspired school spirit, but that's not what it lit in Vina Carpenter.

All these years later I could laugh at it, but it wasn't so funny when I had to march Carly and Susan to Vina Carpenter's house and make them apologize and then supervise them while they replanted her grass and made sure they kept it watered and mowed until it filled in.

"Well, Carly doesn't do that. She still laughs and jokes and stuff, but there's this kind of watchfulness about her now."

That familiar dull ache throbbed for all that Carly had been through. Instead of a carefree childhood and rambunctious teens and twenties, Carly had lost everything and then put herself in dangerous situations. I wondered if she'd ever have an easy life. "Might take her a while to get traction under her wheels after last year." Then I thought of Dad and his before-and-after Vietnam experience. Maybe Carly would be forever changed.

Susan tipped the rest of her beer back and stood. "Whatever that was. She won't say much. Except sometimes things slip out. Like how hot it is in Dubai. Dubai! What the fuck? And how Chicago deep-dish pizza is the best. Like, when was she in Chicago?"

I slapped a five on the bar. We both waved at Twyla and got a chin wave back as she filled a mug from the tap.

"We'll probably never know what she was up to, and we're going to have to accept that." Although I had more information about Carly's activities than anyone else in the family. Except Diane, who had a ton of secrets of her own.

My information came from Baxter. If I let myself think about that too much, I'd curl into a ball and not want to move. All those phone calls over the last several months. That nearly physical connection that grew with each minute we spoke. And the one night in Wyoming, when the promise of a future together burned so bright it nearly blinded me.

Now there was nothing. I couldn't blame Baxter for severing the cord. But I felt certain I'd feel the loss for the rest of my life. I hadn't yet learned to carry it without the pain taking my breath away.

A young couple met us at the glass door. Classmates of Susan's who'd just gotten married last summer.

Susan turned to me. "I'm gonna stay and have a beer with Zoe. I'll be home in a while."

After a few exchanges with the newlyweds, I left them and trudged across the highway, down and up the railroad right-of-way, and back to the house.

Summer held on by the tiniest grasp, and fall was closing in fast. When I'd left the house, I hadn't needed a jacket, but now, goose bumps erupted up and down my arms. The smell of a wood fire wafted in the air. As much as I loved summer and dreaded the long slog of winter, I always felt a sense of comfort as October marched in. Like a cozy blanket pulled up when you settle into a good book.

By this time, the lot beside the house we all used for parking was empty except for Susan's little wreck of a red car, Elvis, my 1973 Ranchero, and Mom's 1983 Vanagon.

I let myself through the side door into the kitchen. A soft light over the stove revealed scrubbed and sparkling countertops. A few dozen jars of salsa cooled on the butcher block island, and Poupon lay with his head on his paws, staring at the door I'd entered through. He didn't jump up to greet me but stared at me with resentment at his state of abandonment.

Maybe because so recently the house had buzzed with activity, now it seemed deathly quiet. Using the term *death* brought back the horror of the man in the basement. How would Mom ever be able to work down there again?

Thank heavens Dad was here with her. There'd be some kind of hell to pay for him leaving in the middle of a trip, but he'd work it out with BNSF. They had to have provisions for family emergencies. I didn't know because I was fairly certain that where most railroaders missed a call or two in their careers, Dad hadn't laid off for any reason in the over forty years he'd been on the rails.

But he was here now. Whatever Twyla wanted to believe, Mom and Dad had a rare connection. For their whole marriage, Dad had been gone for thirty-six to forty-eight hours a couple of times a week. So many railroad families fell apart under that kind of schedule. But Mom and Dad seemed like the most stable couple I'd ever known. I'd never heard them bicker or complain to or about each other. When one of them entered a room unexpectedly, even after all these years, the other's face would light up. It was the kind of love I hoped to find one day.

And thought I had. But now it was gone.

I whispered to Poupon to come. I'd leave Mom and Dad to the quiet and hope they might find some peace and sleep.

Though it was barely eight o'clock, Hodgekiss had gone to sleep except for the Long Branch. The ride north to my house took ten minutes, with only the sound of Elvis's wheels on the pavement, which shifted to pings on the undercarriage during the last two miles of dirt road.

Poupon and I climbed out of Elvis. No lights shone from my house, and there wasn't enough moonlight to brighten the night. Stars punctuated the dark sky in a way they'd never see in a city. I reached for my phone before I realized I couldn't call Baxter and tell him about it.

It was only the twentieth time I'd done that today. Maybe I'd grabbed for the phone twenty-five times yesterday. Last week it was probably thirty. "We'll survive this," I said to Poupon.

He walked away from me and lifted his leg on one of the cottonwoods lining my small yard. At least I could always count on the unconditional love of my dog.

Even though I took a shower and climbed into bed, sleep was a long time coming. Every time I closed my eyes, I saw the dead man in Mom's studio. Saw her holding the gun.

Susan said Mom had a secret phone. She lied about who she called. Mom had been prepared. Almost as if she expected someone. She said the caution was born from a tarot reading. But did it all add up?

9

I was dressed in my spiffy sheriff browns and scarfing toast and coffee while enjoying the morning on my front porch when my phone rang. With eight brothers and sisters and being the only law enforcement officer in a county the size of Rhode Island, even if the population was less than five thousand, a phone call at any time wasn't unusual.

I jumped up from the porch step and retrieved my cell from the table inside my front door. Susan's smiling face showed on the ID. "Morning, sunshine."

"They're gone." She sounded freaked out.

My toast stuck in my throat. "Who's gone?"

"Mom and Dad. I thought they were in bed when I came home last night and didn't think anything about it. But when I got up just now, there's no coffee or tea or anything, and I checked their room and they're gone. Where would they go? Why didn't they tell me?"

All good questions. "Hang on. I'm on my way."

I tugged Poupon's collar to urge him off the couch, where he consistently ignored the rule about no dogs on the furniture. Furniture Baxter had picked out and shipped to me as a housewarming gift. But there was no way I was going to think about that.

Where would Mom and Dad go? In my memory, they'd never gone to the Long Branch for breakfast or taken a morning stroll together. I doubted they'd start that kind of innocent mission today. My mind turned somersaults while I waited for Poupon to do what dogs do in the morning and we loaded up for town. After the short drive where I kept asking Poupon what was going on and he refused to venture a theory, I pulled up at Mom and Dad's.

Susan threw open the kitchen door and met me halfway up the sidewalk. Except for the shaved side, her hair was tangled and wild. She wore wrinkled pajama pants and a stretched pink tank top. "Where could they go? They didn't take my car, and Mom's van is here."

I whipped around to see she was right. They'd probably been gone when I stopped in last night. They weren't settled into bed, Dad comforting Mom, as I'd assumed. "Someone drove them. Call Douglas. I'll call Robert."

She spun around and rushed back into the house with me on her heels, already dialing. Robert answered while Susan grabbed her phone from the counter and started poking buttons.

I didn't wait for him to do anything more than say hello. "Hey, have you seen Mom and Dad?"

"Today?" The baby cried in the background, and Sarah's voice spoke over it.

"Well, today or last night. But if you haven't, then you're not the one I need to talk to. I'll call later."

"Wait—"

Susan was hanging up at the same time. I pointed at her. "Michael. I'll call Louise."

We both focused on our phones. Susan started talking while Louise's phone rang three times until it switched to voicemail. Since Louise took pride in being available at all times, that didn't sit well. While Susan still talked to Michael, I searched for my niece Ruthie's number. As the oldest of Louise's five kids and a senior at Grand County Consolidated, she had her own phone.

She sounded cautious when she uttered, "Hello?"

Timid and skittish, Ruthie needed a gentle hand I didn't have time for. "I'm trying to get hold of your mom. Is she there?"

When I was greeted by silence, I chastised myself for being too abrupt. She finally answered. "Um. No. She's. Um. I'm driving the kids to school, so I've got to go."

"Wait." Again, too forceful, but she didn't hang up. "Where is she?"

A slight pause and then a distraught voice. "I'm not supposed to tell you she's gone. But she packed a suitcase, and then she left. She promised she's coming back."

Frog turds. I tried to sound casual. "Of course she's coming back. Don't worry. Your dad is still there, right?"

It sounded as if she might start crying. "He's at work, but yeah."

"Okay, then. Everything's fine. Have a good day." I hung up, cringing at my sign-off as if she were picking up an order of burgers.

Susan stood in front of me. "Michael said Louise asked Lauren to pick up the twins after school and keep them for a few days."

That sealed it. "Louise drove them someplace."

Susan replaced her panic of earlier with a flare of anger. "Where? Why? And why Louise?"

I sank onto the picnic table bench. "I don't know, but we need to trust Dad knows what he's doing."

Susan glared at me. "I'm not trusting for shit." She slammed on the tap and stuck the coffee pot under the stream. "As soon as this coffee is done, I'm heading back to Lincoln. You can wallow in your secrets. I've got a life to live."

I stayed at the house and drank coffee while Susan showered and threw her clothes into a bag. She ranted a bit about Mom's selfishness and Dad always letting her walk all over him. I objected here and there. I didn't agree with her but didn't want to alienate her any further. After a hug, which was way more physical affection than usual, and a promise to keep her updated, though she swore she didn't care, I watched her drive away.

Because I didn't know what else to do, I loaded Poupon into the sheriff's cruiser and we went to the courthouse.

We parked behind the red brick building that had been built in the 1960s. The front of the building opened onto a sparse front yard with no trees or benches, just a concrete sidewalk leading to double glass doors.

The back door opened into the basement level that housed the boiler room and a big activity room. The sheriff had a dedicated parking spot in back.

We clambered up the steps to the main floor, where most of the county business took place. The courthouse wasn't big, but Grand County didn't need much. The treasurer's and assessor-clerk's offices faced off across a hallway of shiny linoleum the color of caramel on the west side of the foyer. A large meeting room where the commissioners officiated each month and the public restrooms took up the east side. And my office, which contained two small jail cells, occupied a cramped corner at the east end of the hallway.

The smell of scorched coffee and floor wax hung in the hallway as Poupon and I tried to sneak to my office. But, as I'd dreaded, we didn't make it far.

The smack of the pass-through gate that separated the office from the five-foot reception area of the treasurer's suite hit me two seconds before Betty Paxton's voice. "Kate. Wait a minute. I want to talk to you."

I stopped but hesitated a second before turning. Poupon sat by my side, probably understanding we'd be here a minute.

A shuffle of slippers on the linoleum and an accompanying *humph* told me the assessor-clerk, Ethel Bender, had joined us. This wouldn't be fun.

When I faced them, Ethel, all blue hair and soft body, shapeless black sweater and slacks—and the slippers she changed into as soon as she got to the courthouse because her feet tended to swell—gave me an expectant glare.

Betty Paxton, her dyed blond hair spiked in the same fashion she'd rocked for thirty years, wore a flashy jersey wrap dress that hugged the extra forty pounds she'd added since that first spiked do. She liked to shop with her teenaged granddaughters, and I suspected she let their tastes influence her. She smiled at me. "I heard your mother shot a man. Now I know that can't be right."

Ethel folded her arms across her rounded chest. "They say she blew him away with a shotgun and left holes in the kitchen walls."

Betty moved slightly in front of Ethel. "I know how rumors get to flying. I actually heard he was stealing her artwork and she caught him red-handed."

I looked from one to the other, wondering how long they'd try to outdo each other. These two battle-axes had been running Grand County going on forty years. And in all that time, I doubt they'd ever passed a friendly word between them. Their feud went back so far no one remembered what caused the rift, maybe not even Betty and Ethel. But they were dedicated to it.

When Ted and I ran against each other for sheriff, Ethel had sided with Ted, and I got Betty. Ethel seemed hell-bent on keeping the grudge against me. Not because she didn't like me, I suspected, but because she resented that Betty's choice had won.

Ethel ignored Betty but took another step toward me. "Does she have artwork worth stealing? I bought a butter dish at a silent auction for that little Dugan girl a while back. It's fine. But I wouldn't break into a house to steal it."

Betty rushed to my defense. Or rather, Mom's defense by proxy. "Of course Marguerite has art worth stealing. She's famous. But only to people who know about art. That butter dish was probably a mistake she wanted to get rid of."

I stopped them with a firm correction. "Mom doesn't get rid of mistakes by donating them to an auction. I remember that butter dish, and if it's signed, which I'm sure it is, it'd sell for seventy bucks at a gallery in Santa Fe. And yeah, she does have valuable pieces. The truth is, we don't know who the guy was and what he was after. We're thankful Mom was prepared."

Ethel and Betty both looked whipped, and I felt bad for coming down on them. "I'm sorry. A man came into her studio and threatened her with a knife. We don't know who he is and what he wanted. She shot him with a pistol, and we're all sorry a life was taken. But it's clearly self-defense. The investigation is being handled by the state patrol." That ought to cover it.

Betty put an arm around my shoulder. "You poor dear. It must be hard."

Ethel frowned at us, then reached into her trouser pocket. She pulled out a plastic sandwich bag, and the rattle brought Poupon to attention. She pulled out a bit of grisly meat and held it out for him without bothering to ask if it was okay.

Poupon stepped forward and first sniffed, then delicately accepted the offering, as if it were his due as royalty.

Ethel's voice took on a babying tone I'd only ever heard her use with him. "There you go, pretty boy." She glanced up at me, and her face hardened. "We got a bad cut from Dutch's grocery store. I ought to quit buying meat from him. That's the second one we've had that we can't eat."

With that, she whirled her bulk around and shuffled back to her office.

Betty watched her and turned to me with a superior shrug. "Nothing's ever good enough for her."

I'd had my share of bad cuts from Dutch's myself and so wasn't one to comment. I employed a diplomatic nod and started down the hall.

Betty stopped me with a timid call. "Uh, Kate. Can I talk to you?"

Uh-oh. Had I forgotten budget papers or a receipt for reimbursement? "Sure."

She came to me and tossed a furtive look at Ethel's office door, probably making sure she was good and gone. She lowered her head and spoke to the ground. "Um. Well. I don't know what the state patrol will need to investigate at your mother's house and such."

Where was she going with this?

"But, well, it's been a long time now. In fact, it was right after I'd started, maybe the first week. And I didn't know what I was doing and…"

She was going to drag this out. Poupon might as well sit.

"Your mother came in. I didn't know her. She'd only been married to your dad for a couple of years by then. But she needed something authorized or something. I honestly don't remember what it was. But it called for her birth certificate number. I notarized whatever it was. But then, maybe a couple of months later, whoever it was sent a certified letter saying that birth certificate number wasn't valid."

She glanced at me, clearly upset and nervous.

"I'm sure it's fine," I said.

She fluttered a hand. "Well, probably. More than likely a number got transposed. But back then, I was kind of afraid of your mother. She was so, oh, I don't know, sophisticated or sure of herself or, well, just not from around here. I should have contacted her, but I never did. As far as I know, nothing ever came of it."

I figured Betty needed the whole bucket of exoneration, so I patted her arm. "I don't think Mom and Dad are planning to apply for passports anytime soon. If they need her birth certificate, they can figure it out. Don't worry about it."

She dropped her shoulders, and her face relaxed. "Whew. I'd never let something like that go nowadays. It was a different time then."

10

Relieved to be dismissed, I continued to my office and let us in. Poupon ignored the dog bed I'd brought in and went straight for my office chair, hopping up despite being too big to fit comfortably.

I tugged his collar. "When are you going to get the message, dude? Furniture is not for dogs."

"Katie."

I yelped at Dad's voice coming from the doorway. He stepped inside quickly and pulled the door closed.

Hand on my chest, I said, "I didn't know you were there."

His tired face eased into a wan smile. He looked gray and exhausted. He'd showered since I'd seen him but hadn't shaved the grizzle from his face. He wore clean Dickies, a hoodie, and his work boots. His brown hair, generously sprinkled with gray, was longer than he normally wore it, and it brushed his hood in back and flopped on his forehead. "I didn't want to run into Betty or Ethel."

"Good call. What are you doing here? Where's Mom?"

He snapped his fingers, and Poupon hopped out of the chair and his nails clicked the few steps it took to reach his bed and flop into it, heaving out a sigh of pure put-out.

Dad dropped into my chair as if he didn't have the energy to stay upright. His brown eyes that always seemed attuned to what any of us needed now seemed steeped in worry. "She's fine. She's with Louise." He gave an unexpected chuckle, and an affectionate twinkle filtered into his eyes. "You gotta know this is what Louise has always wanted, an excuse to mother Marguerite. She's clucking over her, and Marguerite is letting her. Louise even got your mother to eat scrambled eggs this morning."

First shooting a man, then our vegan mother eating eggs. We probably ought to be heading for a bunker somewhere because the end of the world was obviously at hand.

I sat on the edge of a hard wooden conference chair I'd purloined from the commissioners' room. "What's going on?"

He rubbed a hand over his face, the callouses scratching on graying stubble. Anxiety returned to his drawn face. "I don't know. She's terrified. Says she needs to hide. But she won't tell me from what or who. She says she doesn't want me to be in danger."

"So, you took her someplace, like a line shack or calving barn? Hiding her?" I tried to think of places I knew where they could hole up for a while. Without effort I could list a dozen. We're not talking luxury accommodations, but a primitive stove and a cot were available at almost any ranch. And Dad knew them all.

He lifted one eyebrow at me in warning. "Don't bother trying to figure out where she is. She doesn't want anyone to know."

"Louise knows, so it won't be a secret for long."

"She's promised to keep it to herself." He ticked his head in acknowledgment. "But she probably won't be able to last more than a couple of days."

That jarred me. "How long do you expect to let Mom hide out?"

Worry pinched the skin around his eyes, the expression so like Louise fretting about one of her kids. "I wish I knew." He slumped more. "I need your help, Katie."

For the first time, I worried about the age on Dad. He wasn't a big man, but like his sister Twyla, he tended toward the lean and scrappy side. I always thought of him as the softest leather, the buttery kind that was tough but felt like satin. Now I focused on the deep lines around his mouth, the soft skin under his eyes, the network of wrinkles on his face.

I wanted to do whatever I could to lighten the load that weighed him down. "What do you need?"

He settled deeper into my chair. "Your mother is terrified."

"Of what?"

He closed his eyes and let out a deep exhale before opening them. They held sadness. "I don't know. Something in her past. This man, the one who came here, he isn't a fan, like they keep saying. He's someone she knew."

"From where? No one recognized him, so he's not from around here. Mom never went anywhere. How could she know him?"

It sounded as if he dragged his voice from the bottom of a marsh. "She's been to a few shows over the years, but I think this guy is from her past. We need to figure out who he is so we can protect her."

Mom needed protection? None of this sounded right. "Past? As in before she met you?" I couldn't imagine a young Mom in a world without Dad.

"I have to think so."

So many questions whirled around in my head. "Did you ask her about it?"

He hesitated, then shook his head. "She won't tell me, and I know she won't tell you."

I sat back. "Hold on. You want me to help. Protect her somehow from something that's scaring her. But I can't ask her what, and you don't know anything."

"Yep." His face carried such a heaviness. "When we met, we made a pact to leave the past behind us."

"Sure, in all your twenty-something wisdom, it was the romantic thing to do. But forty-five years later, there's a reality you both need to deal with."

He ran his hand over his face again, maybe trying to wipe away his frustration. "I told her that. It made no difference."

"You've been married forever. Raised nine kids. Have twelve grandkids. And you're telling me you've never discussed your past with each other?"

A hint of a smile appeared and vanished. "We agreed to start our lives together without our burdens."

I snorted. "That doesn't seem fair. You brought her where everyone knows your history and isn't afraid to talk about it. Like, I know Uncle

Chester put you on a green broke filly when you were five, and that's when you decided to be a saddle bronc rider."

He smiled at that. "Served Chester right. Twelve years later, I won the all-around at Cheyenne Frontier Days and he didn't make the eight."

"See? That's only one story. So, Mom knows all about you. But you don't know about her."

He grew serious again. "She doesn't know it all. No one does. And no one ever will. She gave me that gift of taking my secrets to the grave. And I promised the same for her."

"Except now you want me to dig around in the dirt." I didn't often challenge Dad, and it didn't feel good.

"Someone tried to kill her. Her safety is at stake."

"This is crazy." We sat in silence for a few seconds. "Or maybe she's crazy." I spoke barely above a whisper.

Dad locked eyes with me, and I saw his mind searching. Now he looked more like Diane with her quick mind studying a problem. He finally looked away. "No. I don't think so. Marguerite has always been different." A hint of admiration touched his voice. "While we see the world in three dimensions, I think she views it in four or maybe even five."

I loved Mom, and even if she did see the world in an amplified perspective, it didn't mean she didn't have a few loose hinges. "Come on, Dad. We can admit she's maybe not that grounded in the real world."

"You're wrong. I think she's too aware of reality. Something happened to her when she was young. It hurt her so deeply she chose to withdraw from society rather than take the chance it would happen again."

Susan might be right. Dad was making excuses for Mom's weakness. My doubt must have shown on my face because Dad spoke with uncharacteristic speed. "You don't think she would have loved attending gallery openings? Chatting with people who appreciate and understand art would have been heaven for her, instead of staying isolated in this place where our idea of art is the Ace Reid cartoons."

"She never acted like she wanted to go anywhere. It seemed like she only needed her art and her family." Probably in that order of priority.

His face softened. "You don't see her through a realistic lens. Kids don't always pay that close attention. And they shouldn't. It's our job to take care of you, not the other way around. I'm not surprised you didn't see the way she pored over the catalogs highlighting her work. Or notice how she saved every one."

"That didn't mean she wanted to be there."

He got a faraway gleam in his eyes, as if seeing a younger Marguerite. "Maybe not so much in the last few years. But those first few shows, I could see how much it hurt not to be there."

"Then why didn't she go?"

Again, his hand wiped across his face, and he grimaced as if fighting himself. "I. Don't. Know." His clipped words cracked with frustration, maybe even anger, and seemed to surprise him as much as it did me.

This wasn't a side of Dad I'd ever seen. With us kids, he always kept an even, if amused, tone. I guess he relied on us never wanting to disappoint him. As far as I could see, it worked.

His tolerance for our antics seemed boundless. He only called us out for foul language. Aside from that, he usually stood by with a hug to cure a skinned knee, a pickup engine running for a quick trip to Doc Bunner, the vet, for stitches. A calm "work it out yourselves" when we ran to him to referee a fight. As we got older, he offered a cup of coffee and an ear to listen to our woes.

"Are you okay?" I asked, suddenly more worried about him than I was Mom.

He drew in a long breath, held it a second, then let it swoosh out. "I've got to go to work."

That brought me straight up in my chair. "Now? Can't you lay off for a trip or take family leave or something?"

He stood. In an abrupt manner worthy of Diane, he said, "I have to go. I can't sit around here and not be able to help her."

"But..." Was he abandoning her? Dropping this in my lap and running off? That wasn't the Dad I knew.

It took two strides for him to reach the door in the cramped office. "She...your mother has moments." He searched for a way to explain. "I call them breaks. That's when she needs me." He ran a hand over his forehead. "I stand in the gap while she pulls herself together. When she does, then it's time for me to leave. Louise will make sure she's fed and rested. All I can do is what I've always done, give her the space she needs."

I jumped up and stepped toward the door but couldn't bring myself to accuse him of running away, though that's what I wanted to do. "What do you want me to do?"

He stopped with his hand wrapped around the doorknob and turned to me, a dark cloud of worry settling on his face. "Find out why he came to kill her so I can protect her from what's next."

11

The office door clicked shut, and I didn't hear Dad's boots retreat down the hall.

I spun around and located Poupon curled on his bed. His eyes focused on me but not with any great concern. "Scared? Of what? Or who? And why is this *my* problem? He's her husband. He should be the one figuring this out."

Poupon blinked slowly, then closed his eyes for a nap.

I grabbed my phone and dialed Louise's number. She didn't answer, and I hadn't expected her to. "Why is it up to me to uncover her past? He's had forty-five years to suss it out."

I paced, a matter of two steps, and turned in the little office. "Like he said, they're my parents. He should be the one figuring this out."

Once upon a time, not even that long ago, I could have discussed this issue with any number of people. My husband, Ted, who, even riddled with narcissistic tendencies, usually came through in a crisis. He loved my family, even my goofy mother. He enjoyed a good puzzle and had a knack for brainstorming. But he wasn't on my lifeline list anymore.

Diane, who wasn't really someone I turned to often, but knowing she wasn't available made me feel the loss.

Sarah, who would listen and sympathize but who didn't have a lot of give-a-damns to spare these days since she had a newborn to stress about.

Oh, let's face it. The only person I really wanted to call was Baxter. He'd talk me through this. Remind me that everyone in my world was safe and that I should be grateful Mom knew how to protect herself. He'd tell me to let Trey take care of the investigation and that Trey would tell us if we needed to worry about someone else coming to harm Mom.

Or would Baxter say any of that? Maybe he'd get involved in the mystery of who the guy was and why he showed up here. Baxter might home in on Mom's secret phone and the mysterious someone she spoke to when she thought no one was around. He might encourage me to go snooping in Mom's studio, where no one ventured unless invited.

"Come on," I said to Poupon.

He opened his eyes, raised his head off his paws, and studied me as if deciding whether I was serious.

I reached over and opened my office door. "Stay here if you want, but who knows when I'll be back."

Dogs can't roll their eyes, but he probably wished he could. He stood and after two steps, lowered his front legs to stretch, gave his back legs one for good measure, and sauntered past me into the hallway.

With Susan on her way back to Lincoln, Mom's Vanagon kept lonely vigil in the parking area next to the house. I let myself into the kitchen, where the smell of cleaning fluid hung in the air. The house seemed to echo with emptiness. Though, in reality, most days it would be silent like this. With all of us kids moved out and Dad on the railroad, it would only be Mom and the ghosts that haunted her.

She'd told me when the house was empty, it filled with ghosts. Maybe they were from her secret past, because I felt only a sad sense of abandonment. My footsteps sounded like hoofbeats as I walked across the kitchen and started down the stairs to her studio. The cleaning smell intensified, but the boys had done a good job eliminating the blood and even Louise's vomit. The studio still contained Mom's work, the trinkets she'd collected, everything that made up her art, but it all felt too tidy. The mysterious energy created by her mayhem seemed contained and subdued. They'd even cleaned off the pottery wheel.

Poupon had followed me to the top of the stairs, but he'd opted to stay in the kitchen. I imagine he smelled more than cleaning fluid.

I thrust open the French doors to the crisp morning. It was another of those brilliant fall days where the sun shouted for attention against a sky of cornflower blue. Bookended by chilly mornings and evenings, these rarefied fall days only numbered a dozen or so every year. They were like gifts to treasure before winter dropped down with wind and gray.

Mom would be somewhere in the country without noise and distraction, probably sitting somewhere sunny, her face turned toward the light. Dad would be on the train, window open, watching the sparkle of light on lakes he passed. And I was standing in the middle of Mom's studio, hands on hips, trying not to envision the man lying in a pool of blood on the concrete floor.

"Okay, what secrets are you hiding?" Still, I didn't move. Living with eight brothers and sisters piled into a small house with two tiny bathrooms, I'd learned early to appreciate privacy. My job often called for me to rummage through people's belongings and lives, but going through my mother's things seemed like breaking a law.

What if she wasn't crazy and someone was really coming for her? If that was the case, I needed to protect her, and the only way to do that was to determine what was going on. And to do that, I needed to search through Mom's things for clues.

The studio had been created long before I came onto the scene. Although Dad had done the initial construction to dig out the backyard to make it a walkout basement and installed the French doors, the interior was all Mom's doing. She'd built the shelves and bricked the space for the kiln, hammered together all the tables and work surfaces. It wasn't a space put together for show. Everything in the room was designed for work. Photos, images torn from magazines, odd bits like leaves, seed pods, dried flowers, and rocks were tacked up or resting on the shelves.

Wide shelves lined the room, some filled with art supplies and tools of her trade. Dozens of pieces in various stages of development crowded most of the space. Mugs, saucers, dishes of every variety from dinner plates to salad bowls. Some glazed and looking ready to ship to one of the galleries that carried her work. The kiln was settled into the far corner lined with bricks up the walls and along the floor. Dust from thousands of projects covered everything except where the boys had scrubbed yesterday.

Two towers on rollers held bright lights that Mom could arrange around her work at a long table with a stool.

So many paintbrushes for someone whose main medium was clay. Stretched canvases stacked in a crevice between a shelf and wall waited for her inspiration. One whole area of the basement contained heavy shipping boxes stacked and ready to be folded and secured with strapping tape. Rolls of bubble wrap and tape, newsprint, and other forms of packaging along with labels. She had a whole manufacturing business going on down here, only requiring her to haul boxes to the post office, a chore she usually relegated to Dad when he was home.

I spent several minutes studying the room and walking along the periphery, bending over and stretching up to see onto the lower and upper shelves. I surveyed the work surfaces and floors. Nothing but supplies and art.

Shoved into a corner away from the door, she'd constructed an office of sorts. She'd sawed an old door in half. A heavy bit of oak, it had a groove outlining a central panel. She'd sanded the truncated edge and set the top on a sawhorse of her own construction and a two-drawer file cabinet. A cheap desk lamp with an adjustable arm lit up the surface she used as a desk. She kept a rickety secretary chair on rollers in front. I'd never paid much attention to it, but now I wondered why she hadn't made a more comfortable office space.

I'd never questioned anything about this side of Mom. The studio and her work represented the worst aspects of sibling rivalry. It took her away from us. Not only when she was in her heated fit of work but also for days after as she moved around in a mood so low it seemed she didn't know or care if she had children. She'd come back to us eventually. She'd share insights and humor. And then the cycle would start again.

Everything felt sad and tight inside me. A door slid closed on the image of me at six years old, standing at the top of the basement stairs, feeling the wet heat of tears sliding down my face and Glenda taking my hand to lead me away. I didn't want to remember how Mom had let me down that day or what she'd forgotten.

It didn't matter. Mom had done her best. She loved us. There was nothing to be gained from holding on to the times she'd disappointed me. I was lucky to have Glenda and my other brothers and sisters. And Dad. Even if he was gone a lot.

Working. Because the railroad required you to show up no matter what was going on in your personal life. The railroad provided one of the best jobs around, and Dad needed a good job to take care of us. I never questioned that going to work might have been an escape for Dad, a way to avoid the chaos and responsibility of a houseful of children and a dysfunctional wife.

Until today.

"You're an adult. You survived your childhood. Honestly, it wasn't a bad way to grow up. You had family and love, plenty to eat, a safe place to sleep." My voice startled me. Sure, I frequently talked to Poupon, which was a lot like talking to myself. But it seemed weird to give myself a lecture in the middle of Mom's studio. Living alone might be getting to me.

Not having Baxter to talk to was probably more the problem. I kept that realization inside rather than declare my loneliness to the gravy boats and casserole dishes.

The secretary chair wobbled a little as I sat and snugged up to the desk. The top file drawer was a mass of loose papers. It shouldn't surprise me that Mom's filing system was more improv jazz as opposed to a classical symphony. I pulled out shipping receipts and invoices for supplies. Check stubs were tossed in among the pandemonium of paper, and I was shocked to see the totals. It seemed Mom was making a good deal of income.

Could that guy be after her for money? Where did Mom deposit those payments? Did Dad know how much money she made and where she kept it? I wouldn't be able to ask him until he returned in forty-eight hours or so.

With heaping handfuls, I pulled the papers from her drawer and dropped them on the desk. The empty drawer gaped at me, nothing more to reveal. I shoved it closed and jerked open the bottom drawer.

This one contained torn newspaper clippings, maybe niblets she kept for inspiration. They seemed random topics from nature articles and climate change to political rants. Maybe this drawer more than anything showed how her mind worked...or didn't. No form or function, no organization, just impulse and inspiration. If this drawer was any example, I'd say we were lucky she managed life as well as she did.

I scooped up the miscellany and was holding the handful over an empty spot on the desk when something heavy shifted and slipped out, landing with a thunk on the desk.

I stared at it for a second, then tossed the paper in my hands back into the drawer. The phone sat on the desk like a rattler coiling up and ready to strike.

"Come on." I let out an irritated breath. "It's probably an old phone she tossed into a drawer when she got a new one." Except it looked more like a burner phone than an obsolete model. And *stop talking to yourself!*

I gripped the device and flipped it open. The face lit up. Fully charged, like no old phone would be. It took a few seconds to study it and find the recent call button. One number. Over and over. Last call two days ago. Area code 773.

Susan was right. And when she found out, there'd be no living with her.

I hit redial and waited. After one ring, a man picked up and said, "Thank God. I worried when you didn't call yesterday. Are you okay?"

Stunned, I struggled with what to say. *Who are you* was my first question. But if I opened with that, he'd know I wasn't Mom. If I started with "She's okay," it might give him ease to speak. Whatever I would eventually have settled on, I waited too long to decide. The two-second silence must have spooked him, because he hung up.

I dialed again, and he picked up but didn't say anything. I waited and he did, too. "Hello?" I finally said.

The line went dead. Another try rang ten times before I gave up. No voicemail.

I needed to ask Mom about this and the man on the other end. I called Louise, and when her voicemail answered, I nearly shouted. "Tell Mom she needs to call me. Or better yet, tell me where you are because I need to talk to her."

Then I dialed Dad and was immediately shunted to voicemail. "You need to tell me where Mom is." I hung up in frustration before giving him any more details.

Damn it. I strode from the studio into the dazzling sunshine and calm day. I stabbed at my phone again, and Trey picked up right away. After hellos, I said, "I need to have a phone number traced."

He made a smacking sound, and when he spoke with a full mouth, I realized it was lunchtime. "Sure. Can't you get that done?"

"I need it immediately and thought you might have better connections."

There was a crinkly sound, like maybe a burger wrapper, and my stomach gave a sudden rumble.

"Used to. But not anymore. My guy worked at Verizon, but he's at Best Buy now. Someone at a phone company can probably get what you need, but if you go through the official way, it'll take a long time. With all your brothers and sisters, doesn't someone have a friend at a phone company?"

My stomach clenched.

"Who's the number for?" He sounded as if the words came through a full mouth, and again I thought about lunch.

I didn't want to tell him about Mom's phone because I had no idea what it meant. This probably had nothing to do with the intruder yesterday, anyway.

"Checking up on my sister. I think she's got a new boyfriend she's not talking about." Wow. The lie slipped out, maybe not with ease, but without too much trouble. I was getting way too good at this.

Trey's laughter barked through the line. "You're the worst liar I've ever heard. But it's okay. You'd tell me if I could help."

He couldn't see me color, but my face burned. "Sorry. Thanks for understanding."

More paper rustled. "Good luck."

When we disconnected, I wandered up to the kitchen and rummaged in the fridge for lunch. Lucky for me that Dad lived here and did most of the grocery shopping. Mom survived on smoothies and other vegan delights. I scored some thin sliced ham and cheese for a sandwich and even discovered Dad's stash of chips. A quick glance in the freezer netted a bag of chocolate chip cookies no doubt delivered by Louise and deposited there, untouched, by Mom.

While I stood next to the butcher block in the center of the kitchen and chomped on my sandwich, I thought about tracing the number on Mom's phone. This silly, hopeful notion tickled the base of my spine.

I tossed bits of my sandwich to Poupon and watched him catch them in his jaws, showing more animation than his usual regal boredom.

Baxter had all the resources to help me. He had a detective on the payroll. Even if Baxter had let him go after Carly had resurfaced, Baxter's news organization had researchers thick as flies on a carcass. Tracking down a phone number would be nothing for them. Finding the identity of the caller was a legitimate need, a real reason to contact Baxter. Not just some lame excuse to hear his voice.

But, oh, I wanted to hear his voice.

I indulged in a daydream. Baxter's personal phone ringing. He'd be sky-high in his Chicago office building of glass and steel, in deep concentration at his computer. At first, he wouldn't register the interruption. Then he'd realize he hadn't heard that phone ring in weeks. His face would freeze, damming up the surge of emotion. While it rang again, he'd fight with himself. Should he answer it? Should he let it go?

We'd grown so close over the last year and half. I knew he'd let me into his life and had come to depend on my presence as much as I had his. He'd told me he loved me. And God knows I loved him. Losing him left a crater in my life, and I believed it left him equally empty.

He'd stare at the phone, maybe with a slight frown. His amber eyes, so much like a lion's, would show the pain I'd caused but also light with a tiny spark of hope. It had been long enough that he'd have learned how much he wanted me in his life.

On the third ring, he'd finally admit to himself that he at least needed to see if we could find our way back to each other, and he'd reach for the phone.

And my heart surged with the romantic fantasy of our first words. Our tangled apologies. Our relief at speaking and reconnecting.

I even reached for my phone and opened my favorites list.

Then I came to my senses. I remembered the last time he'd turned those remarkable eyes on me. The look so hard and cold and impenetrable, it'd buckled my knees.

I'd hurt him, and Baxter wasn't the kind of man who forgave easily. Or at all.

This wasn't the first fantasy that had swept me along, like falling into a rushing river. At first it seems exciting and fun, but then you're dashed into the sharp rocks and your flesh is shredded and you're left gasping for air, barely alive. Somehow, I had to purge all thoughts of Baxter from my brain, or I'd slip under the current and never survive.

I washed my dishes and wiped down the butcher block. With Baxter out of the picture and Trey unable to help, who did that leave?

To be honest, I'd come up with the solution when Trey had mentioned a brother or sister with a friend at a phone company. But I'd turned somersaults around the answer, hoping I'd come up with an alternative. The more I thought, the bigger the lump in my chest grew until the ham sandwich dropped to the bottom of my stomach in a hard ball of dough.

Damn it, Dad. Do your own dirty work. My fingers drummed the counter next to my phone, and I scowled at it. This went on for a few more seconds before I grabbed it. "Quit being a baby."

I entered Diane's number and waited. It rang five times and gave me the curt Diane voicemail. "I'm not available. Leave a message."

I hung up and dialed again. And once more. Might as well stop. I'd never out-stubborn her. I could call one of the other Foxes and tell them to have Diane call me. But then I'd have to tell them why, and I didn't want to share that I was investigating our mother on behalf of our father. And it wouldn't work, anyway. Diane wouldn't call me.

It took a few minutes to find the number for her bank and navigate the phone system of automated and live customer care to finally get to Diane's assistant. "Is this Diane Fox's office?" I tried to sound as if I barely controlled my panic.

He sounded young and impatient, perfect for Diane. "Yes. I'm Patrick, her assistant. How can I help you?"

Breathy, I said, "It's her daughter, Kimmy. She's fallen and hit her head. We're not on the school premises, so I don't have Kimmy's emergency contact, and she's too confused to recite her mother's number. I called the bank and hoped I could get through."

Now I had his attention. It took a real monster not to understand a child emergency. "Of course. One moment."

In half a moment Diane's voice demanded, "What's happened?"

She sounded frightened, and I felt a tinge of guilt. Until I'd heard her wail of pain at seeing her dead ex-husband, I hadn't credited Diane with a wealth of emotion. At least, not the kind that involved love and nurturing. She had plenty of the driving competitor kind.

"Kimmy's fine." That out of the way, I plunged forward, knowing I had less than a second to jar Diane enough she wouldn't hang up. "Mom's in trouble, and Dad needs us to help."

"You asshole. How dare you scare the shit out of me like that. I didn't answer your goddamned calls because I don't want to talk to you ever again." But she hadn't hung up.

"Dad thinks someone is after Mom to kill her, and I need you to call that neighbor of yours, the one who works at Verizon."

She didn't say anything, and I pictured her in her office. Polished bamboo floors, glass desk, a bank of windows with the Rocky Mountain view that would distract mere mortals to the point they'd never get anything done. In my mind, she wore a black pencil skirt and silky white blouse, her pumps just shy of evening wear. If the image wasn't exactly right, it was close enough to how I'd seen her when I stopped at her office once.

She let out a long-suffering breath. "What the hell are you talking about?"

I had her. "There's no reason to tell the rest of them about this." Meaning we wouldn't spill this to our brothers and sisters.

She didn't hate secrets as much as I did, so I didn't expect resistance. "Fine. Now what?"

I let her in on everything I knew. She'd never help me otherwise.

She didn't seem to balk at the idea of someone wanting to off our mother. Not for the first time, I wondered about Diane's involvement with the group who called themselves the Legacy.

A collection of prep school grads had formed two generations ago and used their considerable wealth to extricate Nazi resisters in WWII. Made up of the descendants of those first members, the Legacy still did similar work. Carly's grandfather, and then her father, had been involved. As was Diane's ex-husband.

That thought made me go cold. The Legacy had sucked Carly in and exposed her to danger, nearly getting her killed. I suspected Diane knew more about them than she admitted.

"Poor Mom," she said. "Can you imagine being incarcerated with Louise looking after you?"

"Maybe she'll get Mom to eat and rest. She's got a better shot than the rest of us. And Louise must be in her glory." It was almost a conversation, and she hadn't said she hated me. I counted that as a win.

"You know I hate you." Said with a frosty voice colder than the wind on the top of Mount Everest.

When would I learn the devastation of hope? From now on, I would assume the worst. "But you'll help me."

"No. I wouldn't throw you a rope if you were drowning. But I'll help Mom and Dad. What's the number?"

I recited it, and she hung up without goodbye. I could only hope she'd get back to me.

12

I spent the afternoon doing what county sheriffs do in the Sandhills. I drove up to the high school and watched football practice for a few minutes and chatted with a few of the old-timers who enjoyed the afternoon in the stands watching the young men batter each other and commenting on the chances of beating Bryant High School at homecoming in two weeks. With the brilliant fall sunshine highlighting the yellow leaves of the cottonwoods and bringing out the deep green of the grass, there were worse places to keep a finger on the pulse of Grand County.

Bill Hardy needed a vehicle inspection on the new pickup he'd bought in South Dakota, and we spent a while discussing last summer's hay crop and how the spring rains had helped. We added the obligatory lament about the Husker offensive line not holding up like the good old days and ended on the ever-hopeful note that this was a building year and as soon as the new coach's recruits got acclimated, we'd be on top.

Poupon and I had just settled into my office when Diane's call came in.

"I got the address and the guy's name." Guess we didn't bother with greetings now.

I grabbed a pen. "Thanks. What have you got?"

"Two seats on a flight to Chicago that leaves at eight o'clock."

I stammered, trying to figure out what she meant. "Tonight? Flight? Two?"

"Jesus, Kate. If this guy means something to Mom, we need to see him. And I don't trust you to get it right. If you go alone—I don't know—he might end up dead."

Ouch. No point in reiterating that I didn't kill Vince. I glanced at the wall clock. "That's about five hours. It's a three-hour drive to Denver from here."

"Then you'd better get started. I'll text you the flight information."

My chair swiveled and slammed against the desk when I jumped up. This must be how Diane ran her department. She took charge, issued orders, and expected obedience. Since I couldn't come up with a good reason to slow down or back off, I simply said, "Okay."

"Try to pack something that doesn't make you look like a field hand." And she hung up.

I glanced at Poupon and quickly ran through his options. He usually stayed at Mom's if I was away. "Jeremy it is."

Ted didn't balk when I asked him to handle sheriff emergencies in Grand County. He didn't ask for details. That meant either he felt he owed me for taking care of his baby when Roxy went AWOL in August, or he was storing up a favor for later. Knowing Ted, I'd pay for taking off this time.

After the tornado turbulence of getting ready and heading out, the three-hour drive to Denver was uneventful. Parking the car and getting to the terminal was all just a matter of the ticking clock and wondering if I'd make it through security on time.

Managing the ticket kiosk stymied me. I'd have figured it out, but a helpful attendant stepped in and tapped the screen quicker than I read the prompts. While I waited for my ticket to print, I glanced up to see a sleek, well-coiffed Diane glide by in navy pants and clicking heels of only two inches. A small suitcase rolled behind her as if controlled by magic. With my ticket in hand, I hurried after her, duffel hanging from my shoulder and banging against my hip.

Of course, I didn't catch her as she sashayed through the VIP line and I joined the rest of the plebians in the cattle yard security line. By the time I made it to our gate, she sat at a tall counter with her tablet open, a steaming cup of coffee at her elbow and her fingers tapping furiously. She spared a flick of her eyes in my direction, and the goalpost lines between her eyes deepened slightly. As Grandma Ardith would say, she'd better be careful about making that face or it would freeze that way. Diane would definitely not be happy with permanent frown lines. Of course, she'd buy smooth skin if that happened.

The loudspeaker called first class boarding, and Diane snapped her tablet closed and stashed it in a leather satchel. My ticket had me boarding with a zone number so high it practically matched my age. That gave me enough time to zip to a shop and grab a cold sandwich for the flight. I was sure Diane had enjoyed a fine dinner at home before getting a ride to the front doors of the terminal.

A couple of hours later, stomach unsettled by a bulky sandwich, nerves, and general travel hubbub, I was surprised to find Diane waiting for me when I disembarked. I wasn't the last person off the plane but pert near it. She focused on my forehead as if still denying my existence. "I booked hotels near where the caller lives. Some southwest suburb, so we might as well share a ride." She spared a disdainful sweep of my jeans, lightweight hiking boots, and cotton sweater.

"Who's the caller? Where does he live? You know it's a man?" I tried to keep up with Diane. Even though she wore heels that somehow clacked loud enough to be heard in the busy terminal and I wore comfy boots, her long legs gave her the stride advantage. Plus, her bag seemed to float after her, like a fluffy and obedient cloud, while my bag weighed on my shoulders.

Diane ignored me, and I had no choice but to follow. She didn't offer any conversation or answers while we waited for our rideshare, and when she told the driver the address, she pulled out her phone and dialed.

She started her conversation without preamble, obviously demanding after-hours work. Her employees must hate her. "Get the Abrams files to Dan tonight. He's got some thoughts on that. And finish the quarterly earnings report for Amber by no later than noon. I'll check in before then."

She kept firing orders, and the driver had shot out of the airport congestion onto an interstate with as many lanes as Fox siblings. I decided to take care of my own pressing business.

Jeremy answered on the third ring. "Jeez, Kate. I just got to sleep."

I'd lost track of time. It was an hour earlier in Nebraska, but that still made it after ten. "I'm sorry. Just checking up on Poupon. Sometimes he doesn't eat when I'm gone."

The bed squeaked, and I heard a soft patting that sounded like a hand on a fluffy side. "I dribbled hamburger grease on top, and he gobbled it down. Isn't that right, big fella?"

"You aren't letting him sleep on your bed?" That kind of privilege would ruin him.

Jeremy sounded sleepy. "My house, my rules."

Before Jeremy's brush with some really bad folks last summer, finding him at home with space in his bed for a dog would have been a fluke. While he'd had a nose for trouble, and I didn't miss bailing him out, I kind of missed his good-hearted mischief. I hoped he'd find his fun again soon.

Warehouses, residential neighborhoods, retail areas spun like a crazy kaleidoscope of light and color and seemed to stretch into infinity. I pressed my cheek against the cold window and looked up. As expected, no stars made it through the man-made illumination. I already missed the Sandhills sky.

By the time I'd hung up, it was clear Diane no longer spoke to Patrick or whoever she'd peppered with her demands. Her voice had a warm tone I'd never heard from her. "He said what?" She gave a throaty laugh. "You didn't let him get away with that." She listened and laughed again. "That's my girl. Let me talk to Karl. Love you."

An excited voice I recognized as my nephew's threaded from her phone. Diane's whole body had morphed, somehow grown softer, sunk into the leather car seat. Her eyes had an uncharacteristic glint, and her lips seemed fuller and even turned into a smile. She looked so much like Dad in that moment. "An A. I knew you could do it. That hard work paid off."

She blinked and caught me staring at her and stiffened. Those lines reappeared between her eyes. She spoke quietly, but some of that honeyed tone had hardened. I hoped Karl didn't notice. "You both should be in bed now. Tell Ingrid I'm sorry I woke you up and I won't do that again. I wanted to hear your voices. Good night, now. Love you."

She dropped her phone in her red leather tote, the kind mere sheriffs or ranch hands couldn't afford and had no use for. She turned her head to look out the window.

I missed seeing Kimmy and Karl. It had only been two months, and sometimes we'd gone longer than that without being together. But now I knew they were off-limits to me, and it bothered me. "Sounds like the kids are doing well."

Diane snapped her head to me. "Of course they're not doing well. Their father was just murdered. They're a mess. We're all a mess."

"Maybe we should talk about this."

In the dark of the car, her eyes seemed to shoot deadly rounds at me. "I'm not talking to you any more than necessary."

"Come on. We can't keep this up. It's upsetting the whole family. We need to find our peace." I didn't add that I felt as betrayed by her as she obviously felt by me. Once I listened to her grievance, there would be time for me to have my say.

With a voice like a blade, she said, "Don't talk to me about family. You destroyed mine. As far as we're concerned, you're no longer my sister."

Even if she didn't have the power to sever our blood ties, her declaration sliced so deep I was surprised not to see my innards splattered over the back seat. It took effort to keep my breath even. There was nothing to do but let the ride continue in awkward stillness.

Even the driver didn't break the brittle silence over the half-hour journey to suburbs west of the city. Only a short way from exiting the interstate, he pulled into a well-lit but somewhat shoddy Motel 6. It surprised me Diane would go slumming like this.

I climbed out to a night gone surprising cold. I hadn't pulled my down coat from my duffel and was now regretting it. The driver had the trunk open, and I reached in for my bag and stepped back while he slammed the trunk on Diane's shiny roller bag.

Instead of saying anything to him, I walked to Diane's window. She still sat with her seat belt on. I tapped on the window, and she ignored that, so I opened the door, surprised she hadn't locked it. "You're not getting out?"

With her chin lifted and barely acknowledging me with a sideways glance, she said, "Hell, no. I figured this is what you could afford. I'm staying at the Marriott a few blocks further down. You can meet me there at seven, and we'll go check this guy out."

13

I didn't sleep much. Obligation to family and maintaining simple dignity churned until my stomach ached and I got up to check my travel bag for antacid. There wasn't any, of course. The *should* told me to do everything in my power to reconcile with Diane. The *want* urged me to walk away and not compromise and grovel. I had plenty of sisters, so losing one wouldn't be the end of the world. This was where I ran smack into a tangle of barbed wire, because I had already lost a sister, leaving a hole in my world wider than Death Valley.

As usual, worrying about Carly took up its share of dark hours. Since I wasn't sleeping, I might as well fret about her, too. I wanted nothing more for my niece than a few years of rowdy college experiences. Maybe finding a nice guy who treated her well, a career passion, some direction that would drive her far away from the Legacy and intrigue. I feared—with good reason—she now had a taste of adventure and danger and she'd crave that high-octane lifestyle.

And that brought me back to Diane, who seemed to encourage that path for Carly. Okay, I didn't know that Diane and Carly were in touch. But Diane sure hadn't done anything to stop Carly from getting involved in the Legacy. The real burr under my saddle was that Diane knew Carly was working with the Legacy and hadn't told me.

And then I was back being mad at Diane and thinking she ought to stay in Denver in her high-class world and leave us lowly brothers and sisters alone. But I didn't have the power or the right to exile her from the clan.

And if I had any chance of relaxing with all of that going on, it didn't escape my notice that I was in the same city as Baxter. Where was his penthouse apartment? Downtown, of course, and all I'd seen of that was the bright lights and the endless black of the lake as we'd approached O'Hare for landing. I'd been excited by the view but didn't say a word about it because Diane hated me.

And I hated her. And...yep, not a good night.

Made worse because by the time I finally got to sleep, I sank so deep that I was late waking up.

I tromped into the Marriott parking lot feeling like a cold bowl of chili, my bag whapping my hip with every step. I wore my down jacket to ward off the brisk air, but by the looks of the cloudless sky, once the sun climbed high, it would be a beautiful day. I was struck by the proliferation of trees. In the Sandhills, trees were hard to come by, and we nurtured them. They got water delivered by the bucketful and were tended to as if they were our children. Here, trees seemed like an invading army. Beautiful with their leaves turning red and gold, but somewhat intimidating and claustrophobic to this plains dweller.

The constant flow of cars on the four-laned street kept an acrid odor of exhaust filling my nose. The number of lanes, the busyness of the strip, all the businesses and concrete amazed me. I didn't know the name of this town or suburb or whatever they called it, but it seemed as crowded and hectic as any downtown I'd ever seen. All of it created a swirl of anxiety in me, and I craved the sweet smell of clover flowing to my front porch and the quiet call of a mourning dove. Suburbia wasn't for me.

Motel 6 didn't have a complimentary breakfast or even a mini Mr. Coffee machine in the room. My stomach growled, and just because my head didn't ache didn't mean I wasn't desperate for a heaping dose of caffeine.

Before I made it to the Marriott lobby door, a horn honked, and an engine roared behind me. I jumped out of the way for a sleek gray BMW to slam to a stop and the passenger window to slide down.

Diane growled at me. Her artful makeup emphasized her eyes and smoothed her skin without drawing attention to itself. If I hadn't seen Diane without makeup and didn't know every contour of her face, I wouldn't have noticed the magic she'd created to transform herself from ordinary mortal to a powerful woman unaccustomed to the word *no*. She slid sunglasses onto her face. "You're late."

"I had to wait for the traffic light before I could cross—"

"Get in. We don't have time for excuses." She stared ahead, large sunglasses shading the rising sun.

I tipped my head toward the lobby doors. "Nice digs."

She eyed the hotel with a curled lip. "I normally stay at the Four Seasons on the Magnificent Mile. But for one night I made this work. It saves some driving."

I stashed my bag in the back seat, which was where I was sure Diane would prefer I stash myself as well. But I slid onto the buttery leather next to her and clicked my seat belt. "Can you hit a drive-through? I need coffee and breakfast."

She took off from the parking lot, cutting too close to an oncoming car for my taste. "I assumed you'd take care of that before we started."

I didn't put an effort into civility. "My hotel didn't have room service, so you'll have to give me five minutes for a McMuffin or you're going to see me turn homicidal. And you're the only one within strangling distance, so..."

She cut across traffic to the left-turn lane, earning several honks to which she muttered expletives nasty enough to make a pirate jump ship. I was glad for my seat belt.

"*I* managed to make myself presentable." A clear reference to how she considered my appearance. "*And* eat breakfast, *and* rent a car. Maybe you should get up earlier."

"And maybe you should have booked me in a quieter hotel." No way I would tell her the reason I slept in was because I'd been fretting all night, not because the riffraff had kept me awake.

She tapped the wheel while we took our turn in the drive-through line. One good thing about an urban area, on a weekday morning, they knew how to keep the lines moving. Despite Diane acting as if we'd wasted half the day, we were in and out in less than five minutes.

My coffee was too hot to drink, so I launched into my sandwich.

Apparently, my lowlife ways finally got to Diane, and she couldn't hold it in. "That stuff is going to kill you. The fat, salt, preservatives, carbs. It's death in a box."

With my mouth full, I answered her. "But it's delicious. And fast. I don't eat it every day. And...the box is recyclable."

She navigated through the traffic, changing lanes, making turns, as if she'd been driving in Chicago all her life. Even allowing for the high-tech GPS on the dash, I grudgingly admitted she was impressive. Like the airport ticket kiosk, I could have managed the traffic, but having someone else take it on seemed more efficient.

I sat back and inhaled the scent of my coffee since it was still flesh-peeling hot. "Where are we going?"

She pursed her lips and kept her focus on the three lanes of highway we sped down.

"Come on. You may hate me—"

"I do."

"But we're in this together, and you've got to let me know about this call-er." So many other civilized reasons why I shouldn't resort to violence, but needing information was the only one that kept me from punching her in the throat.

She held on for another second. From where I sat, I could see behind her wide sunglasses. Her eyes stayed on the road, but she squinted in supreme irritation. She whipped to the right, then into the next lane and slapped on her turn signal, jerking us off the highway and braking hard at a light, getting ready for a left turn. "As you can see if you look." She indicated the GPS on the dash. "Not far. I looked at it on Google Earth. It's a crappy neighborhood, and the house fits right in."

Diane always could make me feel stupid.

"What do you know about him?" I asked.

The light changed, and she slammed the gas pedal, pulling enough Gs to knock me into the back of my seat. I didn't think she needed to drive in such a herky-jerky fashion, but I supposed she was proving some point. Maybe seeing how uncomfortable or terrified she could make me.

She inserted the BMW into an opening in the traffic flow I wouldn't have tried. "Marty Kaufman. He has a hot dog cart downtown, so that's why I wanted to catch him early, before he leaves for work." She said it with an accusatory snarl to make sure I understood I'd caused needless delay.

Trees with bright leaves waved as we sped down a street with twice as many lanes as Nebraska's busiest interstate. "It's not even eight. I'm sure we're early enough. You know, if you'd have let me know, I could have run his name and seen if there's any history on him."

She let out a raspberry. "I have his name and address. We'll figure out the rest when we see him. That's why we're here."

Inside, I muttered that, as a cop, I could have gathered enough information to be prepared. "You could have come alone. Why bring me?"

She threw me to the side with a sharp left down a wide two-lane avenue. I'd need to monitor the GPS to avoid seat belt bruises.

"It's not good to go into a blind situation alone. I figured you could be useful. If this guy is a danger to Mom, then it won't hurt to have someone to act as a shield. You know, take the first bullet."

Right. I braced myself against the dash so when she gunned it through the next left, I was ready. We wound our way through a neighborhood of cookie-cutter ranch homes built close together with postage stamp front yards. A few of the yards looked cared for with flower borders and raked lawns recently mowed. Most seemed half-heartedly attended to, with browning grass, falling leaves piling up, junk accumulating on porches, and a general state of neglect.

Diane followed the well-modulated directions from the GPS genie and pulled up in front of a one-story, aluminum-sided bungalow. It wasn't the worst of the houses in the neighborhood, didn't have trash and plastic toys rotting in the grass, but no attempt had been made to weed the flower bed in front of the cement-block porch. The house might have once been white, or beige, or possibly a mint green, but now it seemed a faded combination with dents and slashes in the siding.

The sun climbed higher and kept its promise of a glorious fall day. I was glad for my jacket since the morning carried a brisk warning that summer was a fading memory. Trees lined the street, in the early throes of shedding their leaves but getting after it enough to sprinkle the ground with yellow and brown. We might be in a residential area, but my nose still twitched with hints of exhaust and a general sense of man-made life. Nothing like the earthy tones of Stryker Lake and the hills of grass at home.

Diane and I made our way up the driveway, passing a rusted Toyota 4Runner that had started out navy blue but now was as faded as a worn pair of Levi's. The cracked dash showed yellowing foam, and dirt and trash littered the interior.

Up and down the street, neighbors bustled in their morning routines. Kids ran to cars, garage doors rose and descended, cars eased past. No one seemed to notice two women climbing from a fancy BMW.

Without hesitation, Diane marched up the three porch steps and jabbed the doorbell. A few strides behind her, I was irritated she hadn't given me a second to stand with her and maybe brace myself for whatever opened the door.

When no one answered immediately, Diane poked the ringer again, twice for good measure.

I had one foot on the lowest step when the door whisked open and a gravelly voice demanded, "What?"

Undaunted, Diane spit back, "Are you Marty Kaufman?"

I climbed another step.

A slight hesitation as if he considered whether to answer. "Yes. Is this the neighborhood watch? No. Selling magazines or wrapping paper so your kid gets a trip to Europe on me? No. Petition to put a stop sign up the street? Again, no."

She might have come from the third-least populated county in the contiguous United States, smack in the middle of cowboy country, but she sounded as if she'd been spawned on the seventh green of America's most elite country club. "No, Mr. Kaufman, that's not why we're here."

I climbed the last step and stood next to Diane.

Slightly stooped, he'd probably cut a fine figure before age had thinned his hair and turned it a coarse gray and the years had tugged at his shoulders. Jeans bagged on his thin frame, and a faded Grateful Dead T-shirt finished the look of a hippie gone to seed. He frowned at Diane. "Whatever it is, I'm not buying, so—" His gaze slid to me, and he made a choking noise.

Diane jerked her head in my direction, then back to him.

He stared at me, eyes wide enough I noted they were a deep brown, the kind of eyes that would draw a person in and hold them there. His mouth worked as if he struggled for words.

Diane's voice was the equivalent of a finger snap. "Mr. Kaufman. We need to talk to you."

The way he looked at me gave me chills. Spooked, for sure, but more than that. He seemed to know me and was shocked to find me on his doorstep. I resembled Mom, probably looked an awful lot like her when she was younger. That must be the reason for his reaction.

He blinked and studied me a moment longer, then slowly focused on Diane. He lost the junkyard-dog growl and spoke as if afraid of the words. "What is it?"

Diane seemed to appreciate his response and gave a curt nod. "May we come in?"

He drew himself up, losing much of that old-man slouch. His chin came up, and he sounded strong. "I'd rather you didn't."

There you go. He'd shut us down and wasn't going to tell us anything. I opened my mouth to soften him up a bit, see if we couldn't get him to tell us why his number was on Mom's hidden phone.

Diane thrust a foot onto the threshold and pushed open the door.

Obviously not expecting that and completely unprepared for the force that was Diane, Marty Kaufman stumbled backward.

Diane marched past him into the shadows.

Not to get left behind, I leapt after Diane, shoving into the house while Marty struggled to lift his jaw off the ground and slam the door behind us.

His house smelled like withering apathy: odors of cooking meals without spice or flavor, musty air when no one cared enough to open the windows to the autumn sunshine.

My appearance might have thrown him temporarily, but he was back full force now. "What do you think you're doing? Get out of my house."

The bungalow had little to recommend it, as far as I could see. The front door opened into a tiny living room. A brown shag carpet, maybe not original with the house but installed not long into its life, gave everything a dingy, dark feel. A doorway to the right likely led to a kitchen, shut off from the rest of the house, nothing like the open feel of houses built a couple of decades later. A narrow hallway led in the other direction. Heavy drapes were pulled across what looked to be a sliding door into the backyard.

The furniture was equally shabby and about what you'd expect from a bachelor with little means and no interest in home décor. Serviceable and threadbare, a little messy, and the kind of almost-clean smell that could use a good dose of Febreze.

Diane spun to face him. "You've been calling our mother, Marguerite Myers. Why?"

He opened his mouth a split second before he started speaking, clearly readying himself for the lie. "Who? I haven't called anyone."

Accustomed to doing the talking, Diane didn't wait for me to jump in. "You're lying, Mr. Kaufman. *Marty.*"

I studied the room. Nearly as small as my tidy house, Marty's living room was crammed with books and stacks of newspapers and magazines that seemed out of sync with the digital age, though a grime-smeared laptop peeked from under a pile of newspapers. A coffee table, end table, and one corner of the couch were buried several layers deep with papers, books, notebooks with handwritten pages of crabbed writing, along with a collection of coffee mugs and print-smudged drinking glasses with various levels of liquids of different shades.

Not looking cowed by Diane, his eyebrows formed two dark peaks, like a child's drawing of distant birds in flight. He looked as if he wanted to spew words at Diane, but he clamped his mouth closed a moment before growling, "You've no right to be in my house."

Diane folded her arms across her chest and thrust her chin at him. She showed no sign of weakness. "I'm not debating rights here, *Marty.*" The way she kept emphasizing his name set me on edge, and I assumed it was designed to throw him off-kilter. No wonder Diane had climbed to the heights of a competitive field. "I'm here to find out what kind of threat you are to my mother."

A couple of paintings hung on his walls. They seemed at odds with the careless and worn style. These weren't something bought at Sears or Bed Bath & Beyond. They were distinct works of art.

He rounded Diane and stepped toward her as if herding us toward the door. "I don't know your mother, and I'm no threat to anyone." I had to hand it to Marty Kaufman—anyone who could hold his own against Diane deserved a badge of courage.

Despite Marty Kaufman crowding close, Diane gave no indication she intended to leave. "We know you've called her. Why?"

A rickety bookshelf filled the few feet of wall space from the end of the drapes to the corner of the room. I stepped closer to read a few of the titles crammed onto the shelves and stacked on top of other books. Even though a good-sized TV monitor was perched on a low table against the wall opposite the couch, obviously, this guy was a reader. A quick scan of spines showed mostly nonfiction on every topic from the conspiracy of Monsanto to take over third-world countries to global warming, the evil of the military industrial complex, biographies of world leaders, and heavy history tomes.

All of that seemed scary enough, like the kind of literature you'd find in the Unabomber's Montana cabin along with pages of his lunatic manifesto. But from the corner where I stood in front of the bookcase, I had a view down the hall and into the doorway of a cramped bedroom. One bedside table barely fit between the wall and the slice of bed visible. As opposed to the living room, where every surface was cluttered, one single item rested on the bedside table. It stood about a foot and a half tall, and the familiarity dinged at me. At first, I didn't understand what it was, and then the knowledge seeped in. When I finally understood, my heart thundered, and I sucked in a quick breath. We needed to get out of there.

Frustration vibrated off Marty Kaufman, but unless he shoved Diane, he didn't have a way to get her to leave. "If you're so convinced your mother is talking to someone, why not ask her?"

"Let's go," I said to Diane. Even though I tried to sound decisive, they didn't acknowledge me.

Diane didn't actually step toward him, but she seemed to expand and glower at him. "I'm asking you now, *Marty*. Who are you to Marguerite Myers?"

His face reddened, and those eyebrows suddenly dipped, like diving birds. The air charged, and it seemed possible he'd start swinging. "You need to leave."

"Diane," I said, my tone firm, making it clear it was time to beat cleats.

Diane added an arrogant tip to her chin. "Maybe I should call the cops to see what they have to say."

He laughed, but I'd detected a flash of fear at Diane's bluster. "Go ahead. I'll tell them how you forced your way into my house with crazy accusations about me harassing some woman in Nebraska I've never met."

I stomped to the door and flung it open to the brisk morning and the golden sunshine, a relief from the bleak house. "Come on, Diane."

She hesitated and leaned into him. "I'm coming back, *Marty*. If you don't want real trouble involving the IRS, I suggest you tell us what you know. Don't think this is an idle threat."

I had no doubt Diane had the power to sic the IRS on anyone and make them suffer, even if they were model taxpayers. He probably felt the sincerity of her threat.

She stepped back but kept eye contact. "*Marty.*"

A queen, complete with gem-studded crown and ermine cape, could not have exhibited more flair than Diane parading out of the living room and down the front porch steps. Head high, shoulders thrown back, she glided to the car and into the driver's seat.

Like any lesser minion, I scrambled after her.

She had the car in reverse and wheels rolling before I could slam my door and click my belt.

Without a word, she pulled around the corner, wound through the neighborhood, turned onto the busy street, and within a half block, eased into the parking lot of The Home Depot. She stopped in a place at the rear of the lot and shut the car off.

Her face had lost all color. A stream of air pushed from her lungs and rushed out of her open mouth as if she'd held it for a decade, and she slumped, looking like a balloon deflating. "Fuck, fuck, fuck."

14

I hadn't expected this reaction from the Queen of Cool. Without thinking, I reached out and flattened my palm on the base of her neck to show support. It felt clammy against my skin.

She flinched and shrugged me off, giving me the same combative gaze she'd blasted at Marty Kaufman. "You don't touch me. Ever."

Stung, I dropped my hand into my lap. "Kind of a scary guy."

She shook her head, color coming back to her pale face. "I honestly thought he was going to kill me. Chop me up and feed me to a woodchipper."

Either she thought I'd stand by and watch, or she figured he'd kill me too, but she didn't care enough to mention it. "Wow. That's dark."

"You thought he was Mr. Rogers?" she spat at me.

I couldn't help a smidge of a smile. "Maybe not super welcoming, but he wasn't going to murder us."

Her look of disdain burned. "God help Grand County with a Pollyanna like you in charge."

Just because I didn't assume everyone was a killer didn't mean I was naive. My take was that Marty Kaufman wanted to avoid trouble, and getting violent would mean big trouble. No sense in arguing with Diane, though. "He definitely knows Mom."

She closed her eyes and tipped her head back as if gathering herself. Maybe she wanted some peace between us. "Did you catch that last thing he said? Something about a woman in Nebraska. I never said she was in Nebraska."

I guess I'd heard that, but by then, I hadn't needed the clue. "Did you see the paintings?"

She leveled her head and tilted her gaze toward me. "Paintings? While that psycho was getting ready to kill me, you were admiring his art?"

"While you were playing Grand Inquisitor, I was investigating."

Her eyebrows sprang up, and she sounded patronizing. "Oh, really? And what did the great Sherlock Kate discover?"

I wanted to slap that superior smirk off her face, but it felt familiar and somehow more comforting than the scared expression of a moment earlier. "Did you notice the coffee mug on the table?"

"Paintings and dishes. What the hell are you talking about?"

"The mug was one of Mom's."

She dropped that arrogant air and stared at me. "Are you sure?"

I nodded.

"He could have picked it up from a gallery," she said.

"Easy enough. But the paintings. They were also Mom's."

She squinted as if trying to see them in her mind. "How do you know that? Mom hardly ever paints."

Of course Diane would doubt me. I might have had some second thoughts about it as well, but after seeing the item on the bedside table, there was no question. "Mom has a distinct style. The way she uses color in that swirling way. I know, okay? Trust me."

"But I don't trust you."

To be expected. I ignored the verbal chop. "Marty Kaufman knows Mom well enough she has a phone dedicated to his number and her art is all over his house."

Even in the bedroom.

She shrugged. "So what? How does that tell us anything about either of them? This information is worthless."

"If you feel that way, jump on the next flight to Denver." She was definitely getting on my nerves.

That mask of perfect makeup and curated confidence she'd slammed back in place now cracked the tiniest bit. "You think there's something here?"

Something big, though I didn't want to tell her about what I'd seen in the bedroom until I knew what it meant. "The paintings in Marty Kaufman's house were signed Miriam Fine."

"I thought you said they were Mom's."

"They are."

She gave me a snotty flick of her head to say I wasn't making sense, the kind of teen-speak from when we were younger.

I didn't let it irritate me. Much. "Obviously, this Miriam Fine is Mom's alter ego. My first thought is that it's her childhood name. We don't know anything about who she was or what she did before she met Dad on that beach in California."

"And you're thinking she was Miriam Fine with some link to Marty Kaufman in Chicago?" She sounded dubious.

I sat back and gave her a frank stare. "Yeah. I'm going to put Miriam Fine's name through the Illinois Bureau of Statistics and see if I can come up with anything."

That smooth snarky exterior returned. "Oh, the Grand County Sheriff steps into the twenty-first century."

"Knock it off." I let out my inner pit bull. "You grew up in the same place I did. Stop acting like the Sandhills is another planet."

She pursed her lips and huffed. "How are you going to storm the walls of the Bureau of Statistics when you don't have a computer?"

I slid my phone from my back pocket. "You're not the only one with connections."

While Diane drummed her fingers on the steering wheel, I climbed from the BMW and paced across the parking lot, letting the warming sun settle on my shoulders. It took some dodging to stay in the direct light since trees lined the lot.

Trey answered after two rings. "No, we don't have a hit on the fingerprints yet. I found them on someone's desk this morning. They haven't been turned in yet."

I hadn't expected that. "That's going to happen soon, right?"

"I'm on it," he said. "Anything else?"

"I need you to run a name for me. See if you get a hit."

A slight pause, then, "Sure. Whatever you need. But why aren't you doing it?"

How much should I tell him? Would it matter if he knew I was tracking Mom's secrets because Dad thought she was in danger? Would it help me if he knew? I weighed all of this in a second, then replied, "I'm in Chicago. Got an idea that intruder might have come from here or have links to the area."

"Chicago? How would you put that together since we don't know who he is?" Trey didn't sound mad, just curious.

I winced, feeling embarrassed saying it out loud. "It's a hunch. A really wild leap, so I don't want to tell you because it probably won't amount to anything, and I'll be embarrassed."

His laugh was genuine. "The first time we met you were following a hunch, and I thought you were an over-eager rookie. I'm over that. Not all hunches pan out, but I've learned to respect your nose."

After a snootful of Diane's attitude, Trey's words boosted my confidence. "Thanks for that." I gave him Miriam Fine's name, and we signed off.

Diane was swiping at her phone when I climbed back into the car. She'd opened the windows to the bright fall day, letting in fresh air only slightly tinged with car exhaust and the faint smell of frying fast food. She dropped her phone to her lap. "What did you find out?"

"They'll run the name and see what pops up."

"How long will that take?" she fired off as if I worked for her.

"Depending on how persuasive he is, might take an hour or so."

She considered that for a second, then started the car.

I let her drive for a bit as she wove in and out of traffic before zipping onto I-55. Finally, I asked, "Where are we going?"

She glanced in the rearview mirror and at the side mirrors, whipped across two lanes accompanied by the harsh blare of horns, and sped down an off-ramp. "If we've got time to waste, I want to spend it on the Magnificent Mile. There are a couple of stores I always go to when I'm here."

Shopping. My least favorite thing to do. But always a priority for Diane.

"It might not take very long to hear from my guy." A feeble attempt to cut this expedition short.

In about another half hour she was wending her way into the city. We passed signs for museums and Wrigley Field along a busy multi-laned street that butted up to what I knew was Lake Michigan but looked more like the ocean. She was forced to slow as lanes narrowed and traffic thickened and signs pointed out landmarks I'd seen in movies or read about. She exited into a twisty section and eased down an alley, following signs for public parking. She pulled into a garage and stopped, pushing herself out of the driver's side and handing the keys to a waiting valet. Clearly, this was a routine she'd done before.

This kind of extravagance was so far out of my experience I gawped. How much would she have to pay to have someone park her car? What kind of a tip? The whole thing made me nervous.

After pausing for a moment, she said, "This is Navy Pier. Big tourist stop. Get some taste of Chicago. I'll take an Uber to Magnificent Mile." She stomped away from me with only, "Call me when you find out something," thrown over her shoulder.

The valet, a dapper young man in a crisp shirt and tie, gave me a polite but pointed look, telling me without words that he had my number. He knew I wasn't classy enough to use valets.

I flashed my friendliest Sandhills smile and slunk away from the car, following in Diane's wake. I had no clue where I was or how to spend my time. Diane had evaporated into the sights and sounds of one of the world's most dynamic cities. I took a narrow sidewalk from the garage that quickly emptied out to a plaza filled with people who looked like tourists. Navy Pier. The name almost sounded familiar, or at least, sounded like it ought to be.

The day couldn't have been more dazzling. Lit by brilliant sunshine, the leaves flashed their brightest colors. A slight breeze blew off the lake, bringing damp air to riffle my hair and probably make it even curlier, and the waves lapped the concrete pier. Even on a weekday, the sidewalks were packed and young people tried to interest me in boat tours or Segway rentals. I wandered away from the pier, overwhelmed by the crowds, the traffic, the way every square inch seemed to teem with frantic activity.

What I hadn't known—and felt embarrassed I hadn't—was that a wide river ran between iconic skyscrapers down the center of the city. Okay, I didn't know for sure it was the center of the city because I knew nothing about Chicago, but I let that go for now.

Over the last several months, I'd dreamed of coming to Chicago. In those visions, I strolled the city with Baxter. We sat across the table from each other in quiet restaurants. He showed me his office and his downtown condo. The city itself never played much of a role. In a diffused background, I only saw me and Baxter, together, close enough to look into each other's eyes, close enough to touch.

I'd sold the city short, obviously. This place bustled with people of every ilk and description on a thousand different missions. Storefronts and restaurants buzzed with crowds. The river fascinated me, the water sparkling and fast moving. Flat barges bursting with passengers pointing cell phone cameras and straining their necks to take in the tall buildings. I followed their focus and was drawn in by all the windows reflecting sunshine and clouds, skyscrapers as foreign to me as if I'd traveled to another planet. A building that seemed to wave and swerve like water drew my eye, and then another with art deco façade distracted me. If we had more time, if I'd truly been here on a visit and not to protect Mom, I would have enjoyed joining those people floating on the river, getting a taste of Chicago.

Why hadn't I come here before? If I'd visited Baxter here, let him show me his city and opened myself up for change, maybe things could have been different. We might have built a foundation as strong as those of the famous buildings surrounding me. Something that couldn't be shaken. Baxter and I hadn't seized on what we both felt, and we'd let it slip away before it even started.

My fault. I'd been cheated on and betrayed and developed a strong sense of self-preservation. That led me to doubt my intuition. My suspicion about Baxter killed any warm feelings he had for me.

I hadn't been able to let go and trust love. Not like Mom and Dad. They'd met and felt the connections. They hadn't stopped to worry and stew and wonder if they'd ever be able to fit their lives together. They'd joined hands and leapt. Because of that faith in their love, they'd built a life and family to last. Their foundation could hold up an entire city without the slightest tremor.

I didn't know where I was and pulled out my phone to get my bearings. A few clicks later, I found out what I probably shouldn't have been looking for.

I veered off the river walk north two blocks onto a street in search of more coffee. In a place like Chicago, you couldn't swing a rope without hitting a coffee shop. So, I couldn't exactly make an excuse for why I walked several blocks away. I found the perfect shop amid all the others I'd passed and felt antsy waiting in line while everyone ordered fancy drinks that kept the baristas whirring machines and banging cups. When I finally made it back to the sunshine and cool temperature with my cup of regular drip warming my palm, I headed for a low cement wall surrounding a tiny park.

I skirted a hot dog wagon and forced myself to consider Marty Kaufman. Anger seemed to simmer just beneath his surface, but I wasn't convinced he was a dangerous or violent man. Something about the way he looked at me. With recognition and longing. I know it was because I looked so much like Mom. I believed Marty Kaufman loved Mom. When she was younger, sure, but probably even now. He might be frustrated with Diane—and frankly, who wasn't at some point—but he wouldn't hurt Marguerite's daughters. Miriam's daughters. Miriam Fine.

The name seemed so far removed from the person I knew as Mom. The way she seemed to float from room to room, the still air about her, not exactly serene but more like expectant, how she seemed to listen to voices in her head, all of those traits attached to a woman named Marguerite. Miriam Fine sounded like the kind of woman who ran the PTA. Someone who spent her days taking care of all the practical tasks that kept the world running. If she was a mother, she'd be like Louise, keeping everyone fed and getting them to school on time. If she was a businesswoman, a woman named Miriam would know the bottom line and never run out of inventory.

She wouldn't be an artist.

And yet, the paintings on Marty's walls were signed by my mother. With another name.

All the while I struggled with these thoughts and sipped my coffee, my eyes roved over the tall white building across the street. In the sparkling sunlight of midday, it looked like a shining castle with reflections of blue sky winking off the windows. The top floor seemed to be nearly all glass. It must be a magnificent view from up there.

One I'd never see.

I took my time sipping the cooling, bitter brew, not paying attention to it until I realized I'd drained the cup. By now it was early afternoon, and people crowded into and out of the revolving glass doors. I supposed they were going to and coming from lunch. I could sit here all day and it would serve no purpose. I couldn't change anything. Still, I sat on the wall, the cool of the cement seeping through my jeans. I gave up trying to think about Mom and Marty Kaufman and a dead man on the floor of her studio.

I made a pact with myself to wallow in this one moment and never give in to self-pity again. I allowed myself to feel the wrench and twist of lost possibility, the emptiness of a loneliness keener than I'd experienced after my divorce from Ted. It heaped onto my head and pushed down, making me fight to keep from sliding to the chilly pavement. The darkness inside felt bottomless and dizzying somehow. Coming here was a mistake. Picking at the wound that hadn't even scabbed over would only deepen the scar.

I pushed from the wall and glanced once more at the spectacular monument to capitalism across from me. Saying a silent goodbye to what never was and never would be.

And there he was. Inexplicably. He didn't go to lunch. Hardly ever ate it, and if he did, his assistant brought it to his desk. He had very little reason to leave that glass aerie, and that's why I'd felt safe spying on him. Not spying, because I never expected to see him.

I'd known better than to come here.

Unlike the others who seemed to be sucked into the doors or spit out, depending on their destination, Baxter exited the building as if the doors rotated to his will. Power. It appeared he carried the world effortlessly.

I couldn't breathe. Couldn't move. Lost all awareness of the sunshine, the people on the street, where I stood, if I even had a body. Longing, despair, a dark pit of misery so deep and black I couldn't swim through it.

And yet, I couldn't turn away. Some part of me felt elated to see him, to know he lived in the same world as me, to feel him so close.

I hated this moment, this dramatic reaction as if I were some swooning teenager so in love with her rock-and-roll idol she couldn't stop screaming at his concert until she passed out. I wanted to slap myself to straighten up. No one person should have that much control over my heart.

Baxter stood in the middle of the sidewalk and glanced up the street, then down, as if waiting for someone. He must have a meeting, or he'd never leave his office in the middle of the day. Maybe a car was coming to pick him up. I should head back to the river and find my way to the parking lot. But my feet refused to move.

He wouldn't see me. Even if he glanced across the street right at me, he wouldn't recognize me. I'd be a blur of a person, not a woman or man, just a nobody in jeans. One of hundreds walking past. I was sure he didn't think about me, and if, by some stretch of the imagination, he wondered about me from time to time, the last place he'd look for me would be in front of his building on a weekday afternoon.

From my place across the street, with a barrage of cars traveling between us and pedestrians hurrying by, I watched Baxter freeze. As if in slow motion, he turned his head from where he'd been focused down the sidewalk to directly face me.

What force had I sent out that alerted him? How had he known?

So far away but I swear his eyes widened slightly. He recognized me. A sharp surge of energy hit me, knocking the air from my lungs, and for the tiniest moment, I thought maybe he felt it too. Maybe he wanted me as much as I wanted him. A flutter of hope that he'd understand we should give it another try.

My frozen world started spinning again when a woman entered into what I realized had been tunnel vision. She touched his waist, and he flinched. Thin and fit, tight red dress wrapped around her with a pashmina thrown carelessly across her shoulders, she was gorgeous, chic, sophisticated, and everything I wasn't and would never be.

They laughed together. Then connected with a casual kiss, as if they'd been together long enough and were so solid the gesture was habit and yet meaningful.

It was a kiss that gutted me.

A stealthy black town car eased to the curb, and without another breath, Baxter was gone.

I didn't know how long I stood there. Empty and alone. I might have stayed in that same place forever, the park behind me, the building across the street, the rumble of traffic, the wash of conversation, the feet passing endlessly by me, except my phone vibrated in my back pocket.

I startled and reached for it, forgetting the coffee cup I still clutched in my hand. My whole body felt stiff and unused. After a glance at the caller ID, I tapped to accept the call and asked Trey, "Did you find out anything?"

"There were several hits on Miriam Fine, but the dates narrowed it down. And I figured you'd want someone in Chicago. Turns out there was a Miriam Fine born in Chicago in 1952. There's a mention of her winning an art show for teens, and after that, nothing. No graduation notice or death record and no marriage or change of name popped up."

So weird to think of Mom's past in concrete terms. As kids, we'd peppered her with questions about where she was born and what her family was like. She always answered with some form of her philosophy that the past is gone, and we can't know the future, so all we have is the present and we should live it to the fullest. After being told that all my life, I'd accepted it and lived as though Mom was created on the day she met Dad. I couldn't speak for all my brothers and sisters, and I assumed some had more curiosity than others.

"Have you got anything else?"

With a flourish in his voice just shy of saying "ta da!" he added, "I've got the address of Miriam Fine's mother. Who is still with us and still in Illinois. In Skokie, which I assume is a suburb of Chicago. I'll shoot a text to you."

I thanked Trey and called Diane. "Meet me at the car. I've got an address."

"Where—"

I hung up on her with a grim sense of satisfaction. Such a childish grab at power, but a sister could bring out the brat in me like no one else.

1965

Miriam spared a glance behind her. Dale Radford, all six foot one of basketball hero, walked backward with the same casual grace as when he went in for the game-winning lay-up. The cutest grin in the universe sent a million volts crashing through her and zinging in her ears. If she'd had her way, they'd still be kissing in the front seat of his dad's '64 Riviera.

Dale cut it short, saying he had to be home before ten on a school night. The one thing Miriam didn't like about Dale was that Boy Scout streak. She'd teach him how to live a little. Like how she got him listening to the Rolling Stones instead of Herman's Hermits. It was pretty funny. She silently laughed at how an eighth grader was dragging a junior into the fast lane. As her mother said, Miriam was older than her years, maybe the only thing they agreed on.

The streetlights only illuminated the front yard, and the Stedmans, next door, always shut their porch light off at nine o'clock, so navigating through Mom's trailing junipers meant stumbling as she made her way to her bedroom window.

Debbie hadn't wanted her to go out. She always had a cow if Miriam asked her to so much as stretch the truth to Mom and Dad. Were all little sisters such a pain in the rear? Or maybe Debbie was a born goody two-shoes. At any rate, Debbie worried way too much for a sixth grader. When Miriam was that young, she hadn't worried about a thing, except maybe getting invited to Rachel Cantor's slumber party. If she'd been invited, those nitwits wouldn't have got caught TPing Bradly Blum's house.

Miriam brushed against the screen she'd popped from the window earlier, when she'd slipped out after dinner. By then, Debbie had been in tears, begging her not to go. Debbie didn't realize how lucky she was to have Miriam to take the risks and figure this all out so Debbie could follow in her footsteps when her time came.

Miriam had tried to reassure Debbie, but Debbie would calm down when Miriam returned and proved everything was fine. Then Debbie would want to know all the details about Dale's kisses and what it felt like to be held tight in the dark.

Miriam had used her most confident tone. "All you have to do is go to the living room in an hour and say good night. Tell them I'm already asleep."

Debbie had squeaked back, "What if they check?"

She had been a baby about it, and Miriam was already irritated she'd had to wait this long to sneak out. She didn't have time to waste if she wanted to make it to the game before halftime. "They won't. But if it makes you feel better, stuff my bed with blankets so it looks like I'm sleeping."

Miriam had brought a Black Cow from the concession stand to make up with Debbie. Miriam would tell all about parking with Dale while Debbie ate only half of the sucker because that's how she always did it, saving the rest for later.

Reaching onto her tiptoes, Miriam tried to slide the window open. It didn't budge. Must be stuck from yesterday's rain. Except it opened easily enough when she'd snuck out. The frame dug into Miriam's fingertips as she put her weight into it. She yanked her hands back in frustration and thrust her fingers into her mouth to ease the sting.

"Darn it, Debbie," she whispered, and considered keeping the Black Cow for herself. She tapped on the window and stage-whispered, "Open up."

Nothing.

Miriam tried the window again, and when it didn't give, she tapped harder. "Come on, Debbie. Let me in."

When Debbie still didn't open up, Miriam thought through her options. She had only one. Use her house key on the front door. It'd be okay. Mom and Dad always went to bed at ten. If she waited another twenty minutes, they'd be asleep and she could waltz to her room, no one the wiser. Then she'd let Debbie have it.

Miriam sat in a shadow by the side of the house, eating the Black Cow and getting colder by the minute. She'd picked out the sweater and plaid skirt because it made her look cute and older, not for warmth. Her legs grew numb despite tucking her knees to her chest and jerking her coat over them.

She didn't make it the whole twenty minutes and tossed the unfinished sucker into the bushes near the front porch. The key slid into the lock without making a racket, and Miriam twisted the knob as softly as petting a kitten. She leaned into the door and pulled back at the same time so it wouldn't squeak open. With stealthy movements, she worked her way inside and eased the door closed.

She turned and only then noticed the glow of a cigarette in the dark living room. Her nerves started jangling a heartbeat before the lamp next to the sofa clicked on and Mom stubbed the cigarette into the ashtray on the coffee table.

Miriam's brain scattered into a million pieces, then wove itself back together. "What are you doing up so late?" she asked casually.

Ruby Fine's face glowed like the hot end of her cigarette. No taller than Miriam's petite five foot four, her auburn hair cut short and permed into tight curls, she wore a pink fuzzy housecoat and slippers. "I might ask the same of you, young lady."

As usual, Ruby, who Miriam had recently begun calling by her first name, was making a big stink for no reason. "I went to the basketball game. It didn't get over until nine thirty, so I just got home." It had ended at nine, but a few minutes wasn't much of an exaggeration.

Ruby picked up her pack of Winstons as if getting ready for another, then dropped it on the coffee table again. "Was that Dale Radford who walked you home?"

Miriam felt the slap of indignation, especially since they'd taken all the trouble to park away from the house so no one would hear the car. "You spied on me?"

Ruby stood up, already too mad to reason with. "Spied? You're thirteen years old. You snuck out of the house. Maybe you went to a basketball game, and maybe you didn't—"

How could Ruby even question that? "Obviously, I was at the game. Dale is the starting center. He wouldn't be walking me home if I hadn't been there, would he?"

Ruby pointed her finger at Miriam. "Don't you get smart with me, young lady."

Here we go again. Ruby turning a molehill into Mt. Everest. Miriam gave her a look as if Ruby were a toddler throwing a conniption. "I went to a basketball game. It's barely ten o'clock, and I'm home safe and sound. You're overreacting."

Ruby hated it when Miriam sounded more like the parent, and now she was really hacked off. "I've had just about enough of this. If you'd have asked to go, maybe we would have said yes."

Miriam held on to her cool, even though Ruby was losing it. "I doubt it. You seem to think I'm a baby and can't stay up past nine on a school night."

"You're still in junior high and—"

"And you can't tell me you'd have said yes to me walking home with Dale."

Ruby stared at Miriam for a second, then started as if giving instructions on making brisket. "I'm sure Dale Radford is a very nice boy. I've met his mother, and they're a good family. He's just not right for you."

Here it was, Miriam's argument. She folded her arms. "Because he's not a Jew. You are such a bigot."

Ruby seemed rattled, way less dignified in her robe than Miriam, even if she still wore her coat. "Because he's a junior in high school."

Miriam pushed back. "What difference does that make?"

Ruby's color deepened. "You're too young to know about such things. But older boys want things from girls and..." She sputtered for words. "You need to stay away from him. What's wrong with playing with your girlfriends?"

Miriam couldn't help her laugh. "Playing? I'm beyond that stage."

Ruby was losing ground. "You and Debbie had all the Barbies out just last week."

Oh, for heaven's sake. "Debbie's almost outgrown Barbies, too. I was only playing with her to be nice."

Ruby pursed her lips and narrowed her eyes, preparing to up the stakes. "Barry!"

Uh-oh. Now she was calling in the big guns. Time to make peace. "I'm sorry. Next time I go out after dark, I'll let you know."

Ruby wagged her head slowly. "There won't be a next time. You're grounded."

Barry lumbered down the hall, tying the belt on his brown plaid bathrobe. "This can't wait till tomorrow night? I got a sales meeting first thing and need to be sharp."

Ruby skirted Miriam to meet Barry as he entered the living room. She linked arms with him. "We need to tell her now. I want her to know she's not getting away with anything."

The girls' bedroom door creaked open, and Debbie peeked her head out. She'd want to get a front-row view since it was Debbie's fault this had happened.

If Debbie had just done what she'd asked, Mom would never have discovered Miriam was missing. She couldn't stand it that Miriam had friends and was popular when no one wanted to be Debbie's friend because she was a goody-goody who never had fun. She was always trying to get Miriam in trouble.

Barry swiped a hand from his stubbled chin up his face to wipe back his dark curls. That wild hair was his genetic gift, and she loved to wear hers long and free. Ruby never tired of telling her to "take care of that mop or I'll cut it off."

Ruby elbowed her husband. "She snuck into the house after going to the basketball game and walking home with Dale Radford."

Barry shifted his tired gaze to Miriam. "Is that true?"

Ruby sounded unreasonable, so Miriam took the high road. "I used my key. That's hardly sneaking."

As if conserving energy, Barry closed his eyes for a second and let his shoulders sag. When he opened them, he spoke slowly. "Your mother suggested, and I agreed, that we'll be going to Jewish camp this year, where her sister goes in the Catskills. I'll spend two weeks there when I have vacation. You'll be there all summer, starting when you girls get out of school."

That exploded in Miriam's head like an M-80. "You're out of your mind! I'm not going."

Ruby flashed a satisfied smirk.

Barry pulled away from Ruby and started to return to their bedroom. "We're all going, whether we like it or not."

Something uncoiled inside Miriam. She hated the shriek that came out. "It's Jewish camp! Only Jews. It's racist and bigoted, and I'm not going to participate in something so evil."

Barry gave his head a slow roll, already on his way back to bed. "I don't want to hear another word. We're going."

15

Diane showed up with a valet ticket in her hand and her bag slung from her shoulder but no shopping bags. The valet took the ticket and left us standing alone.

I eyed her empty hands. "No luck?"

She kept her face turned away from me, as if I weren't there, and pulled out her cell. But she answered. "They ship them to my house."

Of course. She wouldn't want to be burdened with all those heavy bags.

After a moment that I'd hoped frustrated her, she popped like a champagne cork. "So? What did your source find out?"

The smell of exhaust and oil swirled around us, so not like the fresh air of home. I rattled off the address.

She glared at me.

I tilted my head to her phone and gave her a sunny smile. "Might want to put it into your GPS. I don't have directions."

"And what will we find there? Miriam Fine?"

I batted my eyes at her in a coy way. "If Mom is Miriam Fine, she wouldn't be in Chicago, now, would she?"

Diane didn't take taunting well. She snarled and raised her voice so I'd hear her above the car engines bouncing off low ceilings. "For fuck's sake."

I flipped my hand toward her phone. "GPS. Seriously, I don't know my way around Chicago."

If she were a cleaver and I were a side of beef, I'd have been T-bones by then. With a flurry of huffs, she pulled her phone up and made me repeat the address. "This is about fifteen miles north of the Loop."

I shrugged. "Not my fault."

The valet brought the car, and we climbed inside. It took a half hour to finagle our way from the congested waterfront up I-94 toward Skokie. Diane and I didn't exchange one word the whole way. I stopped myself from commenting that it seemed everything in Chicagoland was a half-hour car ride. I wouldn't say it was a comfortable silence. More like a glacier growing thicker by the minute.

Diane and I hadn't been all that close as kids. She was nearer in age to me than Glenda or Louise, but she always seemed impatient with me. Where Glenda treated me as her personal mascot and showered me with attention, and Louise wanted to mother me, Diane rarely let me hang out with her and her friends. When we did spend time together, it was on her terms. She could be wicked funny and, when it suited her, the most generous of our bunch.

Despite her abrupt manner and the way she issued orders, I enjoyed Diane. She was smart and pulled no punches. If any of us had to be in Denver, we were welcomed to her McMansion and treated to dinners at trendy restaurants. Her hand-me-downs were always the best, and on the rare occasions she relaxed, she told great stories.

Maybe not all families operated like ours, but I always felt we Fox girls were tethered by an invisible cable of belonging. There wasn't much I could imagine I wouldn't do for them, and I'd been certain they felt the same. Probably because of our unsteady parental supervision, we relied on each other. Brothers were part of this cadre, too. And in fact, growing up, Robert felt more like an appendage than a separate person. But sisters...there was something more in the mix.

But there was always a hard edge to Diane, and the rest of us approached her with caution. Now that we were adults, her caustic attitude often had me laughing, and I appreciated the way she attacked life. Although I'd often wondered if that drive of hers might border on unhealthy obsession, she acted fairly satisfied with her life. She'd never even seemed rattled by her divorce.

That was before I'd witnessed that flame in her eyes when her ex came back into her life. I'd been surprised our granite-hearted Diane had such a soft underbelly. And then he'd been shot down in front of her.

Now I feared this woman of unlimited determination had focused that fortitude on hating me for the rest of her life.

The humorless GPS directed us off the interstate at the Skokie exit and then through several turns in a town that looked like so many others. The usual fast food and retailers, the busy streets. The sameness of urban or suburban life baffled me. But I'd heard people stopping at the Long Branch on a trip across the Sandhills remark about the boring drive and how everything looked the same, when, to me, every hill, valley, pasture, and shallow lake had its own story to tell. I supposed there was a place for everyone. Mine wasn't in a Chicago suburb.

The afternoon had started to cloud up, so the cool temperature took on less of a golden glow and more of a heartless chill. The leaves looked duller, the sky gray like a slab of wet cement. Our robotic travel guide informed us our destination was on our right. A high-rise with a curving front drive and large swath of green, lush grass you wouldn't find anywhere in our dry Nebraska prairie.

Diane read the sign in front with graceful cursive lettering. "Sunset Haven." She humphed. "Sounds like a cemetery."

"If this person is Mom's mother, then I'd say it's a retirement home."

Diane pulled up front and raised an eyebrow at me. "Oh, a clue. We're going to see Miriam Fine's mother? She's got to be in her nineties. Probably has dementia and won't be able to tell us anything."

A young woman in black slacks and a white shirt covered with a maroon blazer approached the car. Diane rolled down the window, and the woman spoke. "Are you here to see a resident?"

Diane morphed into a mild-mannered normal woman, as opposed to her usual Wonder Woman persona. "Hi. Yes. We're here to see Mrs. Fine."

She brightened in recognition. "Of course. Is that Betty or Ruby? I suppose it could be Ina, though she's been moved to hospice now. Oh." She let out a peep of shock and covered her mouth with her hand. "I'm so sorry if you are here to see Ina and didn't know."

Diane reached out of the car window and patted the poor girl's arm, and I nearly choked at the kindness. I knew Diane was only faking it, but it still shocked me she knew what to do. "No, dear."

Dear? It sounded like a foreign language coming from Diane's mouth.

"We're here to see our grandmother." Diane wrinkled her nose and lifted her shoulders like a mischievous kid. "It's a surprise."

The girl's eyes lit up. "Oh my gosh! Ruby's going to be so excited. I'm Ashley, by the way. Ruby is a super lady."

Ruby. Our grandmother's name was Ruby, and she had a daughter named Miriam. I didn't know how the girl had figured we were Ruby's granddaughters and not Betty's, but that didn't matter. Maybe Betty didn't have kids and this girl knew something about the residents. With so many important questions to ponder, I let this one go.

Apparently, Diane was happy to seize on the gift, too. She gave the girl an exaggerated sad face. "We live out of state and haven't been here in a long time. Can you tell us what floor she lives on?"

Ashley paused and narrowed her eyes as if recalling was painful. "I'm sure it's a higher floor, but I can't remember right off. I can call the front desk, or there's a directory by the elevator."

"We'll check the directory, thank you."

Ashley seemed genuinely pleased for Ruby Fine. "This will really make her day. I'll park your car if you want to go up. I'll be here when you're done. Can't wait to hear how she reacts."

We spent a few more minutes with Ashley, me mostly smiling and nodding, Diane telling her she lived in Denver and how much she loved Chicago. I had no idea Diane, who was named for Diane Keaton, had acting chops to rival her namesake. She actually looked as if she'd gained ten pounds from the low-key lifestyle that allowed her to cook for her appreciative family.

We entered the building to a lobby so much nicer than the Motel 6 but probably not as plush as Diane's beloved Four Seasons. The floors were an old tile, clean but worn. A few groups of upholstered chairs, small coffee tables, and love seats dotted the open area, and an elderly woman sat at a piano in the corner playing a classical song. Diane, with all her polish and sophistication, could probably name the concerto or opus or whatever it was. To me, it sounded nice and soothing.

A large Star of David and framed symbols that looked like Hebrew writing decorated the walls.

The furnishings and style looked like it was high society forty years ago but sliding into old age. It smelled of air freshener and floor wax, a long cry from the assisted living facility Grandma Ardith called home. I didn't detect any sour cafeteria odor or that acidic sting that might or might not be urine. Ruby—I wasn't up to calling her Grandma—might not be living on Park Avenue, but she wasn't doing too bad as far as I could tell.

We found the elevators easily enough. Two of them stood side by side with the directory in the middle. We studied it for a moment before Diane pushed the up button.

When the door opened and we stepped into the confined box with a railing around the sides, I pressed 24, just to show Diane she didn't have total control.

And to prove me wrong, she nudged me out of the way to exit the elevator first and strode down the hall as if she didn't need to look at door numbers to know where to go. I stayed right with her as we made our way down a wide hallway. Smells of baking, warm chocolate and sugar, made me think of Louise and wonder how she and Mom were faring hidden somewhere in the Sandhills. The doors of each unit were farther apart than my college dorm, but it still felt confined and crowded to me. In Grand County, our population density was 0.9 people per square mile. This was more like ten people per foot. The air seemed in short supply.

Diane stopped at a door. Like all the others, a mezuzah hung on the doorframe. Mom was Jewish. I'd never considered she might be anything, since she never attended church, didn't talk about God but only the universe. She had her own spirituality and never foisted any beliefs onto us.

Louise and Norm went to the UCC in town. Michael and Lauren were Lutherans, as were Glenda and Brian when they were alive. Ted's family were Episcopalians, so that's where I ended up from time to time. There was no synagogue in the Sandhills that I knew of. Puzzle pieces dropped into our laps that didn't seem to fit with my version of Mom.

Diane locked eyes with me for a second. Maybe she wanted to comment on this revelation. I know I did. But as I opened my mouth to speak, she turned away and jabbed the doorbell.

A soft chime filtered through the door. I had an urge to stand on tiptoes and peer through the peephole. Obviously, that wouldn't do me any good. My stomach jigged and jumped.

What would we find behind this door? I conjured up a shrunken image of Mom, a tiny woman with deeper wrinkles, crazy white waves down her back, wearing flowing silks in wild colors, blue eyes keen, seeing below the obvious, ready to transform the ordinary into art. The woman who had held my mother as a newborn, cooed and sang, taught Mom how to ride a bike, draw her first stick person, sign her own name. Miriam Fine.

My heart hammered out the seconds it took to discern foot pounds on the other side of the door.

Diane's face looked pinched and nervous, a mirror of the way I felt. She bit at her lower lip, something I hadn't seen her do since eighth grade when she'd decided she wanted to be a corporate tiger after renting the movie *Wall Street* on VHS.

The footfalls stopped at the other side. I might have imagined a shadow at the peephole. A chain slid across on the other side, and a bolt pushed. The doorknob lock clicked, and slowly, the door cracked open.

A woman, probably in her late sixties, with dark hair in a short bob and a shapeless plaid shirt over mom jeans, gave Diane a questioning look. Something about her face looked welcoming, and her hazel eyes held a warmth, even if they seemed wary. "Yes?"

Diane drew herself up. "We're here to—"

When Diane said "we," the woman shifted her gaze to me. Her reaction was immediate and violent. Both hands flew to her open mouth, and her eyes grew to about three times their original circumference. A tiny moan escaped, and the color drained from her face.

She whipped her head around to the apartment, then back to us, and she lunged out the door, knocking Diane back a few paces. She drew the door closed and turned to me.

Without a word, she stared at me, panting like she'd outpaced a panther. Her nostrils flared with each inhale as if struggling to get enough air into her body to process the shock. It seemed to take an effort to pull her focus from me to find Diane again. She studied Diane's face as we both stared back.

After a moment, she turned back to me, her gaze intense. Finally, she spoke, sounding winded. "This." She shook her head and swallowed hard, then started again. "Of course you're Miriam's. But I...I have no words for this."

Diane nudged closer to me to be in the woman's sight. "Our mother is Marguerite Myers." When she got a blank look, Diane continued. "The artist. We think she might have been Miriam Fine when she was younger."

The woman blinked. Her hand wandered to her head, and she splayed her fingers as she swept her hand from front to back, frizzing the fine hair that had been smooth. "Marguerite. Of course." She glanced at the closed door and seemed to consider. "Okay. Okay." She gathered herself with each word, and the buzzing electricity of earlier quit sizzling. Enough color came back to her skin she no longer looked like she'd pass out. "Right. Daughters."

Diane sounded subdued and gentle, clearly off her game. "We want to ask you—"

The woman held up her hand. "Not now. Give me a minute to get Mom's dinner finished and make sure she's okay for the night. I'll meet you over at the IHOP." She pronounced vowels in a slightly different way than our western drawl. Sort of nasally or flattened. Different. Not like Mom, who spoke quietly and with careful diction.

"Who are you?" Diane blurted out.

The woman hesitated and looked from me to Diane. A smile appeared out of nowhere, lighting her face in a way that made me feel like the claustrophobic walls of the apartment building fell and the sun came out. "I'm your aunt Deb."

1965

Debbie sounded hopeful as she stared at the crowd of kids hollering in the pool. "Looks like they've got a good game of tag going. Want to play?"

Miriam turned away and reached for the bottle of Johnson & Johnson baby oil. She snapped the pink lid and poured a line down each leg. While she hurried to rub it in before it dripped onto her towel, she let all the boredom of the last two weeks settle into her tone. "No, I don't want to play tag with a bunch of children." She lay back on her towel and closed her eyes, lifting her chin so her chest would tan evenly. She tried to ignore Debbie's fidgeting beside her.

After a minute, Debbie said, "Would you mind if I did?"

Miriam shielded her eyes and looked at Debbie. "Go ahead. I mean, it's okay to leave me alone. It won't look weird for me to lay out by myself, because I have no friends because I'm at this stupid camp where I don't know anyone. Because you didn't do what I asked you to, and Ruby and Barry decided to punish us all by bringing us to the middle-of-nowhere mountains to ruin my life."

"Okay." Debbie responded with more force than usual. "I can't help it that I'm not as good a liar as you are. I already told you I'm sorry about a zillion times."

Miriam almost felt bad when Debbie's eyes teared up. But darn it, this was all Debbie's fault. Dale Radford would be dating some other girl by the time Ruby and Barry drove the Fine mobile back to Skokie.

Miriam had nearly dozed off when Debbie stood up. "I'm roasting. It's stupid to sit here when the pool is so close." She didn't wait for Miriam to object and ran to the edge of the pool, risking the lifeguard's shout of "No running." She executed a clumsy cannonball into the water.

It didn't bother Miriam to be alone; she'd only wanted to torture Debbie by making her miss out on the fun. In a way, she was glad her little sister showed some chutzpah.

Miriam rolled over and grabbed her *Seventeen* magazine. All the girls in the pages had smooth, blond hair. No one looked like Miriam with dark waves going every which way. Maybe she should cut it, even if it was what Ruby wanted.

A shock of cold water splashed across her back, pocking the pages of her magazine. Those stupid kids. Miriam whipped around, ready to let somebody have it. What she found whisked her breath away in a shock bigger than the frigid wave.

Debbie stood in the four-foot part of the pool, laughing. Her hair all slicked back. But Miriam hardly noticed her.

With his arms folded on the side of the pool and his chin resting on them, a boy flashed her the cutest, most mischievous grin. Even wet, his hair stayed wavy. Body golden tan, he was the most gorgeous boy she'd ever seen.

"Hey, Miriam. It's hot out there. Looked like you needed to cool off."

He knew her name. Probably from Debbie. And for that, Miriam forgave Debbie every offense, including being born.

Only one thought made it through the flash of recognition and ringing in her ears: *This is the man I will marry.*

16

We got a booth at the nearest IHOP and ordered coffee. Smells of French fries and burgers made my stomach growl. I hadn't eaten since the McMuffin earlier, and the coffee I'd drained while watching Baxter's building had eaten a hole in my stomach. I considered ordering a pancake while we waited but settled for adding four of the little plastic cups of half-and-half to my cup. I'd rather eat on my own, even if it meant pizza delivery to my hotel room, than eating in front of the sullen sister across from me.

Diane had positioned herself to face the hostess station and the front doors. I sat with my back to the entrance, jumpy and attuned to sound, every second expecting Deb, my aunt, to pop up behind me, and knowing it would take her some time to arrive.

I tried once to talk to Diane. This whole thing was flipping and flopping around my brain, and I wanted to discuss it. Like poking a bruise, I thought about Baxter. And the woman in the red dress. And the kiss.

I needed to mull this over with someone. Holding it inside with Diane facing me, the words piled up behind my closed lips and turned my milky coffee to acid in my stomach. I couldn't process finding out Mom's original name, meeting a man who obviously loved her but not knowing their relationship, finding our grandmother, even if we weren't allowed to meet her.

And now, waiting here to talk to our mother's sister. "When did Mom leave here? Why?"

Diane's eyes focused on me for a second, then she blinked and watched the waitress scurry past, as if bored by my presence.

I'd had enough and, in a steady voice, said, "I didn't kill Vince."

She kept her gaze placid and attention outward from our booth. No answer.

I leaned back in frustration. "He planned on killing Carly. Probably murdered Brian and maybe two other men."

In a lightning-quick move, she grabbed her bag and pushed out of the booth. With purposeful strides, she headed for the restrooms in the back of the restaurant.

The waitress stopped at the table to refill our coffee cups. She wore shiny black slacks and a polyester top with her name badge, Sue, pinned on her skinny chest. With straw-like hair pulled into a scraggly ponytail, she could be anywhere from age forty to sixty. "Can I get you anything to eat?"

My stomach growled. "An order of pancakes." Why not?

After making sure I didn't want eggs or a side of bacon or ham, or pigs in a blanket or any of the specials, she seemed disappointed and hurried away.

I didn't know what Diane was doing in the restroom to keep her there for the next ten minutes, but the pancakes arrived. I slathered the whipped excuse for butter over them and poured maple syrup. Pancakes might be the ultimate comfort food, and heaven knows I could use a little comfort. I dug in. They were probably perfectly fine, but to me, the dough tasted like wallpaper paste and the syrup curled my tongue. It all landed in the bottom of my stomach like a depth charge. Too much was going on for me to enjoy them, and I pushed the plate away just as Deb suddenly appeared in the aisle at my shoulder and slipped into the booth in Diane's place.

The whole gloppy pancake mess lumped into a sour ball in my stomach. I pried open my mouth and had just enough wherewithal to utter, "Hi."

Deb's round face had a pasty pallor. Her lips were colorless and drawn in a straight line. Apparently, we were both nervous and untethered. She made an attempt at a smile and gave me the same weak reply. "Hi." She let out a pent-up breath. "I'm sorry I made you come here. I couldn't let Mom see you." She stared at me and shook her head. "You look so much like her. It's a shock."

I didn't know what to say, so I opted for a nothing phrase. "It's okay."

Deb's eyes seemed glued to me in wonder. "No. It's not. But, well, Mom never really got over Miriam leaving like that. All those years and no word. And now she's so confused and gets upset easily. I'm not sure she could handle seeing you."

From time to time, I'd wondered about Mom's parents. I had the world's greatest grandmother in Grandma Ardith, so I didn't feel deprived not to have two grandmothers. But now that I knew one existed and her name was Ruby and she was a Jewish woman living in Chicago, I felt a longing to know her. But not at the risk of causing her more pain.

Diane slid in next to me, hip-checking me against the wall without glancing at me. She sat forward, her ribs against the table edge. "Deb Fine? What makes you think you're our aunt?"

Deb drew her head back as if slapped. Then her eyes softened. "For one thing," she said and pointed at Diane. "That."

Diane ticked her chin up as if surprised. "What?"

Deb seemed to relax a little, and she rested her forearms on the table. "Your inflection. The intensity. Even your voice sounds like her." Then she swung her head in my direction. "But you. I never saw Miriam after she left home, but you look exactly like her."

Miriam? Such a prissy name. An uptight name, all hairspray and pot roast. That couldn't be Mom.

"When was the last time you saw her?" I didn't know where to start.

Deb sat stiff, as if bracing herself for bad news. In a voice as rusty as an old hinge, she said, "She's dead, isn't she? That's why you're here. She told you about us on her deathbed, finally acknowledging her family. You came to tell me she's gone."

My hand shot out and landed on her arm, surprising me. I wasn't prone to comforting touches. But she was warm and soft and seemed to welcome my touch. "No. She's alive. She's good."

I searched Deb's physique for some similarity to Mom. Both women weren't much taller than me, at about five-four or five-five. Years of vegan diet and frequent yoga kept Mom from carrying any fat on her bones. Deb looked soft and round, a pillow of a woman who looked as though she was built for hugs. Mom mostly wore a calm expression, neither happy nor sad, her thin face sharp surrounded by clouds of wild gray waves she sometimes tamed with a braid down her back. Deb's chestnut-colored hair fell in a limp bob to her chin, and a telltale shimmer of gray peeked at the roots in her side part. Aside from laugh lines and a smattering of crow's feet in the corner of her eyes, Deb's face, with her rounded cheeks, appeared much younger than Mom's hollowed cheeks. Mom's blue eyes contrasted with Deb's hazel. But there was something about the tilt of her face, the way her arms rested on the table, or the shape of her mouth that reminded me of Mom.

Deb inhaled a shaky breath, as if relieved after she'd steeled herself for the worst. "You're her daughters. Grown up. Oh, how I would have loved knowing you as babies and kids." She teared up, and her voice cracked. "I feel like I missed out on so much. I always wanted kids, daughters especially. And now to find out Miriam had two I never got to know."

Diane didn't seem moved by Deb's emotion. "Five daughters. Four sons."

Deb's mouth formed a shocked O, and she looked at me for confirmation.

I patted her arm once and withdrew my hand. "Yep. Nine kids. We lost our oldest sister several years ago. So now there's eight."

She stared at us in disbelief for a moment, then a deep gurgle of laughter welled from her core. I kind of fell in love with her and the sound of that lightness. So different from our serious mother, whose rare laugh was quiet and considered. Deb withheld nothing, as if she had no secrets, nothing dark and brooding inside.

Diane and I waited for her to get control.

She dabbed at her eyes, though she hadn't brought herself to tears. "I'm sorry. It's just the most bizarre situation I could imagine." Her Chicago accent sounded foreign but kind of nice.

Diane didn't seem quite as smitten with our aunt. "What do you mean?"

Deb sucked in a breath and grew serious. "Miriam wasn't the most maternal person."

Diane went on the defensive. "But you said you hadn't seen her for a long time, so how would you know?"

Deb didn't engage in the battle. "You're right, of course. And people do change. I wouldn't have expected this big of a change from Miriam, though. I mean, even the name she gave herself is kind of...elevated."

Diane scowled. "Marguerite Myers doesn't sound all that fancy to me."

I came down on Deb's side on the matter but didn't chime in.

Deb ran her hand across her forehead and pushed her hair behind her ear. She started off friendly and pleasant. "I didn't mean to criticize your mother. It's just that when we were kids, she hated to play with dolls. She wouldn't let the kitten sleep on her bed." By now, her voice hardened and tinged with bitterness. "She really didn't have much time or energy for anyone except herself."

Diane's voice lowered and gave no quarter. "And yet she raised nine kids and has twelve grandkids so far. Maybe you don't know her as well as you think."

Raising us kids might be an exaggeration about Mom's role in our upbringing. She gave birth to us. She loved us. Sometimes she guided us with philosophy and interesting facts. But when I thought about raising a child, the idea of consistency, reliability, discipline, and even routine entered my head. Mom was Mom, and there would never be another woman like her. I couldn't be sad she'd been my mother. But she didn't so much raise us as witness our growth.

Deb conceded to Diane with a nod. "Sure. She was barely nineteen the last time I saw her. So much has changed." She lifted both hands to take us in. "Obviously, Miriam was a good mother, because you both are lovely."

Very diplomatic, since I wouldn't say Diane had been lovely to Deb.

We sat in silence for a few seconds.

The waitress stopped at our table with a pot of coffee in one fist. She pointed to the half-eaten pancake. "Are you finished, hon?"

I nodded.

"More coffee?"

When we shook our heads, she slapped a ticket on the table, picked up the plate, and hurried off.

Deb touched a spoon in front of her, sliding it one way, then the next. "If

Miriam—or Marguerite—is okay, why are you here? How did you find us? Why isn't she here, too?"

"Why did she leave?" Diane countered.

I gave my sister a crusty look, which she didn't see because she hadn't looked at me since she'd huffed off to the restroom. I tried to soften the interrogation. "Mom has never said anything about her past. She met Dad in 1972 when he got out of the army, and he brought her to Nebraska."

Deb's mouth opened and gaped at me. "Miriam lives in Nebraska? Are you kidding me?"

I guess a Chicago native wouldn't be impressed by the Cornhusker State. "She's an artist."

Deb snapped her mouth closed as if realizing she might have insulted us. She seemed to consider what I said and nodded. "I can see that. She was always drawing or painting when we were little."

"Primarily sculpture and pottery," I said while Diane watched Deb like a hawk zeros in on a mouse.

"Huh." Deb sounded surprised. "And she had nine kids. In Nebraska. And never came back to see Mom or me. She didn't even contact us when Dad died." Again, she choked up. Unlike Mom, Deb's emotions seemed to live right at skin level.

"Was she hiding from something?" I asked.

Deb considered me. "Miriam was always so passionate. Volatile. Oh, the fights with our parents. Miriam had to have her own way, and if she didn't get it, she meted out punishment like you wouldn't believe."

Mom? The woman whose model for life was the *Desiderata*, which included lines like, "As far as possible, be on good terms with all people"?

Diane gave a skeptical *humph*. "That doesn't sound like our mother."

I wanted to nudge her and say, "Right?" But we weren't friends and might never be.

Deb didn't seem interested in fighting with Diane. "As you said, I haven't seen her in...my gosh, over forty years. All I know is the Miriam I grew up with."

"Doesn't sound like you got along." Diane said it with an accusatory bite. What had crawled under her saddle that she was so antagonistic to this poor woman?

Deb's smile faltered, and her hazel eyes carried a deep sadness. "Oh, you're wrong. Miriam and I were as close as you can be. We were less than two years apart. That's why her leaving and never hearing a word from her hurt me so much."

I wanted to put my arm around her shoulder. She seemed so wounded. "What happened?"

She let out a short sob and sucked in air, not allowing herself to cry. "I don't suppose it was much different than a bunch of other stories. This was the seventies, you know. Young people were rebelling and trying to change the world. Miriam felt so strongly about the war. There was no talking to her."

"What about you?" I asked.

She flashed an apologetic smile. "Miriam would get so mad at me. Called me a goody two-shoes. And I probably was. Mom and Dad had rules, and I followed them. After I'd grown up and thought about it, I wonder if I wasn't reacting to Miriam."

Diane sat stone-faced.

"What do you mean?" I asked.

She pushed the spoon to the side again and brought the knife next to it. "I'd see Miriam have these terrible fights with Mom and Dad. Then she'd storm out, and Mom and Dad would argue about it. Mom cried a lot. I hated all the conflict, so I tried to be invisible. Not cause any trouble."

I did love this woman. We had a lot in common.

Diane pulled her phone from her purse and glared at the face. "Look, I have just enough time to get to the airport and drop the car off before my flight. You haven't seen your sister for more than forty years. I can't see you're any help to us." She slid from the booth and dropped two twenties on the table. Without making eye contact, she said, "I'll get the coffee and whatever else you had. I don't have time to wait for the change."

She didn't spare a backward glance as she marched from IHOP and left me stranded in Skokie, Illinois.

17

Deb and I sat back against the vinyl booth and stared at each other.

The corner of her mouth twitched, and a twinkle lit her eyes. Her face split open, and she cracked up.

Because the situation was so bizarre and because her laugh was infectious, I gave in and joined her.

This time, her eyes teared up and shone with good humor. She shook her head, still chuckling. "If I had any doubt she was Miriam's daughter, that removed it. Oh my. The same swagger and temper. That impulsiveness."

She stared at the front door, and I swiveled around to see Diane stomp back in with my bag. She shot a few words at the hostess, dropped the bag on the floor, spun around, and whisked through the doors.

Deb reached for the dispenser at the end of the table and snapped a napkin free and dabbed at her eyes. "I remember once, it had to be when she was in high school, and I might have been twelve or thirteen. We were at Grant Park, downtown. I can't remember why we were there. It was about this time of year, though."

The mirth slipped from her face as she thought about it, her eyes far away. She refocused on me. "I can't imagine Mom would have let us go down there on our own. But anyway, we were there, and some young man was carrying on about Vietnam, and people were gathering around. I don't know if it was impromptu or if it was a planned rally of some kind."

Again, she stopped, and her eyes flicked back and forth as if seeing it all. "I wonder if Miriam knew about it and made some excuse why we had to go downtown." She grinned at me and waved her hand. "Doesn't matter. Anyway, we were at the park, and Miriam tried to drag me over to where the guy was talking. People started to get excited. I wouldn't go and tried to get Miriam to leave. Of course, I knew Mom and Dad wouldn't want us there. It didn't matter what I said, she was determined to go hear that guy. And she left me. Walked away from me like Diane did just now."

I never thought Diane looked much like Mom, but now I considered it. Diane stormed through life like she dared someone to get in her way. Mom moved slowly, as if considering where she placed each foot, maybe not wanting to disturb even the smallest dust mote. Could Mom have ever been as forceful as Diane?

"What did you do?" I asked, wondering if I could call a rideshare or a taxi or if there was a bus or subway to the airport, and what to do about a flight back to Denver tonight.

She wrinkled her brow, the soft chestnut hair slipping from where she'd tucked it behind her ear. "I got a bus back to Skokie. It scared the devil out of me, to be sure. But I figured it out. I told Mom that Miriam was at her friend Rita's house. And then I worried until I was sick. I mean *sick*. Throwing up and all that. When Miriam got home sometime after dinner, she was so excited about 'the movement,' as she called it. She thanked me for not squealing on her, but I don't think she thought twice about leaving me to get home on my own."

"I'm sorry," I said. "I can't picture this person you call Miriam as being the same one we call Mom."

Deb glanced around the restaurant. "I can't leave my mother—your grandmother—alone too long. I assume you need a ride to the airport."

Since I hadn't known how long we'd be in Chicago, Diane had left my return flight open-ended. But Diane was right, there didn't seem to be much to find here that would protect Mom, though I had to admit to a curiosity and a yearning to get to know Mom's sister better. Maybe meet my grandmother.

"Why don't we talk on the way? I'm dying to know how my sister spent the last forty-five years, and I'm sure you want some questions answered."

One problem solved. I reached for my phone. "Let me check flights and see if I can get on one to Denver tonight."

She sat back and waited patiently while I pulled up the Southwest app and clicked through the routine of booking a flight. Not a frequent flyer, I was surprised at how catching a flight was almost as easy as casually riding a bus. But more expensive. My Chicago excursion would make a big dent in my vacation savings, pushing that dream of a scuba-diving trip farther away.

Booking complete, I stashed my phone in my pocket. "There's one that leaves in three hours." Hopefully that wouldn't put me on the same flight as Diane. But she'd be in first class, anyway.

I picked up my bag from the hostess stand and followed Deb from the IHOP to a white Taurus in the parking lot. Though it had seen some years, the inside was spotless, and a floral air freshener hung from a knob on the dash. She slipped behind the wheel and deposited her large handbag in the back seat. She sat up straight, both hands on the wheel, and drove with caution, keeping her attention shifting from the mirrors to the windshield, to the dash, in a constant rotation.

"I suppose you want to know what Miriam was like as a girl, so I'll tell you how I remember her. She was my idol. So pretty, so smart and vivacious. Everyone loved her. She had Mom and Dad wrapped around her little finger. Dad especially. She was the sparkle in our family. She always had something going and made us laugh."

"That sounds like my oldest sister, Glenda."

I must have sounded heavy, because Deb asked right away, "Is that your sister who passed?"

I nodded. "She looked like Mom, too." I lifted my wavy hair. "Some of us got this, and some didn't."

Deb flicked at her own straight hair and returned her hand to the wheel. "All those marvelous curls come from your grandfather."

Grandfather. Wow.

Watching traffic, she said, "I always envied Miriam her looks. What most people didn't know about her, though, is that she had a sadness inside. A deep hurt, and I don't know where it came from. I always wanted to ask your grandmother about it, but we never talked about Miriam after she left. Maybe Miriam was born with it, a kind of chronic depression."

We'd made our way to another interstate. This metropolis was sprawling, but the arteries seemed to keep everything moving at a swift clip. As the sky darkened, the city took on an even more foreign feel to me, adding to my anxiety and claustrophobic feelings.

Your grandmother. It jolted me, hearing Deb slip so easily into calling her own mother, Ruby Fine, my grandmother.

Cars whooshed around us as Deb stayed in the right lane. Glad it wasn't me maneuvering in this traffic, I said, "Mom once told me she had so many kids because she needed us to chase away the ghosts. I don't know when the darkness started, but it's been there as long as I've known."

That seemed to sadden Deb. "Maybe Miriam's drive and passion as a young person were her attempts to escape those ghosts."

I prompted her back to Mom's childhood. "You said you were close."

Deb's smile brought sunshine inside the car, ousting the gloomy dusk. I wondered if she'd sold herself short by giving the spark-in-the-family label to Mom. "We shared a bedroom all of our childhood, and oh, the fun we had. When we were little, we'd build forts and read books and eat peanut butter and saltines all day. By the time we got older, we'd stay up late with our *Teen Beat* magazines and talk about the boys we'd marry someday." Her giggle was lighthearted. "She was John all the way, but I went back and forth between Paul and George."

She included me in her quick glance sequence, and I had to chuckle with her.

At first she didn't seem to mind the memories, but her voice grew darker. "Miriam was always, what we called then, fast. She got a steady boyfriend when she was fourteen. From then on, she shared everything with him and only wanted to be with me when he wasn't around."

Eyes back on the road and sober now. "But then something changed in Miriam. I've heard enough of my friends talk about their teenaged daughters to think it's pretty common. Lots of drama. No one understood her. Shouting, slamming doors. Where she'd always been on the self-absorbed side, she got even more so. It was as if nothing mattered to her but the war and her part in bringing it to an end.”

Her hands gripped the wheel, and her mouth turned down. “Maybe she did have some kind of mental illness. My friend's daughter has borderline personality disorder, and some of her behavior sounds like Miriam. But then, maybe Miriam was just self-centered. I always felt like Mom and Dad spoiled her, letting her get away with everything and caving in to her fits.” Pain and bitterness laced her voice. “I don't know. She didn't give us a chance to find out.”

“When did she leave home?”

“In the summer of 1968. Have you heard about the Democratic convention in Chicago that year?”

I'd heard a little about it. “There were war protests and the police cracked down, right?”

She kept her eyes darting on their survey rotation. She gave me more confidence driving than Diane had. “It was the night everything went crazy. At the end of the summer. She'd just turned seventeen. She'd gone to the protest with her boyfriend, made me get in on her plan. But then Dad saw her on TV, and they had a huge fight when she got home. She ran away but snuck into our bedroom window at three o'clock in the morning. There was blood all over her clothes, and it was like she was on fire. Manic, we'd call it now. All I knew then was that she scared me, like if I stood too close, I'd get burned. She packed a suitcase.”

At this, Deb stopped and laughed. “She took my favorite shirt and cutoffs I loved. You know, just the right length and fit. You never get those back.” Her eyes twinkled. “At fifteen, those things really mattered to me.”

“She took all the money we had, which wasn't much because we were kids. I had about forty dollars from baby-sitting, and I couldn't tell you what she had saved up from working at the ice-cream shop all summer, but not more than a hundred. I snuck a twenty out of Dad's wallet, and Mom had two ones.” Deb's voice that could be warm as butter on a biscuit now grated like it was sprinkled with coal. “She never even hugged me. Just disappeared out of the window.”

The pain in her eyes stung me with the thought of one of my sisters abandoning me like that. I pictured Diane, her back receding from the

IHOP. Our rift was temporary, though. Right? "And you never saw her again?"

She tapped on her blinker and exited at the signs for O'Hare. "I saw her once after that. About two years later, she came to the house when Mom and Dad were gone. She gave me some money and had me go downtown to a creepy neighborhood and pick up something for her. It was in a sealed manila envelope, and I was sure it was a fake ID. She came and got it after Mom and Dad were in bed. That time she hugged me. I think she knew she'd never be back."

"Marguerite Myers?"

We'd made it to the airport complex and slowed as we approached the terminal. Her eyes darted to the curb, searching for a place to pull up. "By then I was so mad at her, I never wanted to see her again. You know, she broke our parents' hearts. Dad got angrier and angrier and smoked more and more. About ten years after she left, he died of lung cancer. She never even sent a card."

Did Mom know about her father's death? By 1978, Glenda, Louise, and Diane had been born. It felt wrong to defend Miriam and what she'd done, but I'd been standing up for Mom all my life.

Deb eased toward the curb and put the car in park. "I don't mean to speak ill of your mother. I'm sure she's a different person with you than she was with us. She must be, because you and Diane obviously love her deeply. You came all this way to help her. And you seem like such a compassionate person."

Dad had been the one who'd drilled duty and caring into us. He insisted we attend weddings and funerals, anniversary parties, baby showers, show up to lend a hand whenever anyone needed it. I hated to think of all the accusations Susan spewed about Mom, but she was right; Mom did exactly as she wanted with seemingly no thought to what was right or expected. "I'm sorry she hurt you so much."

Deb made a sound that was both laugh and sob. She sniffed. "You don't need to apologize for her. But you should know, I think she helped me once when we really needed it."

I gave her a questioning look.

"My Jimmy manages a paper products warehouse. It's not glamorous, for sure. But he's been at it for almost forty years, and he's going to retire next year." She beamed with pride. "But in 1996, he was in an accident. Some stupid man T-boned him in an intersection when Jimmy was turning left. Jimmy had the light, but this guy was in a hurry, I guess. He didn't have insurance, and ours only went so far. Jimmy's company couldn't keep him on payroll when it took him over a year to get back on his feet. I don't know how Miriam found out."

Cars came and went around us, their headlights waxing and waning across her face that held so much emotion. In the course of a couple of hours, I'd seen her face show loss, betrayal, gratitude, wonder, and, always, the sense that she'd be ready to let loose with laughter at the slightest chance.

"Mom had already moved to the tower, and she had barely enough to keep her going. Just when I was at my wit's end, someone left a bag of cash in my milk box. Close to ten thousand dollars. In cash. Sitting in my milk box between the half-and-half and cheddar brick. I mean, I went out to bring in the dairy on Tuesday morning before it's light, and I flip open the lid, and there's this big manila envelope." She shook her head, eyes shining with tears. "It's kind of inconvenient to spend that much cash, but we managed to deposit it slowly over a year so we could pay the mortgage. And we used it for groceries and things."

"How do you know it was from Miriam...uh, Mom?"

She let her hands flop onto her lap. "Who else? Miriam could be generous. On her own terms and always unpredictable, but she could come through in a time of need."

I must not have looked convinced, because she added, "Oh, that's not it. I just knew." She grinned and all but winked at me. "That's all. The same way I've always been sure she's alive somewhere. We have a connection." That laugh burst out unexpectedly. "But I had no inkling she'd ever in a million years have so many kids and live in Nebraska."

I grabbed hold of the latch to climb out. "What should I tell Mom about you?"

Deb's face darkened like a deep lake in the middle of winter. "Nothing. She's gone from our lives, and she should stay that way."

My lips parted, but I couldn't think of what to say. Deb had seemed soft, welcoming, full of comfort and love. This steel wall she'd slammed shut shocked me. "You don't want to talk to her? See her?"

Deb leaned back in the seat and stared out the window. "I don't know if I've ever loved anyone as much as I loved Miriam. Not even Jimmy, but I'd never tell him that. She tore out my heart. Without a second thought. Walked out on me. Left me to deal with our broken parents. Dad always looked right through me, as if angry I was there and not Miriam. And Mom only sees me as a weak replacement for the daughter she adored. So no, I don't want to open myself up for that kind of pain again when she rejects me or leaves me. Because she will."

Deb leaned against her door and pulled herself out of the Taurus. By the time I stood on the curb, she'd made her way to me and threw her arms around me, all darkness gone again. Her hug pulled me into her soft body with determination and surprising strength, and her words vibrated through me. "I'm so happy to have met you. If you'll have me, I'd love to be part of your life."

The lump in my throat made it impossible for me to do anything but hug her back until I could get control. This hug smacked of maternal comfort I'd never experienced and didn't know I'd missed.

If anyone asked me, I'd tell them without irony that I'd had a happy childhood. I never felt unloved or neglected. Surrounded by family, the freedom to roam the countryside, all my physical needs met, a rumpus of a home with laughter and care. But this hug opened up a longing in me I didn't know existed.

We held on for another couple of seconds before we let go at the same time and took a small step back.

"I'd like that," I said, my voice cracking.

She reached into the car for her bag and pulled out a small spiral notebook, one she probably kept for grocery lists. She scribbled her phone number and handed it to me. "Call me. Anytime."

After another quick hug, she scrambled back to the driver's side as a security officer eyed us for overstaying our time in the drop-off zone.

I watched Deb nose into traffic and cruise away. Was it possible Marguerite Myers and Deb Fine came from the same gene pool? I thought of Louise and Diane, me, Susan, and even Glenda.

A dull thud soured my stomach to think of Diane. I hadn't done anything wrong to her. She kept flinging me away. Maybe I should take a note from Deb's life and let her go. It seemed the epitome of stupid to keep opening myself up for rejection. Let Diane wallow in her bitterness. I could hold my head up and move on, like my newly discovered Aunt Deb.

1967

The harsh scent filled the air, so different from the campfire smoke. It gave Miriam a thrill to watch the joint move from hand to hand, slowly making its way around the circle.

Marty's friend from Parkchester was a freshman at Cornell, and he'd invited them to this party only an hour's drive from the summer resort. Ruby and Barry thought it was a pool party at a rich family's summer home. It was one of Miriam's more outlandish stories, but they'd eaten it up. They were so into status and wealth they hadn't pried enough to detect the ridiculousness of the lie.

This crowd, mostly Cornell students, lounged around a campfire listening to two guys playing guitars and singing harmony, "Are you going to Scarborough fair?" The older kids had brought beer, the bottles cooling in the lake. Miriam sipped hers, not liking the bitter taste but loving being part of this cool group. They weren't puking and acting stupid to get attention. Mostly, they discussed real issues, like poverty and racism and, always, the war. Like Marty and Miriam, these people knew change was coming, and they wanted to be part of it.

Sitting between Marty's crossed legs, Miriam leaned back, taking in the warm smell of him, a mixture of his English Leather shaving cream and sweat. Knowing the real smell of his body felt intimate, like a stamp of true love and acceptance.

Ever since they'd met the summer before last, her whole world had been consumed with him. They sent letters to each other every day during the nine months he went to high school in the Bronx and she lived in the prison of the Fines' house in Skokie.

Of course, Ruby and Barry didn't like it. "You're too young to be exclusive. You should be going out with all the boys," was what Ruby said. Dad's answer was, "She's too young. Shouldn't be going out with *any* boys." Both liked that he was Jewish, and they'd met his parents at the resort. But they hated that Marty was three years older than her and had graduated from high school a few weeks ago.

They didn't understand what it meant to have a soul mate. It wouldn't have mattered if Marty was thirty years old or twelve, they were destined to be together. Ruby and Barry couldn't stop that.

Any more than they could stop Miriam from creating the art she was put on earth to make. After the fights about why Miriam couldn't stick to painting landscapes and fruit bowls instead of the abstract and disturbing images that emerged from her brushes, Miriam had started hiding her paintings. The fights stopped, but Miriam would never stanch her creativity. No one could take that from her. She'd even sold a couple of paintings to her history teacher, who'd seen them in the art room.

Marty nuzzled her hair. "Mm. You smell good."

She knew what he wanted. She wanted it, too. He had the rubbers in his wallet. But the only way she'd been allowed to leave the camp with Marty that night was if she agreed to bring Debbie with them. Ruby never wasted an opportunity to screw up Miriam's plans.

If they had known Marty was taking her to a college party on a lake, they'd have had a cow. What they didn't know wouldn't hurt them.

Miriam had to loan Debbie her favorite peasant blouse and bell bottoms so she wouldn't look like such a square. Debbie hadn't been able to stop fidgeting and staring, constantly winding the strings of the blouse around her fingers. In her second-best jeans and fringed vest, Miriam looked cute anyway.

Debbie elbowed her, eyes sparkly with panic. She forced Miriam to sit up and lean close so she could whisper. "That's not a real cigarette. I mean, not tobacco."

Ugh. Miriam knew this was going to happen. "I told you: if you come with us, you have to be cool."

Debbie pursed her lips like an old lady. "I didn't want to come any more than you wanted me to."

The singers launched into "Blowing in the Wind," one of Miriam's favorites. "Just pass it along when it comes your way and try to act like you've seen a doobie before."

Marty nudged her back. "Is everything copacetic?"

Miriam rocked back into his chest. "She's cool."

The joint had made its way around the circle a few times. It occurred to Miriam there had probably been more than one being passed around, and the thought of that set her off into another wave of giggles. Marty had his hand on her stomach, and it occasionally traveled higher to cup her breast, sending showers of tingles over her. Could she drag him into the trees and do what they wanted?

Debbie sat next to her, staring at the fire and looking miserable. She'd better not blab to Ruby and Barry about being at the lake. She wouldn't, though. Debbie and Miriam were sisters, and that bond was solid.

Miriam nudged Marty, deciding they could sneak off for a few minutes. If they hurried, Debbie would be safe enough. She sat forward and grabbed Marty's hand.

"Hey, my man." A guy with stringy blond hair appeared between them and the campfire.

Marty let go of her and held up his hand, and the two of them clasped each other around the thumbs. Marty nodded at her. "Babe, this is Lyle Joffe. The guy I told you about."

What guy? Miriam searched for the right reference and remembered Marty's friend from school, the guy going to Cornell now. "Oh, right."

Lyle didn't pay much attention to her but spoke rapidly to Marty. "My brother finally made it. The meeting with the SDS ran late, but he's here now. Alan's gonna lay out all the dope on the rallies in the city. We're gonna burn our draft cards."

He spared a short glance at Miriam. "SDS is Students for a Democratic Society."

She wanted to shout, "I know," but that would seem childish, so she settled for a terse nod.

Debbie gasped, suddenly wide awake. She flashed Miriam one of her little-girl panic looks, all wide eyes and round mouth.

The way Lyle said it made the whole thing seem real. So far from the resort and its potlucks and golf scrambles. From the Friday night talent shows and the afternoon canasta tournaments. Light-years away from Skokie and homecoming parades and National Honor Society.

Marty perked up but cast a questioning look at Miriam. She knew how he felt about the war. They talked about it all the time. He'd turn eighteen next month, and the possibility of the draft loomed.

Ruby and Barry were dyed-in-the-wool Democrats. But they still supported the war, like it was some patriotic duty or something. When Miriam had dared to argue with them and point out that the United States getting involved in Vietnam was imperialism and an unjust conflict, she'd been grounded...again.

It hadn't stopped Miriam and Marty from informing themselves about the war and the corruption in the so-called democratic government. They'd come to this party for the weed and to escape the insular and safe resort for once. But now it seemed the universe had magically drawn them here.

A guy with a flop of blond hair across his forehead, growing long enough to brush the collar of his short-sleeve shirt, stepped into the light from the fire.

Lyle kicked Marty's foot. "That's Alan."

The first words Alan spoke sparked a passion in Miriam, and one look at the others gathered there showed the same burning.

Tall and confident, Alan spoke hard truths. "The times demand action. We're not simply protesting the war, though make no mistake, we're doing that. But we hold a vision for a whole new world. We're going to do away with poverty, racism, greed, and prudery."

A cheer rose up, and Miriam joined them.

"We're bringing in a time for love, peace, and rebellion."

This was where it was happening.

And Miriam and Marty were about to start really living.

18

By the time I got back to Denver and retrieved my cruiser, it was inching past eleven o'clock with a bright moon lighting the prairie north of the city. Normally, I'd head to Diane's house for a few hours of shut-eye, a strong cup of coffee in the morning, and some sisterly gossip before she jetted off to work and I left for home. But Diane wanted nothing to do with me. Maybe she rejected me first, but I felt confident in my resolve to quit trying to reconcile. It was up to her, and maybe I would or wouldn't forgive her if she made an overture.

I could get a hotel room and head back to Nebraska in the morning, but I doubted I'd sleep much in a strange bed. I'd been to Chicago but hadn't sampled the famous hot dog or deep-dish pizza. I had, however, found a decent restaurant at the airport and indulged in a steak dinner complete with a salad, so I was fueled up. With enough gas station coffee in my system, driving the three hours home didn't seem impossible.

I wanted to call Jeremy to check on Poupon, feeling guilty I hadn't thought about him all day. But Jeremy would be in bed. I felt a tug of loneliness for the silly fluff of fur I'd inherited from Diane. In my stew of grievances, I thought it possible Poupon was the only good thing I'd ever had from Diane.

When I got tired of the radio, I listened to podcasts on my phone, and when I had enough of that, I shut everything off. The rumble of tires on the road, the fellowship of the moon, the growing sense of belonging in my soul as I neared the Sandhills kept me going the last hour until I bounced up my dirt road to home.

My house felt too quiet without Poupon, but despite the abandoned feel, I fell into bed and didn't know another thing until close to seven o'clock the next morning. I could have used another few hours of sleep, but most Sandhillers were hard-pressed to stay in bed past sunrise. I consciously let go of my accusations of laziness at sleeping in and discombobulation at starting my day on delay.

My trip to Chicago hadn't gotten me any closer to IDing the dead man or discovering if Mom was in danger, but it had opened a hole with more questions than answers. What I wouldn't give to be able to call Baxter and discuss it. I'd give a whole lot more than that to quit missing him so much.

Even as hateful as she'd been lately, I'd be grateful to talk to Diane about what we'd learned or hadn't learned to help put everything in perspective. What I had now was my brain in a complete muddle. I hadn't come up with any clues why someone was after Mom, so I couldn't help Dad understand if she was in danger.

But Mom and I had some things to discuss. Of course, I had questions about her leaving her family and what she'd been doing between 1968, when she'd abandoned those who loved her, and 1972, when she'd met Dad. But what really ate at me and had kept me going all night long was Marty Kaufman. The paintings on his wall might have been old enough to be signed by Miriam Fine. The coffee mug sure could have been picked up in a gallery. But the sculpture on the bedside table in Marty Kaufman's house couldn't be more than a year old.

I had questions.

While the coffee dripped—so damned slow—into the carafe, I dialed Louise.

She picked up after the second ring. She sounded as fake as an actress in a high school musical. "Oh, hi, Kate. What are you up to today?"

More to the point, what was she up to? "I need to come talk to Mom. Where are you?"

Again, she used that silly tone. "I'm sure Mom would love to see you. Stop by the house anytime."

"Come on, Louise. Tell me where you are."

A little less sunshine in her voice this time. "I'm at home, as usual. Why do you ask?"

I was getting tired of her game. "Are you with Mom, or are you really at your house?"

This time, she sounded more normal. "I'm at home. The twins need costumes for the homecoming bonfire. Ruthie has them playing the parts of the Panthers and the Longhorns. They'll be so cute in the skit she wrote, but I've got to get these outfits sewed up. You remember homecoming's next weekend, right? You will be there. And Susan."

"I need to know where Mom is."

Her mumbled reply sounded like she held pins pinched between her lips. "You promised you'd be there. The past queens are going to ride in Shorty's flatbed around the track while the band plays the school song. And then they'll light the bonfire."

"I really need to talk to her." ·

She passed the ball back to me. "So, it would be great if you didn't wear your uniform. That dress Diane gave you, the wrap one, it would be perfect."

That stubborn streak ran deep in our clan. "Yes. Fine. I'll be there. Now, where is Mom?"

The pins must have come out of her mouth. "I swore I wouldn't say. You'll have to ask Dad."

Getting to Mom might be trickier than tracking her past in Chicago. "He's at work."

"Guess you'll have to wait, then."

"How is Mom?"

Louise lowered her voice, and I pictured her leaning in, wrapping up in the drama of the moment. "She's agitated. I got her a sketch pad and pencils, and she goes at it like nobody's business, but she won't let us look at what she's making. She paces from window to window but won't go more than a few feet from the house."

I listened hard for clues about where she might be. A house. If Louise could slip into town to get Mom's art supplies, maybe not too far away.

Now Louise nearly whispered. "She really seems off."

"What do you mean?"

Still in that conspiratorial tone, she said, "You know how she gets when she's working? Like, if you ever went downstairs while she's in the middle of a piece and she's all fired up and..." She paused and then flat-out whispered, though I assumed her kids were at school and Norm was at work. "Naked. She's kind of crazy, like there's bees inside her that can't get out."

Deb said Miriam had been on fire. When Mom was in her creative stage, she worked naked, too hot for even a light layer of clothes.

Louise kept going, "She'll barely talk to me. Won't eat anything except tea and sometimes vegetables."

Poor Louise, trying so hard to nurture this mystifying creature that was our mother. "I'm sorry. It must be hard to be with her like that."

A sound like a hiccup came from Louise, and then her voice cracked. "It's okay. She might not be the mother we wanted, but she needs us. Now more than ever."

Good thing I stood in my kitchen, or I'd have surely caught a few flies in my open mouth. I hadn't expected that kind of compassion from Louise. "She's lucky you're on her side."

The moment passed, and Louise refocused on her children. "Esther has a junior high volleyball game this afternoon. I know she'd like it if you can be there. Two o'clock."

I wasn't likely to get any more out of Louise. She might love gossip, but once Dad swore her to secrecy, it'd be tough to get her to cough up Mom's location. "I'll see if I can make it." She probably knew that meant not to count on me.

I donned my sheriff browns, poured the coffee into a ginormous travel mug, and took off to check in at the courthouse and then off to collect my trusty sidekick.

By the time I arrived at Jeremy's house, on a ranch north of Bryant, the sun had climbed high, giving us another of those rare October days. The hillsides burst in a dazzling array of golds and reds, with only a slight breeze to give it all life. The sky stretched into infinity with a blue no painter could dare repli-cate for fear it would look unreal. I could breathe here. No trees crowding in, no rush and grind of ceaseless traffic, only the pure smell of freshness and life.

I didn't blame Mom for settling here and not going back. But what was Miriam Fine hiding from?

Jeremy wasn't home, of course. This time of year, work slowed on the ranch, and a marvelous day like today would be perfect for fixing fence. I guessed he was in a remote pasture, pickup doors open, radio blaring, and him digging postholes and stretching wire.

From his throne on Jeremy's bed, Poupon raised his head when I entered the bedroom. His tail gave one thump, what might be a thundering ovation from any other dog. He waited while I tugged his collar to get him off the bed.

"Glad to see you, too." I ruffled his head, then, remembering Deb's hug, I leaned over and wrapped my arms around Poupon's belly and laid my head on his fluffy, apricot-colored back.

To my surprise, he tolerated it. It might have been wishful thinking, but I detected him leaning into me. I straightened. "Right. Well, we've got places to go. On Thursday, that would be the auction house in Gordon."

Convenient for me since Jeremy's house was halfway there from Hodgekiss, so Poupon and I only had a half-hour drive to catch each other up on yesterday. He didn't have much to say about his stay with Jeremy and showed little interest in my experience, so the conversation didn't take long.

The auction had just started when we arrived. Every Thursday, Willard Stumpf, owner of the auction service, had a sale for estates not big enough for their own sale and for odds and ends that didn't fit anywhere else. He'd start with the most popular items, so I knew I had some time to talk to Newt and Earl before they'd clean up on the stuff no one in their right mind would buy.

Which said a lot about Newt and Earl.

Poupon reluctantly dropped out of the back seat when I held it open. He might prefer to spend his days napping and his nights snoring, but I thought he needed a little exercise. We wound through the crowd of about twenty people gathered around Willard as he rapid-talked through the auction. Not a bad showing for a Thursday sale in the Sandhills. I spotted the camo-clad duo pawing through a box of bolts and screws.

From this distance of a few feet, it was difficult to tell them apart. Faded camo jackets and pants that draped on ropey bodies only a few inches taller than me, they resembled military scarecrows. Gray scruff on their gaunt faces, buzz cuts they gave to each other, and the general look of homeless men, except they lived in the house their mother left them on an acreage not far from Hodgekiss. When I got closer, I distinguished them by checking their ears. Earl, the older of the two by less than a year, had bitten a chunk out of Newt's ear when they were toddlers.

"Hi, boys," I said when I got close enough.

Neither of them looked up, probably because they didn't expect anyone to talk to them. They communicated in their own mumble, and as I approached, Newt pulled his head up and shoved Earl backward. "Ain't so."

Earl covered the lost ground and pulled his fist back. "Prove it."

I used a voice I pulled out to corral Louise's twins when they threatened to turn violent. "Hey, now."

They spun toward me and snapped to attention, all military "ten-hut" without the salute. Earl gave me a friendly tip of his chin and relaxed. "Katie, what are you doing here?"

Newt elbowed Earl. "Sheriff. You got to show respect." He flashed me a satisfied smile, his teeth a gray that made me want to floss mine. "Good to see you, Sheriff."

Newt and Earl were Dad's age. They'd also done a stint in Vietnam and settled back in Hodgekiss to the junking business. No one could pick through garbage quite like the Johnson brothers. They'd declared themselves my confidential informants because they spent so much time slinking behind the scenes, sneaking onto ranches and their private dumps, slipping around when people never suspected they were being watched.

I squinted at Willard, his head visible above the crowd while he conducted the auction from a wooden platform. "Looks like a good sale, huh? Are you after anything special?"

Newt and Earl passed a questioning look between them. It probably constituted an entire conversation. Earl answered, "Regular Thursday sale. What the rest don't know is that some of this stuff that don't look like nothing, you can sell for the metal. Or some of it, you hang on to it and you can make money when it turns into a antique."

No doubt they had piles of junk at their house they'd bought for pennies in the '70s and were holding out to sell for a fortune.

Newt cast around as if to make sure no one listened in. "We got all these old canning jars one time for a dollar for couple boxes of 'em. And we took 'em on down to the Antique Mall in Ogallala, right there on the interstate, you know? And we got five dollars each for them."

Earl curled his lip in disgust. "Course we had to give Tacy James half that to put 'em in her booth."

Newt grinned at me, and I managed to not gag at his smell. The Johnson brothers supplemented their income by trapping and skinning muskrats. Sometimes, they forgot to shower afterward. "But it was worth it."

Now that I had them warmed up, I waded in. "You boys heard about what happened to Mom?"

They turned solemn faces to me and nodded. Newt said, "That's some bad business right there. We heard he was a art fan. Came at her because he loved her too much. I gotta feel for your mom..."

Without a break, Earl picked it up, "Having to shoot at somebody and to kill him. We done that, and it's a hard thing to take."

Newt's face melted into an old sorrow, and I wanted to comfort him, but it would take more than this to get me to touch him. He said, "That war business stays with you. Your dad, he knows."

Earl and Newt made eye contact, and I'd have loved to know what they knew about Dad. Earl came out with a vague statement. "It changes a body. Changed us all. But your dad..." He struggled for explanation. "Well, he ain't hardly the same guy."

Newt elbowed his brother hard enough that Earl let out a grunt.

"How did it change him?" I asked.

Newt's forehead crinkled with trying to put it into words. "Hank was a wild one growing up. Your grandma had her hands full with that one, for sure. Got throwed out of school so many times he pert near didn't graduate with the rest of us."

"Why did he get thrown out?"

Earl took the baton. "Fighting. It's like a day wasn't right if Hank didn't throw a punch at somebody."

Newt shoved Earl. "Don't go tellin' Kate stories on her old man." To me, he said, "Hank wasn't near that bad. But he did have a temper."

"And when he came back from 'Nam, he kind of hid it away someplace," Earl said.

Newt cheered up. "Yep. He come back with your mom. Man, she was a looker back then."

Earl took his turn with his elbow into Newt's side. "You don't say that to a daughter. What are you thinking?"

I kept from laughing. "It's okay. I think Mom still looks good."

Newt had turned five shades of red and couldn't look me in the eye.

"Anyway, I wanted your opinion about something," I said.

Earl widened his shoulders, his eyes glinting with importance, and Newt recovered enough to tilt his head up to squint at me.

"Since we don't know who that guy was, we're kind of worried someone else might get the notion to do the same thing. So, as you know," and I did hope they knew, "we took Mom away for a bit."

Earl listened with full attention. "We thought that was a fine idea. I was sayin' to Newt that same thing."

Newt nodded. "He was."

Good. They knew where Mom was hiding. Now I needed to weed it out of them. "What I want to know is, do you think she's safe there?"

I waited while they gave the question serious thought. Finally, Earl said, "It's a good place. I might have got her off to that calving shack at Bill Hardy's. It's hidden way back there."

Newt scrunched his face. "That's a stupid idea. You have to drive through Bill's yard to get there unless you go the back way, but that road washed out two years ago. And Hardy never could keep his mouth shut. Not like where she's at now. Ain't a word'll come outta that mouth about your mom's whereabouts. They've kept darker secrets than that."

Earl looked to the side and lifted his chin in a royal sign of offense.

Newt didn't seem to notice in his excitement to give his opinion. "You could hide in plain sight. You know, get her a room at the Long Branch and let her live in luxury."

Newt's and my idea of luxury didn't match up. He'd probably think the Motel 6 was living the good life. So far, they hadn't given me any clues about where Mom might be. "I wondered if maybe the road out there wasn't used enough, so all the sudden having tracks might seem suspicious."

They tilted their heads at each other, looking like confused puppies. Earl said, "I don't see that. Maybe after you get past the Autogate, but you'd have to know where you're heading."

"But mostly that big cottonwood shades the intersection most of the time, so tracks is hard to see," Newt added.

An intersection with a cottonwood and a sign. Someone who could keep a secret. That was something. But not enough.

Earl and Newt gave each other another meaningful look before Earl shook his head. "It takes some nerve just to drive on her place, so even if you don't go by the house, you're taking your life into your hands. Course Newt and me have ways to get around nobody knows about."

There it was. The last bit I needed.

1968

"The whole world is watching. The whole world is watching. The whole world is watching."

The words rang in Miriam's ears. Even though her head pounded and she kept swiping at the blood in her eyes, she wanted to keep shouting it.

Marty gathered her closer in his lap, his sweat mingling with hers. He pulled the soaked bandana away from her face and squinted in the lights from the dash, trying to see where she'd been sideswiped by a pig's baton. His voice shook. "It's a lot of blood."

The car carried a telltale scent of fireworks from the tear gas the fuzz had used.

Lyle Joffe gunned the old Buick around a curve, throwing Marty and Miriam into the door. Miriam cracked her head on the window.

"Slow the fuck down," Marty screamed at Lyle. "I think we need to take her to the hospital."

Miriam laughed. She put her palms on Marty's face and pulled him toward her for a passionate kiss. "I'm fine. Head wounds bleed a lot. But it's a badge of honor. Look what we did tonight."

Lyle careened around another curve. Lights from oncoming traffic slid across the windshield, and colorful neon from businesses added to Miriam's excitement.

Marty dabbed at her forehead. He shook his head at her, and a soft smile formed on his lips. "It got crazy." He rubbed at his red, irritated eyes.

Lyle glanced at them with eyes swollen from the tear gas. His shoulders sank from around his ears. "Yeah. The cops, man, they tried to kill us."

Miriam took the bandana from Marty and held it to her throbbing head. Her eyes burned and probably looked as bad as the boys'. "Fucking Daly. Fucking pigs."

Marty grinned. "But we showed them. The whole world is watching."

Together, the three of them chanted a few more times, the thrill of making the country pay attention coursing through them. They were forcing the change. Things would be different from here on out.

Their conversation was a jumbled burst of plans and hopes, interrupting each other, interspersed with kisses shared between her and Marty.

Marty and Lyle had driven from New York to march with the SDS in the protests at the Democratic National Convention. The Establishment got more corrupt and evil, intent on throwing the bodies of young men under the tanks of the politicians' ambition. Since Robert Kennedy's assassination, the Democrats had been lost to them. Miriam and Marty agreed that they needed to be with those protesting the Convention.

Getting away from home had been tricky since she was under house arrest again. This time for spray painting "Make Love Not War" on the recruiter's posters at school. Miriam told Debbie to spend the night with her friend Meg, then they told Ruby there was a slumber party Miriam and Debbie had been invited to at Rachel Cantor's house. Ruby approved of Rachel and her little sister and was thrilled Miriam would be spending time with the most popular girl in her junior class.

And they'd taken off to Lincoln Park. Eventually, they'd made their way to Michigan Avenue and the Hilton. That's when the pigs, courtesy of Mayor Daly, had started their own riot and attacked the protesters. Now everyone would understand the fascist regime they were living under. Miriam and Marty had been part of history tonight.

Miriam felt like she could fly. This was only the beginning. God, she hated the idea of having to go home and pretend she hadn't been part of this fab experience. She kissed Marty and squirmed a little in his lap, enough to let him know she wanted to be with him. "Take me with you back to New York."

Lyle flicked his eyes toward them, then concentrated on driving north out of the city, toward Skokie and her prison.

Marty thrust against her and closed his eyes for a second. When he spoke, his breath was heavy. "Not yet, Miriam. I just started school. I can't support us. We have to wait. At least until you graduate high school."

Miriam struggled out of his lap to the bench seat next to him. "That's two years. I'll die if I have to live under Barry and Ruby's rule that long."

"I'm sorry, babe." He sounded wounded. "I want you with me all the time. But we have to be patient."

The hurt look on Marty's face only pissed her off. "Oh, like if we were patient we'd never do what we did tonight. The whole idea of me living in this middle-class life is so bogus. We don't need it."

Marty put his arm across her shoulders and drew her close. He spoke close to her ear in a way that usually made her wet. "I know. We're soul mates, babe, and living without you every day makes me crazy. Give me some time to figure it out. I promise it won't be long."

Miriam didn't doubt his love. It was the only thing, besides her art, that she knew was hers forever. "We don't need much. I can sell paintings. We can move to Frisco and be with other people who think like us."

He kissed her again and again, promising to find a way for them to be together. They made out the rest of the way to Skokie, keeping it to kissing and light petting because of Lyle being there.

The plan was for Miriam to sneak into her bedroom window. Barry had nailed her window closed three years ago, but Miriam had pulled the nails and came and went as she pleased. Her folks weren't very bright. She'd wait for Debbie to come home in the morning before leaving their room. Ruby wouldn't think twice about it.

But now Miriam had to come up with an excuse for the knot on her head. She'd say they had a pillow fight and she fell out of the bed. This late at night, she instructed Lyle to drop her in front of her house. Ruby and Barry would be out like logs and wouldn't hear the car or her climbing in through the window.

After the most passionate kiss in the universe, Miriam slipped from Lyle's car and started across the yard. She didn't get far when the porch light flipped on. It felt like getting caught in a spotlight escaping across a jail yard. All she could do was freeze and wait for the bullets.

The front door swung open, and it surprised Miriam when Barry stepped out. Even in the dim porch light, his face radiated rage. He roared in a way she'd never heard. "Miriam Fine. Get in this house."

Out of conditioning, she took one step toward him before she stopped.

The car door opened behind her. "Mr. Fine—"

Dad's shoulders expanded, and he fired off at Marty. "Shut up, you lousy piece of shit."

Instant fury erupted in her. "Leave him alone."

Barry stomped down the concrete steps toward her. "I saw you! On the news. My daughter with the damned hippies attacking the cops."

Her vision pinpointed on him, shutting out everything else. "That's right. We're changing the world. And you aren't going to tell us what to do anymore. We're done letting you destroy things."

He grabbed hold of her wrist and jerked her toward the house. "That's it. We've tried everything with you. And now you've finally gone too far. You're going to reform school."

Everything broke loose in Miriam's head. They couldn't lock her up. She'd almost died living with them, being grounded every other week and Ruby demanding an exact itinerary. She couldn't go to reform school. It would kill her. Miriam's scream set off an explosion of panic. She shocked Barry so much that wrenching free wasn't hard.

"Miriam!" Barry hollered and ran after her.

But she jumped out of his way and sprinted toward the car. "Go, go, go!" she screamed at Marty and Lyle. If she didn't escape, they'd choke her with their rules. Chip away at her soul, destroy her art, chain her spirit. Now was the time to break free. Her life depended on it.

She and Marty threw themselves into the back seat. Miriam shoved

Marty off of her so she could sit up and watch her house as they drove away.

Barry stood in the middle of the yard, just out of the circle of light from the porch. She couldn't see his face. But Ruby was clear. She stood on the porch in her fuzzy pink robe, her face a waterfall of tears. She didn't fool Miriam. Those tears were for Ruby alone.

19

Clever Dad. He'd taken Mom only a couple of miles as the crow flies from my house. As soon as Earl said "her," the pieces shifted into place. Not many women had their own place and were as ornery as May Keller. As far as her keeping secrets, that probably referred to speculation that May Keller offed her husband a few decades back. All anyone knew for sure was that he disappeared. If I had to live under May's thumb, I might find a way to escape, too.

We continued chatting for a few more minutes until it was polite to leave, and I wished them happy hunting. Poupon settled into the back seat for the next hour as I drove us back to Hodgekiss and north about ten miles to the turnoff to May Keller's ranch.

In this moment, on this spot in the universe, the sun sent its gift of shining brilliance to underline the shift from summer to winter. Too bad we couldn't stop and enjoy the final warm breath.

I hadn't reached the Y in the road with the cottonwood and the Keller Ranch sign, but the cloud of dust ahead alerted me to an approaching vehicle.

The sun flashed on faded blue metal, and I recognized May Keller's ancient Ford Ranger pickup. As we neared, we each pulled to the right, making enough room for both of us on the road with an inch or two to spare for our side mirrors.

I rolled down the window of my cruiser, wondering how May would react to me on her road. "How're you doing?"

She draped an arm thin as yarn out her window and leaned out. I waited for her gurgling cough to subside. She looked me up and down like I was a 'coon under her porch. "Katie Fox. Hank promised me there'd be hardly any traffic on my road, and here you all are, raising dust and turning it into washboards."

May wasn't known for good humor, so her attitude didn't surprise me. "Sorry about that. Maybe we'll get some rain in the next few days and smooth it out."

"Hmph." She pulled her arm in and turned away, fiddling inside the cab for a second before she popped her head out, unlit cigarette between her teeth. "I've known your dad all his life. Ain't much I wouldn't do for Hank. He's helped me out plenty over the years." A tinny pop sounded from the cab, and she reached for the lighter and held it to the tip of her cigarette. She pulled strong and long and held it in her lungs for a beat before exhaling the smoke to float away. "Never knew what he saw in your mom, but that's not my business."

For an unknown reason, Poupon decided to take a stretch. He stood in the back seat and bowed to the front, then stuck his nose against the window. I rolled it down so he could get some fresh air.

"My hell. What is that?" May's outburst set up a string of coughing.

My best friend, the only one I could talk to these days. "It's my dog."

She pulled her head back and appraised him. "Not much of a cow dog."

"I don't have any cows."

She raised her eyebrows in acceptance. "True enough. But let me tell you something. A dog ain't no substitute for a man."

I started to protest, not sure where I'd go with that but wanting to end the conversation.

She held up her hand. "Oh, I know. Not a man around all the time to tell you what to do. You sending Joshua Stevens on his way was a good thing. He's a nice man, sure, but he's too nice for you. You understand. You're like me."

No, I wasn't. At least I hoped not.

"You don't need a man around all the time. But you need one for sometimes." She wagged her hand as if she'd burned it, just to be sure I caught her meaning. "So, okay, have a dog. I've had a few in my time, too. But I told you this once before, and I'm going to tell you again. Get you some weekend time in Rapid City or Omaha. Have you a good time with some handsome stud with lots of muscles and enough money to buy you a cosmopolitan." She seemed proud to pull up the cocktail name.

Not much I wanted to add to that. "We all appreciate you helping out. Mom's nervous being at the house. You understand." I doubted May had ever been afraid of anything, so she might not understand.

May was already shooting smoke streams from her nostrils from her second pull. "Hank was tight-lipped about the whole thing. What's your take on it?"

Sharing gossip would delay me seeing Mom. I suddenly dreaded confronting her and had no idea how it would progress. What would Mom tell me about Marty Kaufman? "We don't know anything about him."

May waved her hand holding the cigarette. Her face looked like a jack-o'-lantern left on the porch two days after Halloween. "My thinking is that he was a flame from the old days." She bobbed her head as if that settled the matter.

Marty Kaufman and this unknown attacker both? Whatever Mom's vacant spells or her days spent in her studio, I'd never seen any reason to doubt her attachment to Dad. They never fought. They shared smiles across rooms overflowing with their kids and grandkids and moved around each other with an ease and acceptance I always envied. No way Mom could have shared that connection with someone else, let alone more than one man.

I kept my face polite. "I doubt that. Probably a fan."

She scoffed outright. "It's not like she's Marilyn Monroe or something."

Moving along. I figured May kept tabs on everything that transpired on her place. "Has anyone but family been out to see her?"

She sucked up the last of her cigarette and stubbed it on the door of her pickup. Guess it wouldn't damage it any more than the decades of sun, snow, sand, and wind. "Not that I've seen. That sister of yours in her big ol' bus been down a time or two. Now you."

She'd made it seem like a parade had gone through when it was only a few vehicles. "Thanks again for letting Dad use your place. I know it means a lot to him."

She waved it away and pulled down the road without another word.

Part of me wanted to turn the cruiser around and follow her. No daughter should have to interrogate her mother about infidelity. Would I have to choose sides?

1969

Excited chatter arose on the crisp fall air as Miriam gathered at the fringes of a group of about twenty, mostly students. She'd twisted her wavy hair into two long braids, and someone tugged one. She spun around to find Marty holding out half of a sandwich wrapped in wax paper.

He grinned. "It's peanut butter and jelly. There's a lady by the Washington Monument handing them out."

Miriam rose on tiptoes and kissed Marty. "Thanks. I'm starving." She wasn't fond of peanut butter and jelly, but free was her favorite. In the last year, she'd learned to be less picky and more grateful. As long as she had Marty by her side, nothing else mattered. Well, the movement mattered.

Marty's cheeks were rosy as a breeze whisked through the crowds. His jean jacket didn't offer much protection. Next time she sold one of her paintings, they'd make a trip to Goodwill and find something better. His eyes sparked with excitement. "They say there's half a million people here today. More than any of the Moratorium protests in October."

Miriam worked the peanut butter from the roof of her mouth. Her heart beat with everyone here, warming her more than any fur coat would be able to. "That's two Woodstocks."

He threw an arm around her shoulders and pulled her close. "More people, less mud."

"No music."

He laughed. "They said Peter, Paul, and Mary are here."

They'd been in DC for a couple of days. They'd started with a single-file march down Pennsylvania Avenue to the White House on Thursday night, each of them holding a placard with the name of a murdered US soldier. Yesterday had been filled with gatherings and plans, everything building for this rally at the White House. They'd found places to sleep in the Smithsonian last night, but Miriam hadn't rested much.

She wadded the wax paper and stuffed it in the pocket of her peacoat. "Look at this. All of these people. Nixon has to pay attention."

Marty didn't look so hopeful. "He's still ranting about 'peace with honor.'"

That fueled a flash of rage. "Asshole."

Lyle appeared next to her and hip-checked her. He'd been trying to grow a Fu Manchu mustache, but his whiskers weren't up to the task, so he looked like he wore a chocolate-milk mustache. His blond hair, grown long enough to tuck behind his ears, looked grimy.

Lyle had his arm draped on the shoulders of a petite blonde who looked about sixteen years old. "This is Beth."

The cute girl smiled at them. "Isn't this rad?"

Miriam raised her eyebrows in amusement. "Rad. Totally." Another of Lyle's conquests. Heaven knows what he told them, but likely something about being a radical war protester and probably exaggerated his experience to get into their panties.

Lyle nodded toward the center of the knot of young people. "Alan's at it again."

Miriam followed Lyle's gaze to take in a familiar scene. Alan on one knee, almost like a marriage proposal. He leaned forward, his earnest face focusing on each of his audience in turn. He looked so much like Lyle, with a start of a mustache and thin blond hair he usually wore in a stringy ponytail, but his features came together in a slightly different way to make him almost handsome. But it was his charisma that drew people to him. She tuned in to hear what enthralled the group.

"Remember the name: My Lai."

Someone tittered, and Alan frowned, silencing them. "Slaughtered. Women and children, mowed down by American soldiers. Murdered innocent people. We need to stop the war."

A few uttered, "Right on," and "Peace now."

Alan waved an arm to indicate the thousands of people gathered on the browning lawn of the south Mall. "We're gonna march down Pennsylvania Ave and tell Nixon what we think of him and the organizers of this *Moratorium to End the Vietnam War*." He spoke the last words with a sneer in his voice as well as on his face. "They are here to demonstrate 'their grief and sorrow over the war instead of their anger and rage.'"

He seemed to grow in front of his listeners. "I say we need to show our anger and rage and to hell with grief and sorrow. This is all well and good, but it's not enough."

Miriam slid her hand into Marty's and squeezed. Fires lit inside her, she wanted to fight and make love, run and shout, embrace, laugh, and cry all at once. "Yes," she whispered.

When she looked up at Marty, she caught a dark pool of worry in his eyes.

She threw her arms around his neck and forced his head down to hers, planting a deep kiss to draw him to her again and away from his doubts.

"There they are." Alan's voice rose, and a hint of humor lifted his serious tone. "My M&Ms."

Marty and Miriam both turned to him, surprised to be called out. Marty raised his arm in an embarrassed peace sign.

Alan stood up. "They've sacrificed everything to the movement. Marty had to drop out of college. Mimi left her home. They're fighting for our lives. Our rights. Against Nixon's tyranny, the profiteers, the Pentagon."

It had taken Miriam some time to get used to Alan's nickname for her, but she kind of liked it. As far as M&Ms, that was good, too. She and Marty were two parts of the same soul.

Alan locked eyes with her, sending a thrill racing up her spine. "I'm not going to sit around here to show grief and sorrow. I'm going to the Pentagon. Maybe it's time to show some rage."

Lyle's grin split his face. "Hell, yeah!" He reached across Miriam and shoved Marty's shoulder. "Let's go, man."

Marty hesitated, but Miriam grabbed his hand, and he fell into step with her.

20

An enormous metal Morton Building anchored May Keller's ranch headquarters. Not far from that, a freshly painted chicken house was encircled with wire, as scenic as any aviary in a fancy zoo. Her house, a one-story Craftsman with a wide porch, probably built in the late '80s, looked homey with large pots of cheery yellow chrysanthemums on the steps. Her yard was perfectly trimmed and the grass velvety green, with only a smattering of leaves bold enough to settle from the tall oaks shading the house. Neat as a pin, was what occurred to me.

I pulled the cruiser next to Louise's faded maroon Suburban in front of the picket fence and stepped out, taking a moment to look around. The stress of the past few days was weighing on me. It was hard to take in— Mom killing a man, the rush to Chicago and all its shocking discoveries, and not knowing if any of it meant Mom was still in danger.

The bottom fell out of the afternoon as it does in the fall. Compared to summer, when it stayed light until after supper, the sudden drop in temperature from shirtsleeves to heavy jacket in a matter of a few minutes ended the afternoon with the abruptness of a Dear John letter.

The best of both summer and fall were on display in May's perfect yard. Her bright fall flowers and falling leaves contrasted with the lush green of her yard. Even if she didn't have many visitors to share the beauty she'd created, I was sure she enjoyed every bit of it, from the effort of upkeep to the relaxing sip of bourbon while on her porch swing.

As I urged Poupon from the back seat, the front door opened and Mom stepped out. Petite and thin normally, she looked as if she'd shrunk three sizes. Her long gray hair billowed out in wild waves that made her look unhinged. Her eyes seemed huge in her pale, gaunt face. She watched me approach.

I stopped at the bottom of the steps. "You look tired."

It was as if a string holding her upright snapped and she slumped, letting it go. Her eyebrows bunched, and her face sagged. "So tired. As though I haven't slept for forty years."

I started up the steps, and Poupon stayed at my side.

The fear was apparent in her drawn features. "Did they find out who the man was?"

"They just turned in the fingerprints, so hopefully, it will be soon. I know Trey will call as soon as he finds out because he knows I'm anxious to hear. In the meantime, you're safe. May's around most of the time, and no one messes with her."

That didn't seem to humor her at all. "Maybe they'll never find out who he was." It sounded as if she'd be glad if his identity remained a mystery.

I stood close to lend comfort. "What are you so afraid of? If it is a fan, this is a one-off. And if it's not a fan, well, there's really no other explanation. I find it hard to believe an army is coming for you."

Her head bobbed in agreement. "You're right. Of course. Nothing to be afraid of."

But she didn't sound convinced. She looked down at the ground, and tension built across her face until it seemed she lost her fight to control her fear. She drew herself up and reached for my hands. "Take me someplace."

The turbulence in her manner jolted me. "Where?"

She looked around the yard. "Anywhere. Someplace where I can't be found."

I let go of her hands and tried for a joke. "This is May Keller's ranch in the middle of nowhere. She's not likely to tell anyone, and no one will get past her."

Her eyes darted around as if danger hid in May's tranquil yard. "No one can protect me as well as you can."

"Mom." How would I begin? "I've been to Chicago."

Her eyes snapped to mine, and she seemed so brittle a falling leave would shatter her. She watched me closely, as if gauging how much I knew. "I wondered. How did you know?"

I didn't answer her, still not sure if I wanted to find out another thing about her past.

The front door flew open, and Louise burst out like a jack-in-the-box. In her jeans and loose plaid shirt, she didn't quite carry off the authoritarian command of her voice and stern set of her face. "You're not supposed to be here. How did you find us? Does anyone else know?"

"I think you're safe unless someone else can get close to the Johnson brothers." I put an arm around Mom. Her shoulder blades felt like cold rebar. She trembled, and I wondered if her legs would carry her inside.

Louise shoved the door wide for us and followed us in. The house smelled of warm chocolate chip cookies. Inside was as cheery as outside. The kitchen opened off to one side with a family room and a bank of windows. To the other side was a cubby of a room, one of those spaces people call the formal living room, though Sandhills folks didn't do formal and it ended up being a room no one used.

Except Louise decided we ought to make use of it and led us there. May had decorated with surprisingly feminine touches of chintz drapes and an overstuffed couch that looked like it wore a Laura Ashley dress. Thick carpet and dark wood furniture with glossy polish made it all fussier than I could imagine for May's tastes. Maybe Mom wasn't the only one with a hidden side.

Louise dropped into a high-backed chair with upholstery covered in such big flowers it looked like she was swallowed in a garish garden. She must love this room, girly and free from family clutter of toys and sports equipment.

I settled Mom on one end of the sofa. The cushions looked plush but were as hard as a wagon seat. I perched on the rolled sofa arm.

A smear of flour wisped across Louise's plump cheek. "Did I hear you say you were in Chicago? Why would you go there when we need you here?" She tilted her head to Mom and gave her a sympathetic expression. "I mean, I'm glad to be here, of course. It's just that there's so much to do with homecoming next week and Ruthie in charge. I hate to leave her without an advisor. And you don't have any kids, so you wouldn't have to worry about not being home." She struggled to smile, but the strain of being away from her family was tattooed on her face.

"I'm sorry." I really was. "Diane and I were only gone overnight."

Louise fell back in her chair, and her eyes and mouth rounded. "You and Diane? Together? That's wonderful!" She clapped her hands once and spun toward Mom. "Isn't that great?"

Mom looked pale, and her lips quivered. "Diane, too?"

A soft dinging sounded from the kitchen. Louise jerked forward, glanced toward the kitchen, then back at us. She pushed herself up. "I've got to take the cookies out. But I want to hear all about this. I'll hurry."

As soon as she was gone, I turned to Mom. "I met Deb."

Her hand flew to her mouth, and her eyes glistened. It was impossible to miss the love, loss, and longing in her eyes. "Debbie. How is she?"

My throat closed up. "She's fine, I think. She takes care of your mother." My grandmother.

A glint like a knife edge showed in her eyes. "Ruby Fine. Of course she'd have someone care for her. I'm sorry it's Debbie. I wanted more for her."

"Your sister didn't mention that taking care of your mother was a burden."

The skin around her eyes softened. "No. Debbie wouldn't say anything bad about anyone." She sought my eyes. "What did she say about me?"

I probably should go easy on her, but maybe she didn't deserve a soft landing. "It wasn't all good."

Mom stiffened, as if squeezing in her insides so they didn't spill onto the floor. She closed her eyes and let the worst of it pass. "No. She wouldn't have cause to sing my praises, I suppose. Though I'd hoped she hadn't forgotten the bond we shared growing up."

The woman in front of me was Miriam Fine, who'd walked out on the sister who loved and needed her. But she was also the mother who braided my hair with daisies when I was seven. The one who found me the most perfect embroidered jacket, saying it called to her across the plaza in Santa

Fe because it was meant for me. "She remembers. She loved you, and you left her. Why would you do that?"

Mom's cheekbones looked like they'd slice through her skin. She seemed so fragile. "I miss Debbie every day. She was eighteen the last time I saw her. Hair in a ponytail, white Keds and my old Levi's. The image of her standing in the driveway of our childhood home, watching me drive away, haunts me. She'll never know how often I think of her."

"She said your leaving ripped them up. Your parents never got over it."

It took Mom a moment to answer as a swirl of emotions spun through her blue eyes. Sorrow, defiance, longing, loss.

Louise banged pots in the kitchen, then she shouted, "The dough is done, and I have to shape the rolls. Come in here and talk."

I leaned back so she could hear me from the living room. "We'll be there in a sec." That would give us some time. I turned back to Mom and nodded at her to start talking.

Mom had taken the churning feelings and locked them away somewhere. Her face had hardened as she settled on resentment. "Maybe they mourned the loss of the daughter they wanted me to be. They pushed and squeezed me into the box of their ideal. They wanted me to be a teacher. Can you imagine?"

For one of the few times in my life, I wanted to fight against her. "And that was a reason to leave? Seems like you could have worked that through."

She massaged her temples, something she did often when it seemed she'd rather not talk. "You don't know what it was like then. The world was on fire. The Establishment was stealing our young men and sending them to slaughter, all in the name of capitalism." Her face flushed, and her voice strengthened. "Now there are documentaries and books written about it proving what bastards they were. But *we* knew then, and no one would listen." She sucked in a breath. "My parents supported them. They wouldn't listen to me. They forbid me to join the movement. If they could have gotten away with chaining me to the house, they would have."

"But there must have—"

She leaned forward, heat almost searing me. "Something needed to be done. And Debbie wouldn't pay attention. She only wanted to be a good girl and do what Mom and Dad wanted. I had to leave. Can't you see that?"

I tried to imagine a passion that hot. But I couldn't picture anything that would make me turn my back on my sisters or brothers. On my parents.

When I didn't answer, she sat back, apparently moving on. "What about you and Diane?"

I slid from the arm to sit. "We went to Chicago together. But she doesn't want anything to do with me."

She gave me the same look of sympathy as when I was twelve and Danny Duncan told me my hair looked like a crow's nest and, like then, I wanted to cuddle next to her and forget about the cruel world. "You've always been so willing to forgive them all. So willing to think the best of the others. You'll give them your last penny, crawl across the desert to find them a drink. I know you believe they'd do it for you. And some of them would. But Diane is not like you. She's got a hard place inside her. A chamber of granite with a steel door, and if that door is slammed shut, it won't open again."

If she'd smacked me across the cheek with a baseball bat I wouldn't have been more hurt. How did this get to be about me? Deb said Miriam could manipulate. Maybe Mom was more like Diane than I'd thought.

"What about Marty Kaufman?"

Mom quit breathing or moving. Like a bunny in the brush, holding still so a predator wouldn't see her. Then her cheeks flushed, and anger sparked in her eyes. "I won't talk about him."

Marty Kaufman must be who she was afraid of. "Diane and I went to see him."

"You shouldn't have done that."

I clenched my hand in frustration. Getting anything substantial from her seemed impossible. "What the hell, Mom? Who is this Marty Kaufman, and why does he have your paintings hanging on his walls?"

She brushed a shaking hand through her hair and avoided my gaze. "Marty Kaufman. He's someone from my past. And I've got nothing to do with him now."

If she'd been more open, maybe I wouldn't have dropped the bomb on her. "I saw the sculpture."

Her gaze flew to me in surprise. Wide eyes with a hint of panic, it appeared as though gears cranked behind them as she tried to formulate a response.

I waited, watching her.

Louise banged pots. "You said you'd come in here. I can't hear what you're talking about."

The interruption gave Mom enough time to gather herself. She lowered her already quiet voice. "You understand it, I know you do."

I bristled. "Understand what?"

She reached her hand toward me and let it drop back to her lap. "Love. I've seen how it is with you and Ted. Once you give your heart, you never entirely get it back."

My stomach hitched, but not because of Ted. "I don't love Ted anymore. He truly is my past." I'd destroyed my future with the man I loved.

She gave me the sad look of compassion. "Is he really? He betrayed you, and you've made a new life. But I know you, Katie. When you love, it's forever."

Footballs and fudge, I hoped she was wrong. But I feared I'd never be free of Baxter. "We're not talking about me. We're discussing Marty Kaufman. The man who lives in Chicago and whose number is on the cell phone I found in your office."

A lump skimmed down her thin neck, a literal gulp of shock. She pushed her hair off her forehead with a shaky hand, even though no locks fell across her face. With a weak voice, she said, "He is Glenda's father."

Cymbals crashed in my ears, and it took a second for me to breathe again, but I came back fighting. "Glenda?"

She jumped from the couch. "I love your father. We've been together for over forty years, and we share a bond that is deeper than anyone will ever know. I won't be interrogated by you." She walked on surprisingly steady legs toward the back of the house, likely to May's spare bedroom. Before she got there, she suddenly turned and pointed her finger at me. "Or anyone else." I might have expected the door to slam, but Mom only allowed a soft click.

I meant to go after her and demand answers, except my phone rang. I wanted to ignore it, but even if the Sandhills stayed peaceful most of the time, I was sheriff, and not answering my phone wasn't an option.

Marybeth, the dispatcher for the Sandhills regional law enforcement located eighty miles away in Ogallala, started in. "Domestic. Duran ranch. Wife says husband is depressed and drunk and took off in his tractor with his shotgun. She's worried he's suicidal."

Buster Duran stood about six foot five and was built like a grizzly. When Ted was sheriff, he'd been out to Duran's place a few times. Buster and alcohol were never a good mix. "On my way."

Louise stood with a mitt on her hand, the hot tray of cookies suspended. Bright slashes of crimson marked her cheeks. I hoped it was from the heat of the oven and not because she'd overheard me accuse our mother of adultery.

Frustrated I couldn't stay and hash this out with Mom, I sounded terser than I intended as I barely slowed on my way to the door. "I've got to go."

The tray dropped to the counter with a clatter. "Go? You just got here. I hoped you'd stay with Mom so I could pop home and check on things."

Heading out to disrupt a suicide attempt wasn't in my plans, either. I didn't turn around. "Can't. Sorry."

21

Dark clouds gathered on the western horizon. A bit of wind kicked up its heels just to warn us that porch-sitting and sunset-gawking season was buttoning up for the year. Duran's place was about a fifteen-minute drive north from May's ranch. Driving logistics was working out well for me and Poupon today, since if I'd been in Hodgekiss when the call came, it'd have tacked on another ten miles.

Poupon settled in the back seat with a huge inhale and even longer exhale. Not that he was prone to complain if he had a spot where he could nap, but the cruiser's back seat had become his second favorite place after my couch. If I ended up needing to haul in Buster—and I hoped I wouldn't —Poupon would have to ride shotgun. He preferred not being forced to curl into a ball tight enough to fit in the bucket seat.

I'd hit eighty miles an hour when my phone rang. Dad. He must have made it to Lincoln, his layover spot before being called on a return train sometime after ten hours, per FTA regulations. I tapped the speaker button.

He spoke slowly, as if worn down to nubbins. "Have you found out anything?"

I didn't want to spill what I'd discovered about his wife of many years. But he deserved to know, didn't he? Wait. Wasn't it Mom's place to tell him?

There was a reason I spent so much of my formative years reading comic books under my bed. I hated family drama, and this was the worst yet. "Trey is still waiting on fingerprints."

His voice sounded like gravel in a bucket. "You know something you're not telling me."

Dread sloshed like acid inside me. Evening was falling hard and fast. My headlights shone in front of me, and all I wanted was to keep driving into total darkness, come back two days ago, when my biggest worry was Louise nagging me. "Yeah. I found out she's from Chicago." I shut the gate on telling him anything more.

"Katie." The one word dropped heavy with his demand.

I raced through the night but not fast enough to outrun his disappointment in me. I did an end-round from mentioning Mom's infidelity. "Mom has a younger sister, Deb. Mom's mother is still alive. And before she called herself Marguerite Myers, she was Miriam Fine."

His heavy breathing came over the line. Then, "That's not all you found out, though."

I wanted to ask him how he knew that, but Dad could always read me. Apparently, even if he couldn't see my face. No hiding from it now. "There's a man she used to know."

I pictured him rubbing the spot between his eyebrows, as he did when he was upset. After learning he had a temper as a young man, I wondered if that habit was a way to give himself time to calm down. Maybe he counted to five or ten. "*Used* to know? Are they in touch now?"

Maybe I wouldn't have to tell the worst of it. "She won't say anything about him." That much was true.

"But you know some things."

I squeezed the wheel, refusing to answer.

His question speared me like a pitchfork through hay. "Is he Glenda's father?"

I opened my mouth to speak, then closed it. Then opened it again. "I don't want to be in the middle of this. I talked to him. He denied knowing Mom. I'm sure he's not a threat."

Exhaustion vanished from his voice, and it took on energy. "I knew your mother was pregnant when I married her. She never hid that from me. We agreed to keep our pasts in the past, though. I've got things I wanted to leave behind, too. But I truly believed she'd made a clean break."

My heart cracked open. Suddenly it wasn't Marty's face or even Dad's in my mind. I hated that all I could see was Baxter and contempt burning in his eyes.

I blinked to dispel the image. This wasn't about me. "She probably only talked to him on the phone. What else could there be? She hardly ever goes anywhere."

But I knew better. Her art was a smoking gun.

He didn't sound any more convinced of her innocence than I was. "Sure." Another half mile ground under my wheels before he asked, "What's his name?"

Saying it out loud would make it real. I didn't want Mom's betrayal to wound our family even more. "Come on. You don't need to know."

"After forty-five years, I think I deserve that, at least."

But not from me. Where did a daughter's duty lie? Mom did wrong. And Dad was broken. "I'm not going to say."

When he spoke, the hard edge of his voice ripped into me. This wasn't the Dad I knew, and it felt like a rumbled warning. "I want to know his name."

Even though I wanted to spare him more pain, I felt like a kid in the face of his command. I was compelled to confess. "Marty Kaufman."

He sucked in a breath, and my heart banged. "Do you know him?" I asked.

"Marty Kaufman. From Chicago." He paused. "No. Not personally." Another moment of silence. When he spoke, his voice sounded like an amped-up version of himself, as if a gate opened in his throat and let out a flood. It chilled me. "So much makes sense now."

I braked to make the turn from the highway to Duran's dirt road. "What makes sense?"

The phone went dead.

~

The washboard road caused the cruiser to jump and swerve. I managed to keep hold and steer with one hand while I found redial with the other. Dad didn't answer.

I had no time to try again.

My tires rumbled over the Autogate leading to Duran's ranch yard. Lights shone from the front windows of Duran's old stucco ranch house, casting shadows on the front yard covered in leaves.

My headlights splashed across the front porch. The door opened, and Fran zipped out and tripped down the stairs to meet me as I pushed out of my cruiser.

Probably in her fifties, Fran had worked hard all her life and looked like it. Petite enough you'd expect a sneeze might toss her away, and her gray hair reached about chin level with no style to speak of. She wore jeans and an oversized sweatshirt with the sleeves pulled down over her hands and bunched in her fists. "He took off for the south pasture. There's a tall hill out there that looks over a lake. He likes to sit up there."

I confirmed Marybeth's information and followed the scant directions Fran gave me. I'd never been to this part of Duran's place but didn't have trouble finding the hill and spotting Buster's tractor idling at the top. The covered cab was silhouetted against the dark night, and exhaust puffed into the chilly air.

Buster had to know I was approaching. No way to hide it. From his vantage point, he'd have seen my headlights on the road. I assessed the steep hill and the best path up, since there didn't seem to be even a trail road to the top.

Bless my hardy Charger. It didn't balk as I gunned it mostly straight up the hill, bumping over bunchgrass and spinning some in loose sand. I had to tack to keep from stalling out, but my cruiser was game for the tough stuff.

Buster hadn't made any move to drive away or get out to meet me. I couldn't see him in the cab, and that sent a shudder through me. The tractor continued to idle, and cold dread dropped into my belly, afraid he'd taken the shotgun to himself. And if not, there was always the chance he'd take it out on me. I considered most law enforcement protocols about wearing Kevlar vests.

I parked, grabbed Big Dick, my flashlight, and stepped into the drying prairie grasses, even though I'd rather do anything, including talking to Dad, than walk to the cab of that tractor and maybe find Buster... I stopped myself from imagining what I might see. I'd had to deal with more dead bodies than I cared to since being elected sheriff, and I prayed Buster was unharmed. Poupon didn't insist on getting fresh air, and I was glad to keep him in the car.

No shouting, warning shots, or threats as I approached, which I counted as only marginally good news. *Please, don't let me stumble over Buster's mangled body.* A shotgun death wasn't pretty.

There wasn't much moon to light up the prairie, but deep night hadn't yet descended, making it possible to pick my way through the clump grass and soapweeds without having to turn on the flashlight. Diesel exhaust from the tractor tainted the night. Wind raced on the hilltop, cutting through my sheriff-brown shirt and cascading goose bumps from my scalp to my waist.

When I got closer, I saw the tractor door open and Buster sitting sideways on the tractor seat with his feet resting on the step outside and his head in his hands. "Howdy, Sheriff. I 'spose Franny called you."

"How're you doing, Buster?"

As you'd expect from a giant, his voice was low and melancholy. "I know I worried Franny, and I wish she hadn't called you out here. I'm okay now."

"That's good." I kept my tone conversational. The chug of his tractor and my cruiser's engine covered the gentle swish of the wind in the grass. "What set you off?"

He wagged his head slowly, giving him even more of a bear image. At fifty-something and carrying some extra weight, he had a defeated air about him. "Sometimes it all gets too much, and I wonder why we keep at it. But I get up here and see this country." He focused on me and swept his arm to indicate the hills surrounding us. I hoped he took in the stars winking in the sky, the sweet smell of grass and sand. "It's real pretty. And I remember I'm lucky to be able to live here. And even if we're having a hard time making ends meet and I can't give Franny all she deserves, it's still the best living anywhere."

I understood his love of this rugged country. I stepped close enough I could touch his boot if I thought it'd give him comfort. "Glad to hear that. You know Fran loves you more than she'd love anything she could buy."

He swallowed hard. Now that my eyes were accustomed to the night, I could see the tears threatening the big man. "She's a damn good woman. It'd be hell on her if I...well, if I did something stupid."

His love for her floated out like steam from a cup of hot chocolate. "That's the truth."

"So, I'll head back on down and tell Franny I'm sorry to get her so worked up. I appreciate you coming out to check on me."

"I'm always glad to help, Buster." I wanted to fix everything, but I gave him what I could. "The state offers a program. It's free to you. Someone to talk to."

He let out a rueful chuckle. "A head shrinker?"

I laughed with him. "People who are trained to help you when you get sad or feel helpless. It's all online, so you can talk to them from your computer. You have a hookup, right? If not, you can come in to the court-house. You can use my office, and it's totally private."

He swung around to face the steering wheel. "I'll think about it."

I took a step closer and grinned up at him. "I'm going to leave a brochure with Fran."

He reluctantly matched my smile. "That'll fix my wagon."

I waited for him to turn the tractor and head down, then followed him to the house. While he parked the tractor, I stopped in to talk to Fran and leave her the information. Stayed long enough to shake Buster's hand and look in his eyes to assure myself the crisis had passed, then I headed back to town.

On the drive back, I cranked up the heat. It was the time of year to keep a jacket handy, and I hadn't remembered earlier when the day had been so sparkling and warm. I tried Dad again. No answer.

With twenty minutes to town, my fingers tapped the wheel with unspent energy. Mom was safe at May's with Louise. Part of me wanted to storm in and demand she tell me all the details about Marty Kaufman. Starting with what that damned sculpture in his bedroom meant. The part of me that dwelt happily in the Land of Denial didn't want to know any more than I already did. There was the fraction that felt inclined to intervene on Dad's behalf, but to what end? And then the rational bit that told me what went on between Mom and Dad was their business.

But what about Deb? Aunt Debbie. Where would she fit into our new reality? It would be something to pull up a chair in her kitchen and share a cup of tea. She seemed a wonderful combination of Glenda, Louise, Diane, and Susan all rolled into a non-judgy aunt. Maybe I should call her to chat. About what? Not Mom.

Admit it. I wanted to call Baxter.

In the months while we'd been searching for Carly, while on long drives with plenty to work out in my head, I'd talk to him and everything seemed to fall into place. Baxter had only been a part of my life for a short time, but now that he was gone, wind blew through my emptiness like a blizzard on a Wyoming prairie.

Still restless and with ten more miles to go, I jabbed in Trey's number.

His words were muffled. "Do you have some kind of radar that tells you when I'm eating?"

I laughed. "Sorry about that. What's for supper?"

He smacked as if he finished swallowing. "Runzas."

My stomach rolled over and sat up to beg. I suddenly craved the cabbage and hamburger mixture wrapped in soft, steaming bread. "My sister Louise makes the best runzas around."

"I don't know about that. These are pretty good." A woman scoffed in the background, and I remembered Trey said he was dating someone.

Happy for him, loneliness poked at me. Not because I minded being alone, but because I missed Baxter. "I'm checking up on the fingerprints. Wondering if you'd heard anything?" Of course he hadn't heard anything, or he would have called me.

Silverware clanked on dishes. "Oh. Yeah. They handed me something on my way out, but I was late and didn't get a chance to look at it. I'll check now."

I didn't snap at him as I wanted to. I tried to sound patient instead of yelling at him to hurry up. "I appreciate it, thanks."

It sounded like he set the phone down, then the ruffling of pages. "This is interesting."

I kept using my inside voice, despite wanting to shout. "What?"

"There's not much here. Whoever this guy is, his prints flagged the FBI, and this report says it's classified."

My heart jumped to my throat. The man who attacked my mother was someone important to the FBI. Maybe she had a legit reason to be scared after all. "Not even a name?"

Maybe he'd taken another bite, because it took a second for him to answer and his mouth sounded full. "Uh-uh. There's a big red stamp on it. I'll see if I can dig a little deeper tomorrow."

I understood the hint that right now, Trey was off the clock and had better things to do than track down information for me. "Great. Thanks. Have a nice night."

By now we'd made it to Hodgekiss. I craved one of Louise's runzas and thought I stood a pretty good chance of finding some in her freezer. But that would mean driving another few miles to her house outside of town, and I wanted to get after finding out who this guy was and why the FBI wanted him.

I stopped outside the Long Branch and swiveled to make eye contact with Poupon. "Hold down the fort and I'll bring you some dinner."

Blessed stars and stripes, the bar was so busy Aunt Twyla couldn't take the time to play twenty questions. I stepped into the restaurant side and ordered a burger and fries to go for me and two plain patties for my best friend. Uncle Bud waved to me and produced my food in record time.

I made Poupon wait until we made it up to my office at the courthouse before I placed the burgers in their Styrofoam container on the floor. He made them disappear before I'd pulled my food from the bag and set it on my desk.

I'd been sheriff for almost a year and spent plenty of time in the courthouse after hours. Yet the place still creeped me out. My office had started as storage space on the main floor, so by the time it got converted to an office with two small jail cells behind a heavy door, I had barely enough room for my desk, chair, and two file cabinets. The building moaned and creaked at night, and even though it was built in the 1960s and didn't seem old enough for leagues of ghosts, I swear I felt their restless energy around me. Poupon wasn't the kind of dog to throw himself between me and danger, but having him snoring on his bed in the corner helped with the heebie-jeebies.

Since enjoying a greasy meal hinged on the temperature of the French fries, I ate before taking my next steps. Uncle Bud knew I preferred medium rare, and he'd cooked my burger to perfection, the juice mingling with his special sauce (Thousand Island dressing he bought by the barrel), and he'd tossed on a tomato slice and pickles to make it almost as rewarding as one of Louise's runzas. I didn't get through the fries before the cooking oil cooled and turned from deliciously decadent to grossly coagulated.

Hands clean again, I searched my contacts and pulled up Ryan Standage's number, an FBI agent I'd worked with in North Platte. He sounded surprised to hear from me, though with his low-key manner, it was hard to tell if he was pleased or not.

"Don't know if you heard," I started out after the obligatory greetings and health check, "but there was a break-in at my mother's studio, and she shot a guy."

Ryan sucked his teeth. "People don't get shot to death in Grand County every day, or even all of the Sandhills, so yeah, we heard about it."

"They said the FBI is involved, and I'm trying to get a little more information."

Ryan drawled in a slow way. "I heard the fingerprints IDed the guy. Pretty interesting development. Can't believe he finally turned up after all these years and in Nebraska. I mean, the guy was pretty old, but this is like finding D.B. Cooper after all this time."

So far, he hadn't told me much. "I'm concerned he's connected to others who might want to harm my mother."

Again that sound of sucking his teeth. "He's been out of the country for a long time. Frankly, if anyone thought about it, I'd bet they assumed he was dead. Don't know why he'd end up at your mother's place. Unless maybe he was traveling through the area and needed cash. For some reason, he targeted your house. Damn good thing your mother could defend herself."

Except now she acted as helpless as a bunny. "I'd like to do some checking. Can you give me his name?"

Ryan hmmed. "I'm not authorized to do that. But you can be sure he'll be checked out. Eventually, you'll get a report."

"I'm sure it's all okay, but my whole family is on edge. You know how it is. No big deal. Just want to be sure our mother is safe."

He didn't think too long, and his words dribbled out in his usual way. "You know, if it was my mom, I'd sleep better looking into it myself, too. You won't have any trouble finding out his past. He's been on the run for a long time."

I tapped my pen on the desk. "You know about him?"

"Well, after I saw the name, I looked it up. Alan Joffe. You know him?"

It didn't sound familiar, but Ryan continued before I could answer.

"Do you know about the bombing of the office building in Milwaukee in 1970?"

That bit of obscure history didn't register. "No."

He continued with that same enthusiasm. "Yeah, me either. But after I looked him up, I kind of remember seeing a thing on *60 Minutes* or some other show."

I wished he'd cut the background and get to it.

"Anyway, during the war protests for Vietnam, some groups got violent. Like the Weathermen and stuff."

Mom and Dad had come through that era as pacifists; neither seemed like the type to actively protest. But according to Deb, Miriam had been passionate about the war.

"Some splinter group broke off and decided to bomb an office building because they thought that Dow Chemical operated there. I guess Dow was making napalm or Agent Orange or something. Turns out no offices in the building had anything to do with the war."

I couldn't take this wandering and urged him to get to the important part. "So, this guy, Alan Joffe, who was he?"

Ryan seemed thrown off by being interrupted and took a second to get going again. "He was one of the Milwaukee bombers. At least, that's what the FBI thought, since his prints were all over the site and they never found him. They assumed he ran to Canada and was in hiding with all those draft dodgers."

"The FBI has been after him for a bombing over forty years ago?"

"Well, a couple of people died, so there are outstanding murder charges."

Oof. A murderer had wandered into my mother's studio, and she'd shot him. This couldn't be a random act. I fought for a light tone and a way to end the call. "Okay. Thanks for letting me know."

He apparently had more to say. "So, yeah, don't know how he ended up in the Sandhills. But I'll say it again; your mother was lucky she had a weapon close. On the other hand, the guy had to be in his late seventies. You saw the body. Did he look like a threat? I mean, they said he had a knife, but someone that old would be moving pretty slow."

I didn't want to speculate about how it happened. I needed to find out what kind of trouble Mom was in. "I'm sure the FBI will figure this all out. In the meantime, I think Mom will be okay. It's not like there'll be a stampede of old war protesters thundering through Nebraska."

He seemed to consider that. "Probably not. At any rate, the situation is on our radar."

I disconnected and pressed the power button for my ancient and ailing desktop computer. Before I charged out to confront Mom about her past, I needed more information.

The computer stirred to life, and I typed *Alan Joffe* into the search line. Plenty of articles appeared, and I picked one and started reading.

Ryan had given me the barest information. As I read, my heart started to pound.

Working on so little sleep, I'd thought I might doze off with all the reading, but my blood rushed through me until I thought I might never sleep again.

Poupon raised his head and eyed me, and I realized my breathing had grown heavy and quick. I read several accounts, each restating the same thing, and I kept hoping someone, anyone, would refute the facts. But they were consistent.

The night of Thursday, August 5, 1970, there was a deadly bombing. A white van pulled up to a four-story brick office building in downtown Milwaukee. One witness in an apartment across the street said two men got out. Other witnesses confirmed two others waited in getaway cars a block east and west. One light shone from an office on the second story.

The bomb was detonated less than a half hour after the van arrived. Thomas Scanlon, a first-year law associate for a small firm located in the building, was killed in the explosion. He left behind two small children and a wife who gave an account of an ambitious, energetic man determined to make partner in record time. He often worked until the early morning hours. He had nothing to do with the war.

Another man also died in the building. Lyle Joffe, Alan's younger brother. According to the one bomber who was captured and convicted, the bombers hadn't counted on anyone being inside and hadn't intended to kill anyone. They wanted to shine a light on the greedy practices of Dow Chemical, who they said were making money off of murder.

Apparently, Lyle had entered the building to alert Thomas Scanlon. The convicted man swore detonating the bomb had been a mistake. But Lyle Joffe and Thomas Scanlon had been found on a landing, apparently on their way out of the building.

One article written over two decades ago commemorating the twentieth anniversary of the explosion had interviewed the one bomber who had served time, completing a seven-year sentence. He'd been working in Chicago at the time of the interview. The FBI had identified three of the bombers: Alan Joffe, a known activist whose fingerprints were found in the van, his brother, Lyle, who perished in the building, a mysterious third man whose fingerprints were collected from the van but never identified, and the one man who'd been convicted, David M. Kaufman.

22

My ears roared, and it felt as if every nerve poked through my skin. With shaking fingers, I typed in David M. Kaufman until I found the reference I'd been terrified to see. "David M. Kaufman, known as Marty..."

I clicked on the mug shot of Alan Joffe taken a year before the bombing. Stringy hair and a scraggly beard. His eyes had a certain magnetism, but he looked like a scruffy man without much going for him. The other picture showed a younger, but no less morose version of the man Diane and I had cornered in his home in the Chicago suburbs. This article, written twenty years ago, captioned the photo as "The only Milwaukee Bomber to spend time in jail." I couldn't drum up much compassion for the man who might have started out full of passion and confidence but had ended up broken. He'd been responsible for the death of Thomas Scanlon, an innocent man.

Poupon appeared by my desk. He planted his butt next to my chair and turned his gaze away from me. I dropped my hand on his fluff of a head and let my fingers wind into his soft hair. I couldn't talk to Baxter, so I mumbled to Poupon. "A fourth bomber. A man no one has identified. Mom and Marty Kaufman are..." I hesitated because even if Poupon was a dog, I couldn't put that into words. "Involved. Alan Joffe came to harm Mom. But how had he found her after all this time?"

I pondered that for a second. Mom had aged well. "She'd been an artist in her youth, and Alan might have known that. What if he routinely watched the evening news and caught sight of her at the end of the segment? Did they say he was in Canada? But maybe he'd moved back to the US sometime in the last forty years."

Poupon closed his eyes while I massaged his ears with more force than was probably comfortable. I tried to relax my fingers.

"If Mom knew about the bombing and the identity of the fourth man, and Alan feared somehow she'd reveal it after all this time, then maybe he came here to shut her up. And that meant the fourth man might be on his way, too."

Poupon tipped his head back, maybe in annoyance of my rigorous pawing of his hair. He licked my hand.

I looked into his disinterested brown eyes, not remotely as enticing as Baxter's had been. "You're right. I'm riding all around this pasture trying to avoid the obvious."

I pushed back from my desk and stared at the discolored ceiling tiles. I tried to come up with any other explanation. When nothing else made sense, I dropped my head and closed my eyes, clenching every muscle in resistance. With a deep breath of resolve, I raised my head and looked into Poupon's bored eyes.

I needed to do the hardest thing I'd ever done.

23

My foot fell heavy on the gas pedal on my way to May Keller's place. Not a mile went by that I didn't fight to turn the car around. The whole way, I struggled not to have the pieces fitting into place like a jigsaw of the Japanese tsunami, the Honduran hurricane, California's wildfires, and all the world's worst disasters in one.

Dad met Mom in 1972. Pregnant with Glenda, David M. Kaufman's baby. The same man who was arrested that year. A fourth bomber never identified.

I pulled up in front of May's tidy home and dashed through the gate, across the yard, up the front steps, and across the porch. I paused only long enough to knock on the door, open it and announce, "Hello," and thunder into the well-lit kitchen.

May was already up and standing by the table with the remains of meatloaf, green salad, and broccoli. Louise would make sure of a well-balanced meal even in the middle of the apocalypse.

May's scratchy voice shot at me. "Where's the fire? You pert near gave me a heart attack."

Even if I drove everyone into a tizzy, I still almost shouted, "Mom. I need to talk to her."

Louise, who turned from the sink and wiped her hands on a dish towel, might be used to a houseful of confusion and drama because she took my outburst in stride. "I think you upset her, or else she decided to take a nap. Until you showed up, I was making some headway with her to get her to eat regular meals, even if she wouldn't look at the meat. She needs more protein..."

I left Louise to ramble and whirled around to shoot down the hall. My fingers closed on the doorknob, and I twisted it. Locked. My fists pounded, and I shouted, "Let me in."

I waited two seconds and heard nothing, so I backed up.

May stood behind me. "Don't think you're going to dive into that door like you're Matlock or something."

"I need to check on her."

May scowled at the door. "Locked doors, damsels in distress. It's this kind of foolishness that gives us all a bad name. I appreciate at least you don't have all that feminine foolishness about you. But you ain't gonna bust my damned door down. You wait right here, and I'll get a key." She disappeared into what I assumed was the master bedroom.

I wanted to ask why May had installed a lock on a bedroom door that had a key. This wasn't standard issue on homes as far as I knew. But May Keller had a few secrets I didn't want to discover. Especially not tonight.

Louise lumbered down the hall. "If she's not interested in eating the broccoli at least, I can heat up some broth. I flatly refuse to make one of those disgusting green smoothies."

May strode from her room and shoved Louise out of the way. Louise grunted and acted as if she'd like to shove back, but she folded her arms over her ample breasts and clamped her lips tight.

May fit the key into the lock and pushed the door open. "Damn it all to hell. That's gonna take some repair work, and I don't have time for this precious princess's party."

Wind rustled the curtains at the window, and the screen hung from the upper frame, twisted and bent at the bottom where Mom had shimmied out. This room, as with the rest of the house, had been decorated in ruffles and soft baby tones. Some other time I'd try to reconcile May's decorating tastes with her personality.

Louise slapped a hand on her chest and sounded aghast. "She's gone."

"No shit, Sherlock. And she bent the hell out of my screen, and look it, here, she tore my drapes. I'm gonna have words with Hank about all this."

May and Louise could gasp and rant; I had to find Mom. My footsteps pounded as I raced down the hall and out of the house. Wind had picked up, but it wasn't as if I'd be able to track Mom's trail across the lawn and beyond. Light shone from the bedroom window, and I scanned the area around the yard, looking for any clue as to where she'd gone.

May stomped up next to me. "My guess is that little ol' minx hightailed it while I was out checking the west pasture."

"She didn't have a way to get anywhere."

May cackled and pointed across the ranch yard to a garage. "I didn't know she had that much gumption. I ought to be madder than a horny bull in a pen of steers, but I kinda like she figured this one out."

She'd lost me, and my response was to stare at her like she was crazy.

She waggled her eyebrows at me and turned back to the garage. "I don't leave that door open. Funny I didn't notice it when I came home, but I smelled that meatloaf your sister had going, and I guess my stomach blinded my brain. Anyway, looks like your old lady made off with my Scout."

May's International Scout, probably new about the time I was born, was the colorless kind of vehicle you'd never look twice at. I couldn't remember the last time I'd seen May drive it. "It still runs?"

Her scowl deepened, creating a Badlands worth of wrinkles on her face. "Of course it still runs. I don't tolerate things that don't work."

That might explain the disappearance of her husband several decades ago. "They" say he was as lazy as a summer breeze. "They" also suspect he was buried somewhere on May's five thousand acres. Right now, I didn't care about her past. I needed to find Mom.

I sprinted to the front of the house and found Louise, phone in hand, pacing on May's front porch. Lit by the porch light, she looked pale and worried. "I'm sorry. I never thought she'd take off. She's going to Chicago, isn't she?"

I pulled up, my stomach dropping into my boots. "Why would you say that?"

Louise shifted from one foot to another, swinging her bulk back and forth, a rocking motion she used to soothe babies. "That's where this man is. Glenda's father. She'd go to him."

"Wha—" I stammered and started again. "What are you talking about?"

Louise's voice squeaked. "I heard you and Mom talking. But I already knew about Glenda."

The night had grown dark and downright cold, but that didn't account for my chills. "How did you know? When? Why didn't you say anything?"

It looked like her knees buckled, and she plunked down on the steps. "Glenda told me. We were in high school, and Jeremy had just been born. Glenda ran away."

"She what?" This was news to me.

Louise winced as if a sharp pain struck her. "You'd have been seven or eight, and I covered for her. I'm not sure anyone knew she left. Norm and I were dating then, and we helped Brian find her in Omaha. He brought her back, and that was all."

Brian and Glenda were high school sweethearts, and whenever they couldn't get out of it, they double-dated with Louise and Norm, who'd been together since before anyone could remember. Louise was right. At that age, I'd be easy to hide something from.

"All this time you knew Dad wasn't Glenda's father? How did Glenda find out?" There was more to the story.

Louise looked flattened. "After all these years, I thought the truth would never have to be told."

"Now's the time," I said.

May had joined us by then, sneaking up as quietly as a barn cat. She stood in the grass in the shadow cast by the porch light and, surprisingly, said nothing.

Louise sat back and directed her words to the stars. "Dad was on the train when Mom went into labor, so Glenda went to the hospital with her. Mom was in her forties then, and it was a hard delivery. She was really out of it. I doubt she'd taken meds, but who knows where her mind was after all those hours in pain."

"She told Glenda then?"

Louise still didn't look at me, as if she pretended not to spill a secret she'd kept for so long. "The way Glenda told it, Mom was crying and ranting about Jeremy being Glenda's true brother, and then it all came out somehow. I don't know. But Mom told Glenda that she and Jeremy weren't Dad's children."

My knees threatened to give out just as Louise's had. Glenda and Louise had known this, and they'd forgiven Mom. Somehow, they'd kept the secret that could have detonated an explosion to blow our family to bits.

I didn't know whether to be furious at the deception or grateful for the years of ignorance. I plodded to the step and dropped next to Louise. "I'm sorry you had to carry this alone for so long."

Louise grabbed my hand and pounded it on her knee several times, fighting sobs that wouldn't be dammed. She let loose in a torrent, and she kept tapping our clasped hands on her leg. I held on to her warm hand, thinking how much it felt like Deb's.

May watched us from the shadows for a time, then she stepped toward the porch. "I've heard worse. I feel bad for Hank. He's a good man. But I'm not surprised by that bit of fluff he married." She skirted us on the stairs and clumped across the porch. "Don't worry about me saying anything. I know how to keep a secret. You can darn sure bank on that."

When Louise's crying jag tapered off, she released my hand and swiped her sleeve across her face. "You've got to find Mom."

I leaned forward, hugging my knees for warmth. "I don't think so."

Louise patted my back. "Whatever she's done, she's our mother. Nothing has changed from this morning as far as the rest of the family goes. They don't need to know. Especially Dad and Jeremy."

A hard ball of blackness pushed against my ribs. "She's never been the woman we thought she was. Susan was right. Mom is a narcissist who never cared anything about us."

She kept patting my back, a little harder than needed. "Selfish. Okay, I'll give you that. But I think she did the best she could."

I fought for some distance to look at this without the filter of betrayal. "I can't believe you're defending her. You've always complained about the way she mothered us."

Louise resumed her maternal role. "And you always defended her.

Think about all the arguments for why you appreciated her. Use those now. You can't deny she loves us."

Sure. Somewhere in the past, Mom had loved Deb and maybe even Ruby and Barry Fine. But she'd left them, too.

Louise nudged my arm. "You have to go get her."

"Why should I?" Louise didn't know about the bombing, Thomas Scanlon's widow and the children who grew up without a father. The right thing to do would be to call Ryan Standage and have him intercept Mom. But I'd need to refuel my Do-Right tank before I could sic the FBI on my mother. Even if she deserved it.

Louise hefted her bulk from the step and descended to the yard, moving away from the light. She didn't face me. "Because I might have told Dad she ran off."

Dad? He'd been so agitated when I'd spoken to him last. Not at all the calm guy who allowed the chaos of nine kids and multitudes of grandkids to swirl around him without being annoyed. He'd sounded ready to crawl out of a straightjacket. I jumped up and grabbed her arm, making her look at me. "What did you say?"

She shifted her gaze from me. "I didn't mean to. Really. I was upset and worried and guilty because I let her go and afraid she'd hurt herself because she's so unpredictable."

I shook her arm. "What did you tell Dad?"

A hiccup escaped from her throat. "I told him I thought she was going to Chicago." She slapped her hand over mine on her arm. "But it's okay. Because he doesn't know where exactly. I never told him about Marty Kaufman and never said our aunt Deb's name."

Oh, dear dread. "He knows." I grabbed my phone from my pocket and hit Dad's number.

Louise's eyes glittered with fear. "Is he answering? Is he okay?"

Dad answered, and I heard the static rumble of tires and the unmistakable sounds of driving. "I'm not letting her go, Katie. One way or another, this is going to end." Somewhere in that voice was the man I loved more than anything. But it was buried behind a fury that froze my blood.

"Wait. Dad. I'll go get her. We'll figure this out."

"This isn't your mess to fix." The phone went dead, and I prayed that would be the only death this night.

1970

Even with the windows rolled down, the smells of diesel and fertilizer overpowered them in the heat and humidity of the August night. Miriam drove the Econoline van through the empty streets of Milwaukee. As the smallest of the four, she'd held her ground to be the driver of the van, though the manual brakes and steering required effort. No way she'd leave this to Alan. His forte was firing up crowds, not detailed planning. Though he didn't lack courage to do the tough things.

No one stirred at three in the morning. She held back a hysterical giggle. This was serious. The biggest gesture anyone had made so far. It was time for the world to see the evil that greed created. Their action tonight would shine the light on Dow, literally. Even people as ignorant as Ruby and Barry would have to take notice.

In the two years since she'd left home with Marty and Lyle, they'd had plenty of adventures and made more mistakes than they should have. The pipe bombs at the power station had been a disaster. Not only had they not detonated, they'd earned Alan a record and probably FBI scrutiny. Too bad they hadn't thrown his ass in jail. He knew nothing about bombs, clearly.

She and Marty had risked it all to be his getaway drivers. They'd trusted him to know how to make a bomb. But she'd learned from that mistake.

Miriam had managed this plan from researching how to make the bomb, how much fertilizer, how much diesel fuel, to the timing, how long the fuse needed to be, and their getaway route. Alan's contribution had been procuring the dynamite and van. There was no doubt this bomb would work. The explosion would take out this office building, a monument to the greed that fed off the lives of young soldiers in Vietnam.

Alan found out that Dow was operating part of their business from this innocent brick building housing law offices and accounting firms. The letters had already been dropped in mailboxes that explained why they were destroying the building in case anyone didn't know. They'd addressed them to all the major news outlets.

Pay attention, America. You wanted a war? Well, here it is. Only we're not sending our poor and black young men to fight it. And we're not killing little brown people half a world away. We're bringing it to your doorstep. How do you like it?

Miriam sang the Country Joe and the Fish song that everyone loved.

Lyle grinned and joined in.

Miriam glanced in the rearview mirror to see Marty take a left in the Oldsmobile Alan had hot-wired earlier. After they lit the fuse, she and Marty would take off in it and abandon it at a rest stop on the expressway. Alan had procured another nondescript car for him and Lyle. He turned right. Lyle and Miriam would separate and run to their designated getaway cars as soon as they lit the fuse.

One of the few fights Miriam and Marty ever had was over who would stage the bomb and who would drive the getaway car. In her heart, Miriam knew Marty didn't have it in him to strike the match on such destruction. He might chicken out. She'd convinced him that they needed his nerves of steel to drive them away because she'd lose her cool. He'd bought it. Maybe because in his heart, he knew his limitations, too.

"Just you and me, baby," Lyle said as the two sets of headlights peeled off.

Miriam didn't want to chat with Lyle. She didn't like Alan and didn't trust him, but like her, he wouldn't hesitate to pull the trigger. Lyle was all bluster and no commitment. She'd probably end up sending him away before she lit the fuse. She had to trust Alan to keep Lyle quiet. He was likely to brag to some coed so he could get laid, and they'd all be exposed.

But Alan was smart. As the only one with a record, he planned on high-tailing it to Canada and dragging Lyle along. Good riddance.

Miriam drove past the building. *Damn it.* A light shone from a window on the second floor.

She turned into the alley and made her way to the loading dock. Her heart thudded in her chest, and her mouth was dryer than the Sahara in summer. Sweat ran down her sides and back, soaking her T-shirt.

Lyle spun toward her and strained his head to look out the window. "No. Wait. We can't do this. There's someone inside."

See? He had no stomach for this. Alan wouldn't hesitate. Miriam shook her head, her nerves jangling like sleigh bells. "It's three o'clock. No one is in there. They just forgot to turn off the light."

Lyle faced front as Miriam backed to the loading dock. "We should leave. Try again tomorrow."

She struggled with the steering and brakes, maybe that was all that kept her from slapping him for acting like a hysterical little girl. "Let's just get ready. If the light is still on, we'll deal with it then."

He folded his arms. "I think we should scrub it."

A fireball of rage threatened to erupt in her brain. She sent her words in a tight stream. "Alan stole this van. How long do you think it'll be before the owners figure out it's gone and start looking? It's tonight or not at all."

After all the planning, exposing themselves to rent a trailer and driving to three Podunk farm supply stores to get the fertilizer. Her back and arms ached from shoveling fertilizer into barrels half-filled with diesel yesterday afternoon. She and Marty had spent tense and sleepless hours talking about why they had to do this. No way in hell she'd back out now.

Lyle remained in his tall seat while she climbed out and opened the back doors. He pouted up front while she fitted the dynamite into the tops of the fifty-five-gallon barrels. All six of them. While he stewed, she twisted the fuses together along with the ten-foot fuse they'd light. The length would give them ten minutes to get away.

She didn't need Lyle. She'd agreed when they put the plan together that two of them would transport the bomb, set it up, and light the fuse. Two would drive the getaway cars. Alan probably sent Lyle with her because he knew Lyle couldn't tie his shoe without help, and Miriam didn't need help.

When the bomb was ready and Miriam felt like her skin had melted away, leaving her nerves raw and exposed, she walked to Lyle's open window and banged on the frame.

He glared at her. "The light is on."

No time for his squeamishness. Alan knew. She knew. This had to be done no matter what. "We've planned this out. Nixon just increased the troops, and they need us to speak for them. This explosion is going to make it clear that if these bastards continue to make money off killing people, they're going to pay a price. This is the big-time now. Not some SDS protest where we ask the university president, 'Pretty please can we put up a literature table in the student union.'"

Lyle's eyes bugged out a little. "Someone could be in there. We can't blow them up, they aren't killing anyone here."

The time was now. She felt it in every breath, every inch of skin. "They're working for the men who do and should be held accountable."

Lyle stared up at the building, then he grabbed the door latch and opened it, pushing Miriam back. "Okay. Just give me a minute to go inside and get him out."

She considered it. Checked her watch. Almost three thirty. They could spare a couple of minutes. "Hurry."

Lyle's loafers clattered on the pavement as he sprinted for the back door.

She pictured him running for the stairs and taking them two at a time. His footsteps would sound like horses' hooves in that quiet space. The guy —probably signing an invoice to send napalm to tear through the Vietnam countryside, killing and displacing countless women and children, annihilating the jungle—would hear Lyle's approach, and he'd get up from his desk.

She checked her watch and waited another thirty seconds. Her ears roared, and her stomach clenched. She refused to vomit.

With shaking hands, she reached into her pocket and brought out the box of wooden kitchen matches. She'd never been good at lighting matches from the flimsy cardboard matchbooks. Marty always lit the match and held it to her roach. She wasn't taking chances here. These matches were sturdy. Up to the job. Like Miriam.

She paced to the end of the fuse, and her gaze wandered up to the lit window. She had to do it now or they'd lose their chance. Lyle had always been the weak link. Chances were he'd get caught for something stupid, then he'd turn in Alan, Marty, and her.

If that happened, who would be brave enough to carry on the work? If she got caught, they'd throw her in jail. She'd die.

War.

Them or us.

She thought of the young men drowning in rice paddies, slogging through jungles with bullets ripping them apart. The broken men coming home without arms and legs, in body bags, or not coming home at all.

They didn't choose to be soldiers. But she had.

Miriam squatted down, gave one last glance at the lit window, then struck the match.

24

The night had to be cold, but standing in my shirtsleeves in the light from May's house, I didn't feel it.

Louise seemed oblivious to the air, too, as she leaned toward me. "What are we going to do?"

"Dad's..."

She interrupted. "I heard him. God, Kate. He sounded nothing like himself. I'm worried he's going to do something stupid."

I stared at the ground, calculating. I'd left Mom about six hours ago. Lincoln, where Dad laid over, was a five-hour drive from here. Getting Marty Kaufman's address might have been tricky for Dad but not impossible. He spent a lot of time on the internet when he was stuck in hotels on the other end of the road, and he might have skills we didn't know about. Allowing for all of this, it didn't seem crazy to think they'd end up at Marty Kaufman's house close to the same time.

Louise still rambled at me. "They say Dad had a bad temper and something happened in Vietnam—"

"I know." I wanted her to stop talking so I could think. Three hours to Denver. If I could get a flight tonight, it would still get me there too late to intercept them. Even if I didn't have to factor in renting a car, which, in my experience, could take a decade to accomplish.

Nothing like a swan dive from the frying pan into the fire. I pulled out my phone and held my finger to dial Diane's number, then stopped. Whatever Louise was saying, I cut her off. "Call Diane."

She stopped mid-word, her mouth open. While she sputtered, I took off for the kitchen, where I'd probably find her phone on the counter.

May stood at the sink, a plate in one hand, a raised fork in the other. "No need to let this meatloaf go to waste."

I snatched Louise's phone from where it rested next to May, and she jumped as if I'd tried to hit her. One tap to Louise's contacts and another to Diane, and it rang before Louise made it to the kitchen.

Diane answered, already talking. "Whatever Kate told you, I didn't abandon her. She's capable of getting herself back to Nebraska."

"Can you get us to Chicago tonight?"

Dead silence.

I rushed on, not knowing what to say to convince her to help. "Mom took off for there, and Dad is following. I'm afraid he's going to do something stupid."

"Stupid? How?"

I thrust the phone at Louise. "Explain it all to her, and tell her I'll be there in three hours. Text me the plans."

Louise barely caught the phone. "Not everything. She doesn't need to know."

Diane's tinny voice came from the phone. "Know what? Tell me everything."

Already moving toward the front door, I shouted over my shoulder. "No more secrets. I need Diane's help. Tell her."

I rushed back to May. Her hand tightened on the fork as if readying to stab me if necessary.

"I'm leaving Poupon with you," I told her.

She curled her lip. "Poop? What's that?"

"My dog. Feed him. Let him sleep inside." It sounded abrupt and demanding, and I tried to soften it. "Please."

"Just this once. And I don't let dogs on the furniture."

Yeah, good luck with that.

I didn't stick around to hear Louise stumble through the story, but I could imagine Diane's enraged reaction at being kept out of the loop.

25

The three hours of driving hadn't been broken up by anything except a text from Diane to meet her at the Rocky Mountain Metropolitan Airport in Broomfield, a town in the urban sprawl between Denver and Boulder. I'd have liked more details but decided to let it unfold since Diane set it up.

You grow up in the Nebraska Sandhills, you learn a certain patience on a drive. It takes an hour from Hodgekiss to get to a town with any services besides the bare essentials. There's nothing to do but let your mind loop endlessly on whatever worries you. I didn't have any lack of problems on my drive.

I might have relived every incident of my childhood trying to understand how Glenda felt finding out she had a different father than the rest of us. Not all of the rest of the Fox kids. Jeremy, it seemed, was Marty Kaufman's son. Was that why Mom favored him? I felt she was closer to Glenda than all of us, but I figured that was because, as the oldest, she relied on Glenda almost as if she were another adult.

After an interminable amount of time, I dialed in a history podcast and tried to lose myself in the minutiae of life in the colonies in the early eighteenth century. It only worked partially, but at least it gave me something to focus on. Because my mind kept being sucked into a dark hole.

By the time I got to the Denver area, traffic had thinned for the night, and I followed the appropriate exits according to my GPS without incident. The small airport had probably been built in a rural area a few decades ago, but after so many years, a busy shopping mall, several conference resorts, and major office parks surrounded it. I pulled up in front of what Diane had said was an FBO. I assumed that meant it was the place private planes used for a terminal.

A smattering of security lights showed through the glass doors and windows of a pristine building with immaculate landscaping. I shot from the cruiser and trotted toward the front door.

Diane swung it open and leaned out. Sarcasm draped her words. "Did you stop for dinner along the way?" Obviously, she hadn't taken in my uniform and the fact I hadn't even stopped home to change my clothes or get my own car.

I slipped past her into a neat, open room with several low couches and chairs, a counter along one wall, and hallways running off in both directions. A faint smell of popcorn hung in the air from the complimentary carnival popper in the corner. The quiet of the empty place was broken up with quick footsteps approaching from the end of the hallway on the right.

With a growl in my voice, I said, "I got here as fast as I could."

She pulled the front door closed and jammed a key into the lock, jingling several others on the ring when she twisted it. "You've got a light bar. Seems like you could have used it."

Of course, whatever I did wouldn't be good enough for her.

A young man burst from the hallway, and I was surprised to recognize Dolan Ostrander. He'd graduated a few years ahead of Susan. Long and lean, he wore a short-sleeved, white button-up shirt tucked into navy blue slacks and, along with a dark tie, he looked like a maître d' or an LDS kid on a mission. Like most Ostranders, he sported a grin with a protrusion of buck teeth. "Hey, Kate. Ready?"

I blinked from him to Diane. She'd crossed the lobby and wound behind the counter and stood at the glass door leading to the tarmac. "Let's go."

I took a few faltering steps and couldn't help staring at Dolan. "I knew you were going to flight school. I didn't realize you'd graduated."

His long strides rushed me into the chilly night. "About a year ago.

Mom called Diane, and she knows the CEO of Lighthouse Insurance. And she got me the interview. Greg owns the plane with two other guys, and they hired me."

That was a whole lot of catching up in four sentences. Betsy Ostrander, Dolan's mother, was a cousin of Dad's in a family spiral too complicated to relate. When you grow up in the Sandhills, family stretches far, and it's always okay to reach out when someone can help. In this case, it looked like Diane helped.

"And you're a pilot now? And you got up in the middle of the night to fly us to Chicago because Diane asked you to?" I felt like my brain was slumped behind the wheel of my Charger and it had no chance of catching up.

It seemed he narrowed his stride so he wouldn't outrun me. "More or less. But any chance we get to fly this baby, we're all in. I mean, Diane called Greg, and he called us."

"Us?"

He laughed. "Well, yeah. The other pilot is on board doing the preflight."

Floodlights from the FBO made our passage across the tarmac easy. A sleek jet reflected light back to us, and I realized Diane was heading straight for it. With a wingspan of maybe seventy feet, they tipped up at the ends, making me think of a hawk soaring toward an unsuspecting field mouse.

Dolan lifted his arm as if presenting it to us. "Challenger 3500. Bombardier."

Whatever he meant made no sense to me. I assumed we'd be taking a small plane, like one of the Cessnas several ranchers in the Sandhills owned. This looked like something from a movie featuring a jewel thief and an heiress or an international spy who spirited around the world on their private jets.

Stairs descended to the tarmac, and Diane grabbed the railing. "Would you hurry up?" she snapped at me.

Dolan kicked it into gear and galloped ahead, taking the stairs two at a time and ducking into the lit entryway at the top.

I wasn't far behind and tipped my imaginary hat at Diane as I started up. "You really came through."

"I didn't do it for you."

"Clearly." I took an obvious right at the top of the stairs and entered what appeared to be a lounge, with butterscotch-colored leather recliners, bar, and table all resembling the finest RVs I'd had the pleasure of touring at the Nebraska State Fair.

Diane shoved past me and landed in one of the recliners. She reached a seat belt around her and glared at me. "Sit down. Belt up. We're taking off."

And we were. The engines roared to life. The wheels started turning before I chose my seat next to a window and copied Diane's moves.

Diane pulled out a laptop and typed furiously. She kept working for the next hour while I marveled at the take-off, Denver's receding lights, and the always engaging display of stars. They were no less amazing from this altitude than they were from my front porch.

Fatigue pounded behind my eyes and in my head, but I couldn't close my eyes.

With a sigh, Diane snapped her computer closed and rose. She rummaged around in the refrigerator and seized on a bottle of Perrier. With no hesitation, telling me she'd been in this plane before, she opened a cabinet and selected a crystal whiskey glass. One dip into the fridge again and she clinked ice into the glass, splashed the fizzy water, and stashed the bottle away.

Suddenly thirsty, I repeated her process. After a few gulps, I refilled my glass and offered to do the same for Diane. She held out her glass and allowed me to fill it. With my back to her, I started, "What do you think of what Louise told you?"

Her ice clinked.

I shoved the bottle into the fridge and turned. "Mom told me Glenda was Marty's daughter. And it was shocking. But I figured it was before Dad and it was forgivable."

Diane stared at her glass.

"When I found out about Jeremy, and that Glenda and Louise knew all along..." I stopped and let my gaze wander to the window before finishing. "I'm lost here. I could use some sister talk."

She spit her words at me. "What do you want? All of a sudden, I'm good enough to be part of your circle? Screw it. Screw the whole damn family."

"You don't mean that."

"You don't know what I mean."

I sipped at the cold sparkles, glad to have something to cool my nerves. "It's a pretty big deal to wake up the owner of an insurance company and ask him to borrow his jet and pilots."

She blew a raspberry. "Greg is an old friend. He owes me a couple of favors."

"See?"

"What?"

"You're right. I don't know. I don't know anything about you. You keep it all hidden from me. From all of us."

She wouldn't look at me. "Glenda knew everything about me, and after she was gone, no one else cared."

That wasn't true, but now didn't seem like the time to crash her self-pity party. "Tell me now. I'm asking. Why do you stay so distant from us?"

She eyed her water. "I'd need something stronger than this to tell the story."

I gave her a lopsided grin. "You don't think I'd love an IPA after that drive? But we don't know what we're going to find. I think we ought to stay as sharp as possible."

She sniffed in reluctant agreement.

"Come on. We've got a long flight. Just tell me the Diane story, and then we never have to talk again."

She checked the diamond-studded watch on her wrist and took a drink. "I was the third daughter. Glenda was the queen. She had that confidence and charisma."

I didn't interrupt to say no one had more confidence than Diane.

"Everyone loved Glenda and would follow her to the ends of the earth. All the family and the kids at school. She was one of those people who have to die young because they're so perfect you can't stand the thought of them disappointing everyone." She eyed me. "As you know they always do."

I quietly moved back to my chair and lowered into it.

"So, then there was Louise, who always wanted to please. She had to take care of everyone. A little mother. She's not a leader, but when Glenda died, it's like she had to fill that spot. She was never going to do it. And, honestly, I wish she'd quit trying."

I was surprised at the kindness in Diane's tone. Who knew she cared about Louise?

"I didn't want to be Glenda and sure as hell didn't want to be Louise. Three girls seemed like plenty to me, but then Mom and Dad were like some kind of baby assembly line. I hated it. All the noise and sharing clothes and beds, babysitting, or fighting."

I couldn't help but add, "Yeah. I love everyone, but there's a reason I married young and love living in the country alone."

Diane pointed at me in a I-know-what-you-mean way. "That's the difference between you and me. I wanted out of there. Away from everyone and any reference to being a Fox from Hodgekiss. I wanted to be my own person. Self-made."

She'd succeeded in spades. Might as well take a leap into the heart of it. "How did you end up with Vince?"

She glared at me, and I thought I'd blown it. She'd never tell me about Vince. She rattled her ice at me, and I got up to pour her more Perrier.

With a heavy tone, she said, "You let Ted pick you."

God, I hated that everyone in the family knew my MO.

"Because you wanted the peace and you wanted to be someone's one and only. But you've always been so tied into the family. Little Katie, always taking care of everyone."

"No, sir." Sometimes, you never grow out of those old standby phrases, especially with people you've known your whole life.

She sniffed again. "Everyone relies on you. You're the glue."

"Am not. That's Louise." There I went again.

"She just irritates everyone. You keep everyone even."

"So, Vince."

Her eyes sparkled. "Vince. He's dashing, of course." She stopped and gave me a deadly stare. "Was." She let her point sit a moment. "He was not like anyone I'd ever known. The money was a bonus. Absolutely. If I'm honest. I can make my own money, though."

She seemed to have forgotten me, so I stayed silent.

She held her glass up as in a toast. "And I do a damned fine job of making money." She sipped. "But I'd always be a nobody. Even if I was a rich nobody, I wanted more. Vince had that old-money thing going on. There were weekends and parties you're invited to with old money that the nouveau riche never knows about. Plus, Vince's family has the kind of wealth that's deep vein, where my money is only surface. I can buy a big house and afford luxury travel, but nothing like the status you have with generations of pedigree."

She focused on me. "Do you think Greg 'Lighthouse Insurance' is friends with me because I'm a banker, for fuck's sake? There were a few weekends in the Hamptons that sealed this relationship."

Connections, secrets, favors. Diane lived in a world I was only too glad to not belong in. "So, you married Vince for a pedigree?" I sounded as dubious as I felt.

She pointed at me again. "You'd think that's enough. But the real reason I married Vince is that he loved me. All of me. He wasn't threatened by the powerful, driven me, the one with thorns on the outside. The bowling-ball me who knocks all the pins down. But he's the only one who ever protected that little me. The one no one took the time to love and cuddle."

We all had scars from our wild upbringing. Diane had been better than most of us at hiding them. "Did you ever show that side to anyone else? I've never seen it."

She laughed. "All my years of therapy, and here you come along and nail it on the first go. The answer is no. I haven't made my vulnerability public knowledge. It's not the Fox way. Which one of us ever shows our needs?"

I shrugged. "Douglas?"

She grinned at me. "Only because he always had Michael to take care of him."

I conceded that point. "Why did you divorce Vince if he loved you?"

"I didn't. He divorced me. Wanted someone younger, prettier, more exciting. Got tired of my job, the home, being tied down. He seemed unhappy all the time. A premature midlife crisis, I guess. I always believed he'd come back to me."

The clunk of the wheels lowering distracted us. Dolan's voice came over the intercom. "Better belt up, ladies. We'll be landing in a few."

Diane thrust her glass at me, and I jumped up to stow it and mine in the kitchen.

I'd just clicked my belt when Diane's words smacked me.

"But you killed him. Now I'll be alone forever. I'll never forgive you for that."

26

The sun hinted on the eastern horizon, bringing a milky feel to the dawn. I couldn't tell if the sky was overcast or if this time of day always sagged heavy in Chicago. Chilly air billowed up from the tarmac through the open door of the plane. I had no luggage, but I had my trusty sheriff-brown jacket to match my always stylish uniform.

Diane wore wide-legged black pants and a long sweater that all seemed to flow around her. Soft leather flats and her hair in its always perfect style made her look like a magazine cover for comfortable and chic travel.

"You've obviously traveled like this before," I said.

She couldn't have acted more regal if she wore a crown. "A time or two."

"So what's FBO stand for? Like, private terminal for very special people?"

She snorted in disdain. "Fixed-base operator. For private planes. So yes, very special people." She obviously didn't mean me.

Dolan stood at the top of the stairs, and I half expected him to smile and say, "Buh-bye." Instead, he asked me how I enjoyed the flight.

Enjoy wasn't the word I'd use. I'd started off confused and alone, somewhere over Iowa I'd soared with hope that I might get my sister back, and ended feeling like bird poop hitting the tarmac from three thousand feet. "Like a good wine, smooth and mellow."

He grinned at me, showing those Ostrander buck teeth. "Hope you got some sleep."

Diane breathed down the back of my neck. "Is the car here?"

Dolan stepped back to let me descend the stairs. "Yep. FBO arranged it. They said it's out front. Don't think they were excited to have to come in early, so I'm sure they'll make you pay for that."

Diane laughed as if we were on a lark. "I'm sure."

He sounded uneasy. "We've got to take 'er back in about two hours. Greg needs to go to Fort Lauderdale. So, I guess…"

Diane sounded chipper. "No problem. We can catch a commercial flight if it's going to be any longer than that. Don't wait around. We appreciate Greg loaning you to get us here. Sorry about the timing."

Just a friendly Sandhills guy. "Don't worry about it. We're used to weird hours. After you got me this job, it's the least I can do."

I hit the tarmac, and Diane was right behind me. She spoke over her shoulder. "You got the job, Dolan. I only made the introductions."

She swung that expensive leather tote over her shoulder and took off at a near gallop, her sweater swirling around her like Maleficent's cape.

Even at this early hour, a young woman manned the counter in the FBO. In her crisp pastel blue shirt with a name tag identifying her as Emily, with hair in a bouncy ponytail, she didn't look old enough to drive, let alone handle the demands of travelers and pilots. She smiled at us when we approached. "Welcome to Midway International. Ms. Fox?"

I was so surprised to hear my name, I answered at the same time Diane did, then realized it wouldn't be me the woman addressed.

Diane spared an irritated glace at me before smiling at the woman. "Do you have keys for the car?"

Emily set a fob on the counter with no key, along with a form on a clipboard. "It's the champagne BMW out front. I just need you to sign here."

Despite treating me and Louise like we were as useful as a solar flashlight, Diane had a way of making Dolan and Emily feel respected. "Thanks for taking care of this at such an ungodly hour."

Emily beamed. "It's what we do. Have a great visit, and welcome to Chicago."

All the pleasantries out of the way, we took off in the spotless BMW with a ripe new-car smell. Diane drove and located Marty's address from her recent locations on her phone.

"Let me guess," I said. "It's a half-hour drive from here."

She huffed at me in annoyance.

"What if Mom isn't here?" I asked.

"She is." Diane's talkative stage must be over for the trip.

This didn't help me at all. We were a meteor hurtling toward the planet, and we'd explode on impact. "What are we going to do if she is there?"

"Take her home."

Even if I didn't know about Alan and Lyle Joffe and what Marty Kaufman had done, taking Mom home seemed too easy. "What about Dad?"

She frowned and looked up at the roof of the car, let out a long-suffering breath, and said nothing. Conversation ended.

After another harrowing drive jumping onto and off of I-55, I recognized Marty's neighborhood. Even with what was probably light traffic for the city, the cars whizzing past wound the spool of my nerves even tighter.

Diane's hands turned white from squeezing the wheel. She wasn't as cool and unattached as she'd like me to think.

We turned the last corner onto Marty's street, the sun a hazy orb in the milky sky but high enough to herald full morning. A sharp breeze ripped leaves from the trees and scuttled them across the street.

My stomach did a loop and plunged into icy dread when I spotted May's Scout parked in front of Marty's house, half on and half off the curb. Marty's front door opened into the dark house, and the screen flapped in the wind.

Diane braked behind the Scout, and we both jumped out.

Marty appeared in the doorway, a cardboard box in his arms. He stopped and gave us a shocked stare before turning his head back to the house and saying something I couldn't make out.

Diane marched toward him and up the porch. "Get out of the way."

He widened his stance. "You shouldn't have come here." His eyes flicked to me, and a crater seemed to open into his heart. He looked away quickly, as if seeing me burned him.

"Yeah?" Diane raised her eyebrows at him. "Well, we're here. And we want to see our mother."

Marty lowered his head like a bull on the fight. "I'm not going to let that happen."

Diane might be all class and sophistication these days, but she was every bit as scrappy as the rest of us. She'd thrown her share of punches and wasn't accustomed to being handed things without fighting for them. Marty ought to go on the offensive or he'd lose before he even started.

Diane's shoulders rose as if ready to join the battle.

A white hand landed on Marty's shoulder, and Mom pressed between him and the doorframe. She wore the same yoga pants but had wrapped a plush cape around her thin body. Her hair looked like a wild animal trying to nest on her head.

In a voice overlaid with serenity, she said, "It's okay, Marty."

His speech was rapid and breathy. "We don't have time. We've got to get up there before they figure out who you are."

This was where I should have said I knew who she was.

Mom patted his shoulder. Their eyes connected in a way so intimate it scalded me. What a betrayal. "They're my daughters. I may never see them again."

That hit me like a fist to my belly. I didn't want to detain her officially, but she was leaving me no choice.

Marty cast a wary glance at Diane and stepped from the doorway. He seemed reluctant to pull away from Mom, but it also seemed clear he'd do anything she asked.

Mom retreated inside. Diane gave Marty a look with teeth sharp enough to break skin and stomped past him.

Marty watched me approach. He didn't say anything while I stopped and searched his face. His eyes were deep brown. Thinning hair, mostly gray but still wavy. None of the sweetness and caring I saw when I looked at Dad. Sadness and loss seemed sunk into the deep wrinkles on his face. Did I see Glenda in his eyes? Jeremy in his smile?

What I felt for him was like a hot coal in the pit of my stomach, smoldering, choking, and oh-so-hard to put out. His eyes went soft around the edges, and it looked as if he wanted me to read what he felt in their depths.

I turned away. Not interested.

Mom and Diane stood in the shadows of the cramped living room, already arguing.

Mom had never seemed old to me until that morning. At home, she'd take long walks, coming home with armfuls of sunflowers or cattails, along with fall grasses of reds and golds. After a snowstorm, she'd often go outside naked in the dead of night and make snow angels. Her mind tripped with colors and ideas, new creations meant to flow from her fingers.

But this morning she looked spent, washed out, slow and numb. "I can't go back."

Diane had lost the corporate image and sounded like a lost little girl. "Why? Dad loves you. He'll forgive this." Diane waved around the room, taking in the whole situation. "He doesn't need to know about Jeremy. Come home where you belong."

Mom glanced over Diane's head and caught my eye. She arched her eyebrows as if begging me to understand. "I gave your father and you children the most productive years of my life. Forty years. Children and so much love. I've got so little left."

Diane pleaded, "I know you're tired, but we'll take care of you."

I wanted to crumple to the floor and disappear in a puff of ash. Mom was going to force me to do the unthinkable. "She's not going home," I said, surprised my voice had any heft.

Diane spun around to look at me, so much fury in her eyes. If I'd had any hope for a reconciliation, I'd kill it with what I needed to do.

Mom shook her head, eyes wet but no tears falling. "You don't have to do this." She spoke so softly I mostly read her lips.

I felt like throwing up. "Yeah. I do." Then with a jab because I hurt so badly, I added, "Because I'm my father's daughter. He taught me right from wrong."

Mom lifted her chin and drew her lips taut, as if battling a sharp pain.

An exchange of voices made us turn to the door.

Deb walked in. Her hair looked newly washed, and she wore dress pants and a nice white blouse, much more put-together than when we'd surprised her. She'd obviously taken some care with her appearance to meet her sister.

Marty stepped in the doorway right behind her. He spoke to Mom. "She said you called her? Miriam, this is a bad idea. We have to go."

Mom floated a silky look to Marty, a mere second but clear acknowledgment of his concern. And a tenderness for him that made me ache for Dad. A micro breath of an argument between two hearts in union.

A sledgehammer smashed into me, flattening my world.

Mom's movements were smooth as she glided to Deb with open arms. "It's you. Oh." She threw herself on Deb, wrapping her frail arms around Deb's neck. She looked so much older than her younger sister. She seemed shrunken and sucked dry. "You came. Thank you."

Deb lightly patted Mom's shoulders, nothing like the bear hug she'd given me. She straightened and pulled away. "I'm here, Miriam. But I'm not sure why."

Mom's voice deepened, and she stood straighter, pulling her head back in an assertive way that reminded me of Diane. "You're my sister. I wanted to see you."

Deb's tone, full of affection and humor with me, scraped like a shovel on concrete. "After all these years, why now? Why not when you had any of your nine children? Why not when Dad died or when I had to move Mom to the apartment? I don't suppose you're here now to help me with her growing dementia and to take some of the burden when it's time to make the decision for her to go into long-term care."

Mom had always been like a quiet, lapping shorefront with us. I'd have expected her face to soften with compassion and guilt. Instead, she answered with a defensive shake of her head. "There are reasons I couldn't contact you. I wanted to come back, and I understand why you're so resentful. I've missed you every single day since I left. We were so close. You can't tell me that's died away."

Deb's eyes glared with acrimony. "After what you did to us, I find it hard to believe you ever cared for anyone except yourself."

A weird energy surged beneath the exhausted exterior of Mom's face, as if she held back an explosion. "It was impossible for me to so much as contact you. It would have put you at risk."

Deb let out a snort of disgust.

Mom doubled down with sincerity. "I never stopped loving you. I sent you money when Marty told me you needed it. Didn't that tell you I cared?"

Deb hesitated, and the hard edge melted. Tears shimmered in her eyes, and she sniffed to hold them back. "I couldn't even tell you thank you. And I wanted to."

Across the room, Diane watched the exchange with intensity. If she felt anything like I did, she was caught up in a surreal parallel universe where suddenly, the artist mother named Marguerite was now a seventy-year-old revolutionary from Chicago who had destroyed her family.

Marty stood by the front door, still holding the cardboard box, and he seemed uncertain whether to allow the confrontation to continue.

Even though Mom was shorter than Deb, she seemed taller and in charge. "Marty didn't want me to call you. He said you hated me now. But I didn't listen. I know you, Debbie. You love me as much as I love you."

Deb's eyes narrowed in disbelief. "Marty was right. We've got nothing left between us."

A bit of Mom's façade crumbled. "You're hurt that I had to hide. And rightfully so. But I'm leaving the country, and this will probably be the last time we see each other. I need to make it right between us before we're lost forever."

Deb folded her arms over her chest. She spoke with quiet intensity. "I knew your name. Did you really think I wouldn't look in that envelope? I could have found you anytime."

Another piece fell from Mom's wall. "Why didn't you?" Her voice cracked. "I needed you."

Deb's nose twitched as if smelling something sour. "Oh, *you* needed *me*? You weren't here when I needed you, and I learned to survive without you. I definitely don't need you now. Just go."

Mom stared at her, and neither moved for a second. Then Deb said, "I know you were in Milwaukee that night. Marty served his time. You deserved to go to jail, too."

Mom's eyes sharpened, and she snapped her head toward the door as if afraid of being cornered.

Deb's chuckle had no humor. "Don't worry. I'm not going to call the Feds."

Diane jerked her head back and flashed a questioning look at me. All I could do was answer her with a slight nod.

Mom grabbed Deb's wrist. "Please. Debbie. We're sisters. Family. We'll always be a part of each other."

Deb shook her arm free. "You broke our family, and it's too late to put it back together." She turned from Mom and strode toward the door.

Marty stepped back to let her pass.

Before she disappeared into the morning, she paused. Slowly she turned around and started back into the room.

Mom straightened and smiled, lifting her arms in a welcome hug. "I knew—"

Deb didn't look at her but walked directly to me. In an astonishing move, she threw her arms around me and pulled me close in a hug so full of acceptance and homecoming I choked up.

She jerked away and met my gaze with a shy smile. With a scratchy voice, she said, "I hope we can get to know each other better."

She turned to Diane and tipped her chin. "You, too."

Diane's jaw loosened, and her eyes rounded. A lump traveled down her throat. She managed to whisper, "Thank you."

Mom's mouth opened as if she'd been rammed in the stomach. She gave a proprietary complaint. "They're my daughters."

Deb walked out and dribbled the words behind her. "You're leaving, but I'll still be here."

1971

Soft rain pattered on leaves as Miriam stood at the railing of the cabin and stared at the heavy sky. Midday and it felt like twilight. She hadn't seen the sun in a week. Or two, maybe. All the days melded together here.

Doug and Bob appeared from a break in the trees, their faces smeared with dirt, hands black with mud. Always cheery, Bob waved and shouted, "Is lunch ready?"

The smell of savory stew mingled with the aroma of warm bread on the thick air of the forest. She and three other women had baked and chopped all morning. "On the table."

They tromped around back to wash before joining the rest of the people gathering from their various duties for the noon meal.

A couple emerged from the shed where they did the laundry by hand until the People of Peace saved up enough to buy a washer and dryer, which wouldn't be any good until they ran utilities, which wouldn't happen until they built more cabins, which they couldn't afford unless a few more people joined the commune. Preferably people with money to contribute. The young woman, June, wore a faded bandana to keep her blond hair back. Denim overalls two sizes too big draped her partner's thin frame, his shirtless shoulders cutting the damp air. They held hands.

June's friendly face focused on Miriam as she climbed the porch steps. "That bread smells so good. It's been torturing us all morning. Thanks, Marguerite."

"Enjoy," Miriam said, now accustomed to her new name. She turned her attention back to the forest.

Finally, Marty trudged out of the path in the trees. His face, weary seconds before he spotted her, broke into a smile that burned through the clouds.

She bounded down the steps and into his arms. "You're late."

He pulled her close. "Not late. Just not early."

She ran her hands through his waves, reveling in his handsome face, lingering in the loving gaze of his brown eyes. After a couple of seconds, she pulled away and fitted her hand into his.

They walked toward the cabin. "Whenever you're not with me, it's late." They had their work assignments. On Wednesdays, she and Marty washed laundry together. Thursdays, she had kitchen duty and he worked in the gardens. Her favorite days were Fridays, when they went to Seattle and she sold her paintings and the handicrafts of the others and Marty picked up odd jobs at Pike Place.

She waited while he washed from a bucket and dried his hands on a grimy towel. "I'm dying to see the sun."

He leaned down and kissed her, as if he needed to make up for missing her all morning. Then he gave her a lopsided look and repeated a well-worn line. "I'm sorry. But we're safe here."

She lowered her voice in imitation. "We're safe here." She sighed. "It's been a year. Maybe we can find a small town someplace where they don't follow the news. We aren't headlines anymore."

He focused on something in the trees behind her. "It's not just the Feds."

She laughed. "*Just* the Feds."

He didn't laugh. "Alan. He blames you for Lyle's death."

They made their way to the cabin. Before Marty took his place at the table and she returned to her duties in the kitchen, she said, "Alan's in Canada. He can't come back to this country, so he's going to have to get over it and start a new life. And so do we." She placed her hands on his cheeks and gave him a quick peck on his lips.

Marty's work-calloused hand tugged on hers until she gave him her full attention. "He's not going to forgive you. You heard Leah…"

"Yes." She spoke sharply in her impatience. "I heard." One of the People of Peace who had welcomed Marty and Miriam had gone to visit friends in Vancouver last month. From a friend of a friend, the way news traveled among the draft dodgers, she'd heard Alan Joffee, one of the Milwaukee Four, had vowed revenge on the unidentified bomber, who he swore knew his brother was in the building when she detonated the bomb. Leah was all in a buzz that he'd revealed the other bomber was a woman.

She pulled Marty's face down to hers. "No one in our world is going to tell Alan about us, even if they figure it out. We're heroes to those of us who believe in the movement."

He pulled her close in an embrace that took her breath away. "I love you, Miriam."

She leaned her forehead to his. "We're soul mates. Together forever."

That dark edge of worry that seemed always to be in Marty's eyes deepened before she turned away.

27

Marty followed Deb out, maybe to load the box in his old 4Runner or maybe to make sure she was gone.

Mom turned to me and Diane with desperation darkening her eyes and pulling at her face. "I know you don't understand."

The conflict inside me rose until I felt like it would split me in two. I had to stop this. "I do understand. I know who Alan Joffe is and what you did."

Diane found her boardroom control, and she sounded ready to make decisions. "Who is Alan Joffe?"

I didn't take my eyes off Mom. "I'm a law enforcement officer. You know I can't let you go."

Miriam had left and Marguerite was back, soft and vulnerable. "Katie. Whatever you've been told, stop and think. I've been a mother for over forty years. Nine children contributing to the goodness of the world. All the love and caring. As a young woman, did I make mistakes? Yes. Terrible, terrible mistakes."

Diane stepped closer to us. "What are you talking about?"

I couldn't break the connection with Mom to answer her. "Those mistakes were deadly."

Mom winced. "I know. I've lived with it every day since it happened. Do you have any idea what it's like to wake up to that guilt each morning?"

It must have been awful for her, but what about Thomas Scanlon? Did she think how terrible it was for his wife and children? I couldn't bring myself to say those things even as her narcissism grated in my ears.

"The only relief I had was in my art."

That must have hit Diane square in the heart because she fired at Mom, "Your art was the only relief?"

Mom realized her omission and leaned toward Diane. "And my family. You children were my redemption. You set the scales right."

Diane looked away. She might not know all the details, but she showed her doubt in Mom's sincerity.

Marty stomped through the open doorway. "If we don't leave now, we aren't going to make the connection."

Diane glanced from Marty to Mom. "Are you leaving with him? You're going to abandon your husband, your children, and your grandchildren to run away with this?" She flicked her hand toward Marty in a gesture of disdain.

Mom's bony fingers fluttered at her throat, and she sounded strangled. "I have no choice."

"That's not true." I jumped in, startling them. "Stay here. Face it. We'll be with you."

With Deb, Miriam had been unyielding. Mom took a different approach with me. She looked at me with a melting gaze. "I can't go to jail. It would kill my soul. I can't be confined."

I watched Marty to see if he resented Mom's remark. He'd picked up another box that looked like outdoor gear and walked out without comment or any more reaction than obvious impatience.

I pointed after Marty. "He did seven years. You can't sacrifice that amount of time for us?"

Mom backed toward the door, her focus flitting around the room as if terrified. "Look at me, Katie. I'm an old woman. I've paid my debt. Stayed hidden in Nebraska. I was a good wife and mother."

Diane snorted. "We were a sentence for whatever awful thing you did?"

I fought to wrangle my emotions and hog-tie them, but this was too much.

Mom flinched at Diane's reaction. Another chunk of armor dropped away. "I did my best."

Again, Diane let out a grunt.

Mom's hair tumbled into her face as she lowered her head in defeat. She sounded weary. "I know I wasn't the kind of mother your friends had. But I loved you fiercely. You must believe that."

Everything inside me felt like glass, and small cracks snaked across the surface.

Diane had obviously reached her limit. "I might have believed that if not for Jeremy."

Mom recoiled and held her breath.

"We know he's Marty's son. You lied. To Dad. To all of us. You're nothing but a fraud. I don't know what you did to make Kate want to throw you in jail, but I say go on. We don't need you. Leave us like you left your sister and parents. You're not worth any of us caring that you're gone."

Mom's mouth dropped open as if she hadn't the strength to hold it firm. She closed her eyes and swayed, and I wondered if her legs would give and she'd fall.

But I didn't step in to help her. Part of me wanted to comfort her, but the rest of me wouldn't make a move.

Seemingly in slow motion, Mom started to reinflate. She opened her eyes, and I could almost see her gathering those pieces that had fallen from her shell and fitting them into place. She straightened her shoulders and raised her chin. "All my life I've done what I had to do to survive. I've lost almost everyone I loved along the way. They've all turned their backs on me except Marty. Now he's all I have."

With a show of dignity, she bestowed a look on us like a monarch sending us into exile. She bent to heft a case of art supplies and walked out the door.

I wanted to let her go. She was my mother. I owed her my life. Even though she hadn't cheered me on at the spelling bees or been the one to lay a cool washcloth on my fevered head, she'd given me love. In her own way. Always in her own way.

Diane's harsh voice brought me around. "Let her go. I don't know what she did, but you don't have to be the one to set it right. Not this time."

"Miriam Fine is wanted for the murder of two people. I can't let her leave." I turned from Diane and strode out the door.

Mom and Marty stood at the back of the 4Runner, and Marty slammed the tailgate shut.

Diane kept with me as we tromped down the stairs and across the grass. Clouds scuttled across the sky, and the neighborhood was waking up. A few cars drove down the street, and garage doors and curtains opened up in houses nearby. For most of these people, the day was like any other. Their worlds weren't crashing into rubble.

"Mom." My voice sounded determined.

Diane commanded me in her big-sister way. "You'll hate yourself if you do this. What if you send her to jail and she dies there? No one will forgive you. You won't forgive yourself."

She was right. But what else could I do?

Diane grabbed my arm, and I whipped around to confront her. She put her face close to mine. "Do you want to end up like Debbie and Miriam? Two sisters who don't know each other. Don't love each other. Not family."

Battered by so much conflict, I muttered, "You're already gone. You won't forgive me for Vince's death."

She threw her head back and huffed out a steamy breath. "For fuck's sake. I know you didn't kill Vince, and I'm not blind to what he was. I was hurt, okay? I needed to be mad at someone besides myself for bringing him into the family."

For a second, this confession overpowered the situation. "You punished me, and you knew it wasn't my fault?"

"I just said so. And I'm sorry." She lifted her eyebrows. "Are we good?"

Stunned by this and how she thought we'd move on in a heartbeat, I couldn't answer.

But she didn't need me to. "So let Mom go. It's the best way for all of us to heal."

Marty made a move for the driver's side, but Mom hesitated. She started to come toward us.

Diane turned her back on Mom and faced me. "Please."

At the sound of a car roaring down the street, we all turned as a beat-up

Ford pickup, more rust than paint, squealed to a stop and came danged close to ramming the champagne BMW.

"Oh, shit." Diane said what I was thinking.

Mom let out something that sounded like a moan. "No." Then, with urgency as she hurried to the passenger door of the 4Runner, "No, no, no."

She was running away from Dad. The man she'd been married to for forty-five years. The father of most of her children. I'd stepped into a horror show with each scene bloodier than the last.

1972

Miriam shouldered the macrame bag, the strap soft on her bare skin. She placed a hand on Marty's tanned chest and leaned in for a deep kiss. She lifted her other fist and forced it into Marty's hand, leaving the crumpled five-dollar bill. "That's it, babe."

The smell of the ocean, salty and damp, mingled with sun on pavement and the grease from the hamburger stand half a block away from the seawall where they sat.

Marty's long hair hid his face when he dropped his head to see what she'd given him. He looked up, and when his gaze met hers, they merged into one. "We're at the end, you know that."

If he needed her to be strong for them both, she could do it. Leaning in closer, she cherished the feel of his arm circling her bare back just above the tie of her halter top. "Don't give up now. We can get to Canada. We know people up there who can take us in."

The seagulls shrieked and dove, snatching bits of hot dog buns from the sidewalk and fighting over them. The waves, too far away to interrupt their conversation, broke against the beach now crowded with families and young people. A soldier walked by in uniform. He looked hot and tired and defeated. He could definitely use a friend. If she and Marty weren't on the run and in so much trouble, she would have invited him along to find someone willing to share a joint and some food.

The look of defeat in Marty's eyes scared her. "Alan is up there. He's poisoned everyone against us."

Miriam wove her fingertips into his beard along his chin. "Canada is a big place, and they'll believe us. I didn't know Lyle had gone inside. I thought he'd taken off to meet Alan. I would never have lit the fuse if I'd known anyone was in there."

Marty kissed her slowly, all his love bleeding into her. "I know. But you know how Alan gets people to go along with him."

A growing desperation beat in her stomach. "We can go somewhere else. I can use that five dollars to buy some supplies and I'll paint. We'll get enough to go to Mexico." She stepped back and flung her arm out toward the sea. "We love the beach."

"Miriam." It came out like a sigh.

She pulled his hand. "No. No. We can keep going. I'll make it okay."

Tears wavered and threatened to spill down his haggard cheeks. How could she have not noticed how exhausted he was? "No, babe. I'm tired of living like this. I want more for us. We need a home. We can't keep running. Not now. Let's serve our time, and then we'll be free."

For seven years she'd looked into those eyes and seen the whole world reflected there. She and Marty belonged together, their souls twined together throughout time and countless lives. Soul mates. This was the first time she'd ever doubted him. A cold, dull edge split her heart, and she gasped for breath. "You know I can't do that. If they lock me up, I'll die."

He crumbled in front of her. "I don't think I can live without you. But I know I can't keep doing this."

She tugged his arm again, desperate to make him stand away from the seawall and walk to the ocean. "Let's cool off. Take a minute to figure it out."

"It's too late." His whisper seeped from him like air escaping a balloon.

No. He couldn't. Her love. Her life. How could he betray her? "What did you do?"

"I called the FBI. They're on their way."

Ice encased her, and her thoughts burst apart like glittering glass.

Marty's voice floated to her from the next planet. "We'll face it together and come out the other side. Free. With our lives ahead of us. We'll have kids and a home. We'll teach them love and peace. Please, Miriam. It's the only way."

When she'd gathered the scattered pieces of her mind, she looked around at the sun glinting off the blue waves, gulped in the salty air, and felt the warmth of the sun soaking into her skin. She studied Marty with his thick hair she loved to run her fingers through, those brown eyes so full of passion. She began snipping every thread that held them together. "You were the love of my life. I believed in you. But now I know I can only trust myself."

Now the tears ran into his beard. "We're soul mates. I love you."

She placed her palm along his cheek in a gentle way to soften her words. "No. If you truly loved me, you'd know I can never go to jail. Never."

She left him at the seawall. He wouldn't follow her. He'd give her that much. Maybe she'd learn to forgive him. Someday. He had always been a little weaker than she was, always a bit more hesitant. But oh, how she loved him.

Miriam tossed the strap of her bag over her head so it tapped against her hip as she made her way down the sandy beach. She needed to get out of LA now. She needed money and a place to hide where the fuzz wouldn't find her, a secret location where no one knew her and even if Alan came to claim the revenge he'd sworn, she'd be safe.

Around a large rock outcropping, she spotted the sad soldier from earlier. He stared at the water, looking lost.

With a serene smile, Marguerite strode to him. She pulled the strap of her bag over her head and reached up to untie her halter top.

His eyes widened in surprise, but he quickly focused on her face, clearly trying to read her intent. Such kindness and strength. His smile grew, and Marguerite felt sure she'd found safe harbor.

She tugged on his arm. "Don't just stand there. Let's go for a swim."

28

Dad blasted from the pickup, leaving the door open and the engine rumbling with an erratic staccato. His graying hair stuck straight from his head as if he'd been pulling it for the last eight hours. His face bloodless and eyes so fiery they glowed; he ran straight for Mom.

Diane yelled something, but I was already on the move to intercept him.

But Marty appeared out of nowhere, as if he'd teleported to Mom's side. He didn't stop next to her but continued racing toward Dad.

It was like two rams on a mountainside determined to claim their mate.

With her wild curls flying, Mom shot after Marty. "Stop! Please. No!"

Marty held his arms straight in front of him, ready to shove Dad back. He had the height and weight advantage over my five-foot-eight rangy father. But Dad was more Tasmanian devil than dedicated pacifist. He ducked Marty's barrier and came up between Marty's forearms. A lightning-quick fist shot out with a punch to Marty's nose. Blood gushed immediately.

With what looked like supernatural speed and strength, Dad grasped Marty's upper arms and wrenched him like a cowboy bulldogging a steer.

The move threw Marty off-balance, and he lost his footing, toppling to his side and hitting the grass with a loud *umph*. Blood from his nose splattered the grass and his shirt.

Mom screamed, and maybe Diane did, too. It's possible I contributed to the chorus. With a few more steps, I inserted myself between Dad and Mom, hoping Dad wouldn't do me as he'd done Marty.

Mom sounded close to hysterical, shrieking as I'd never heard from her. "Hank. Stop it. I need Marty. I have to go."

Dad halted in front of me, lungs heaving, his arms dangling at his sides. His eyes hadn't lost that deranged gleam. It was the scariest thing I'd ever seen.

Even his voice, raw with rage, sounded as if it came from a different man than my loving father. He lasered Mom with his terrifying eyes. "You're not leaving. Not with him."

Marty sat up and struggled to get to his feet.

Diane stood over him and shoved him to the grass. Once a Fox, always a Fox, ready to jump into the fray. "Sit your ass down."

Marty focused on Mom and pushed himself to sit, leaning back and propping himself on his arms. He was a man in his mid-seventies, and he didn't look like he worked out much. His spirit seemed willing to fight for Mom, but his flesh looked played out. Blood surged from his nose, and some ran into his mouth. He spit, leaving a bright red stain on the grass.

Knowing I'd never be able to make this okay, I gave it a try anyway. I placed a hand on Dad's chest. "Come on, Dad. I've got this. I'm not going to let Mom leave."

Marty started to protest, and Diane planted one of those expensive leather flats on the inside of his elbow and pushed. Marty collapsed backward.

Mom bounced a pleading look between me and Dad. "I can't stay here."

In a voice bloody with torment, Dad said, "Don't leave me like this. I can't live without you."

It felt as if a thick fog fell on the world around us. Mom sounded heartbroken, and it was possible she thought she was. "Oh, Hank. I love you. For the years you've sheltered me. For our family. You've been my safe harbor, and I wouldn't have survived without you." She sounded like the woman I'd known.

Dad's breath hitched. He heard the "but" coming as surely as I did.

"But our time has ended. Our circle is complete. I didn't intend for this to happen. Alan found me in the most obscure way imaginable, and I can only assume the universe orchestrated this."

It looked as though Dad's whole world narrowed to the woman before him. He didn't seem to notice me standing between them, or hear Marty grumbling and Diane answering him, the pickup barking at the curb, or even if he breathed. Mom consumed him. "Marguerite..." His eyes filled with such pain it seemed to swallow him. Without him moving, I felt his heart reach for her.

Mom's face arranged itself like a satin sheet smoothing over a bed. She had that low, one-with-the-earth tone to her voice. "Not Marguerite. Miriam. I've come back to who I really am. I love you, Hank, you know that. But Marty is my soul mate."

I wanted to scream at her to stop lying. There was nothing in this woman that was real. My life's foundation collapsed with an actual roar in my ears. Jagged edges sliced into me. This wasn't happening. It couldn't be.

In my periphery, Marty rolled to his hands and knees and shoved from the ground, barreling into Diane and sending her flying. She shouted, "Bastard!"

Marty was on the run toward Dad, low and powerful.

Even this didn't break Dad's focus on Mom. He had turned the gray of a dead man and didn't seem to have any bones underneath his sagging flesh.

"Dad! Watch out!" I tried to jump in front of Marty but wasn't quick enough.

He hit Dad in the kidneys, driving them both several feet and crashing to the ground.

A tether broke loose in Dad, and he let out a terrifying war cry. My blood curdled, and I lost a few breaths. It was the sound of a jungle beast fighting for his life.

In a fury of moves and twists, Dad managed to throw Marty onto his back and straddle him. Marty tried to defend himself, but Dad's fists flew fast, pummeling Marty's face, making pulp of more than Marty's nose before I could react. I tried to grab onto Dad's wrist to keep him from smashing Marty's face again, but he wrenched free without much effort to land another blow into Marty's eye.

Dad let loose crazed bellows, no words but a depth of horrible rage.

Mom screamed, but I didn't make out any words.

Diane appeared and struggled to grab Dad's other wrist. Between the two of us, we finally overcame him and dragged him off Marty.

Mom threw herself beside Marty on the grass, sobbing and wiping away the blood streaming from his face.

Diane and I fought Dad while he struggled to his feet, and together we pushed him toward the front door. We each had one arm, and even then, it was a battle for every retreating step.

He stayed focused on Mom and Marty, that primal roar erupting from him and sending chills over my skin. Between the grunts and shouts, he managed to shout, "Marguerite! Stay. He won't protect you."

While he pleaded and yelled, Diane and I struggled with a series of yanks, pushes, pulls, and shoves, which made for slow progress up the stairs. We eventually stuffed him through the front door.

"Go," I huffed at Diane. "Get an ambulance. I'll take care of Dad."

Diane spun away and slammed the front door behind her. With both hands on Dad's chest, I tried to keep him from advancing.

Again, he let out a sound like an injured grizzly. In a sudden move, he quit fighting against me, stepped back, and drew his arm above his shoulder. If someone had asked me, I'd have said his next move would have been impossible for my father. But that man wasn't here with me.

He pulled back and swung his bloody fist. It struck me on my chin, snapping my head back with a force that vibrated down my spine.

Shock and electric pain all at once and I fell away, slamming my back against the door and crumpling. I'd taken blows before. With eight brothers and sisters, sometimes roughhousing got out of hand. I'd been kicked by calves and rammed by cows, thrown from horses, and once, Sarah had accidently run over my foot with her pickup.

But the agony of being clocked by the man I respected and trusted most in the world shredded me. I tried to sweep together the bits of me that had shattered because I had to stop Dad from leaving. In this state, he'd kill

Marty and maybe Mom. He might believe his life was over without her, but I wasn't willing to buy it.

Using the shaking muscles in my thighs, I pushed myself to stand and face Dad.

Both of his hands were curled into fists, his eyes still flaming. A snarl lifted his lips, and his chest rose and fell. The image of a bull again. This time, aimed at me.

I held up my hands in surrender. "Dad."

He kept heaving, nostrils flaring in and out. But recognition sparked deep inside his eyes.

My voice broke. "Dad." I'd lost the words to say how much I loved him and needed him. I'd lost so much, Glenda, Baxter, Diane, Mom. I couldn't lose him, too. He was the only person anchoring me. "Please."

He stared at me with rage-filled eyes and then blinked. His jaw loosened, and his eyes flew open as awareness hit him. The horror that rushed into his already pale face and the sudden spark of tears ripped my heart in two. He dropped his hands. "Katie. Oh my God. What have I done?"

29

I'd never seen Dad cry, and his sobs were like a thousand hornets stinging me. He sobbed out the words, "I'm so sorry, Katie."

I had my arms around him and squeezed tight. "I know. It's okay." I mumbled a bunch of other stuff that made no sense and I was sure he didn't hear.

The front door swung open, and Diane stepped through it. Despite high-quality makeup that no doubt promised to hold up to any emotion, a rivulet of mascara tears striped her face. She sagged, even her perfect hair drooped.

I released Dad. Alarm bells clanging. "Is the ambulance here? Do they have Marty and Mom?"

Diane sounded surprisingly firm. "They're gone. We have to let them go or they'll destroy the family."

I ran to the door and wrenched it open. The driveway was empty. Dad's pickup was silent, had maybe run out of gas or finally given up the ghost.

I might have shouted. "She's a fugitive."

Dad's tears had subsided, and he looked numb. The sorrow hung on his shoulders, sucked the blood from his face, stole the life from his eyes.

Diane lasered on me in that way she did whenever she wanted to change my mind. "Is she? I mean, is someone actually looking for her?"

I'd need to explain to Diane and Dad about Lyle Joffe and Thomas Scanlon. But right now, I had to do the right thing. Grabbing my phone from my back pocket, I stomped down the stairs to the front yard. The sun made a feeble effort with the clouds but remained weak, giving so little warmth it might not have bothered rising.

Ryan Standage answered right away. I explained the situation and Marguerite Myers's real identity. "They're going to try to make it to Canada. They haven't been gone long."

It took a second or two for Ryan to respond. Admittedly, there was a lot to unpack. "We won't have probable cause to suspect your mother until we get her prints and run them against the database."

I rubbed my forehead to ease the pressure.

"In the meantime, I can issue an alert, but I'm not optimistic. They have a jump on us and connections. Sounds like they've planned it out. Might already have disappeared. There's a network of activists and draft dodgers, even today. And there's a hell of a lot of miles of border between us and Canada. Maybe we could find them, but it'd be a long shot."

Ryan would get the wheels turning, but there probably wasn't much to be done now. I figured I'd be well advised to sign up for video counseling to deal with this whole situation. All I wanted to do was lie down and pull a blanket over me and sleep until this all made sense. Maybe a hundred years. But I wasn't finished yet.

When I returned to the house, Diane had Dad seated on the sagging couch. Clumps of dirt and dried grass stuck to her black pants, and her skinned elbow showed through a hole in her sweater. Smudges of mascara accented her eyes that showed the same devastation I felt. She stood next to Dad, probably trying to soothe him.

He jumped up when I closed the front door, and I turned to him. "Oh, God, Katie. Look what I did to you." I'd never seen such remorse etched in the lines on his face, lines I'd have sworn weren't there the last time I'd seen him in Hodgekiss.

I dabbed at my chin, heat rising from the welt. I'd probably have a bruise to brag about, not that any of this felt good. "It'll heal. How are you?"

He fell back on the couch and folded in on himself. "I swore I'd never let my temper get loose again. But I couldn't stop it." The fire had vanished from his eyes, leaving them red-rimmed and haunted. "I'm so sorry."

Diane rested a hand on his bent shoulders. Her touch more comfort than words.

His brokenness ripped the heart from my chest. "This is awful. I don't blame you for any of it."

His Dickies were smeared with blood and dirt, the T-shirt stretched and stained, the sleeve nearly ripped clear of his flannel shirt. He slumped as if his bones had dissolved. He didn't seem to have enough energy to lift his head, but his eyes sought mine. "You blame her?"

Diane fired up, her head snapping toward Dad. "Damn right we blame her. She left us. She lied for all of these years."

Dad squeezed his eyes closed in a sign of unbearable pain. His words wheezed between his lips. "Not now." He buried his face in his hands, his fingers working on his temples as if trying to dig out poison.

Diane and I stood like guards keeping watch over Dad for several minutes. I searched Diane's face, trying to compel her to look at me. To make contact and throw me a lifeline. I was swirling in a whirlpool of loss and felt like I might drown.

When I couldn't take it any longer, I spun around and hurried into the bedroom closest to the living room.

There it stood. The testament to Mom's lies and betrayal. She'd laid it out plainly for everyone. I couldn't see Dad from where I stood, and he wouldn't have seen this monstrosity. He knew Marty Kaufman's blood flowed in Glenda. I'd never noticed it made any difference to him. He acted as if he loved her with the deep devotion he'd showed all of us. Did Dad know about Jeremy? How much did he need to know?

Diane's silent footsteps carried her into the bedroom.

She shouldn't leave him alone. I whipped my head back to check on him. He hadn't moved.

Diane leaned close and lowered her voice. "He needs to be alone. We'll see him if he tries to leave."

She was right. He seemed too defeated to do more than breathe in and out.

"Tell me why you wanted to arrest her," Diane said.

No reason to keep Mom's secrets. "Before she met Dad, she was a Vietnam war protester."

Diane's voice sounded flat. "And yet she married a vet. A protester and soldier turned pacifists. That's irony."

Ironic, maybe. All I felt was sad. "She and Marty Kaufman, along with two other men, planted a bomb in an office building. When they discovered Thomas Scanlon, an attorney working late, was in the building, one of the bombers went in to get him out."

Diane stared at me, clearly dreading what I would say next.

"The bomb went off, killing both men. The bomber who was killed was Alan Joffe's brother. Alan Joffe is the guy who came after Mom."

Diane hadn't put it all together. "Why would he want to hurt her?"

"My guess is because he blamed Mom for killing his brother."

"But Marty—" She stopped when she came to the same conclusion I did. That Alan knew Mom had detonated the bomb despite knowing there were people inside. After a moment, she said, "Are you going to tell Dad?"

"Nope."

Diane folded her arms and studied the sculpture. "She's an amazing artist, isn't she?"

"Yep." Though this piece would never be my favorite.

"I'm not sorry I let them go," she said quietly.

"I don't suppose you are." Maybe later I'd feel resentment that she'd gone against me in this. But all my hurt was wrapped up someplace else.

There was slight pressure in her quiet voice, as if she pushed her words out. "She's already done so much damage. If we're going to salvage this family, we can't do it with her around."

Steel bands tightened around my chest so I could barely breathe. Diane didn't want to be my sister. Dad was broken so thoroughly he might never recover. Glenda had been gone for years. We were scattering, and maybe that was how it ought to be. "Maybe the whole idea of our family was an illusion. Why try so hard to keep it up?"

She stuck her hand out toward the sculpture. "Do you think this makes any difference to Dad? To me?" She stabbed me with her gaze. "It goddamned shouldn't to you."

I stared at the image, trying to keep the loneliness and loss from bubbling up my throat. Three birds rising from what clearly represented a womb. A smaller version of the installation at the University sculpture garden. Three birds, not nine. Glenda and Jeremy.

I let each word scrape my throat raw. "He served seven years in prison. He was released in 1980. I was born in 1981." Twyla and Susan had listed Mom's favorites. Glenda, Jeremy. And me.

Diane considered the sculpture for a few more seconds, then she lunged toward it, raised it with both hands, and smashed it against the doorframe, cascading shards of clay across the dingy shag carpet. She lifted her leg and brought her foot down on a nearly intact wing, crushing it.

I leaned into the doorway to check on Dad. He had flopped against the couch, his face slack with a sickly yellow pallor. His scruff of whiskers seemed white, making him look ancient. He stared at the ceiling, giving no indication he was aware of the world around him.

I kept my voice even. "Sorry. Just dropped something." It was enough to keep him from coming in.

Diane shrugged at me and gave me a lopsided grin. "Another thing he doesn't need to know about."

Nothing in me could share her smile. I was hollow without my identity as a Fox.

Diane dropped her head back and sighed at the ceiling before giving me that exasperated big-sister tone. "We're sisters. Always and forever. That means I love you even when I hate you. And it means I can hate you because I know you'll always be there when I'm done hating you."

I worked my throat, but words wouldn't come.

"Okay, yeah. Maybe I didn't think that before. But I don't want to end up like Miriam and Debbie Fine. Old ladies who've lost the best gift life has to offer. Mom and Glenda are gone. But there's you and me and Louise and Susan. And even Robert, Michael, Douglas, and Jeremy. And that's a whole lot of love and hate right there."

She wavered in front of me, tears clouding my vision. Still, I couldn't move or speak.

"And Dad. It's going to take the mighty power of the Fox clan to pull him back from this."

I nodded, the well inside me filling with a slow trickle.

She took one step toward me. "Yesterday I hated you. Today I love you. And I know you'll forgive me because out of all of us, you're the one who never forgets: Family is the most important thing."

DOUBLE BACK
Kate Fox #7

Is she a harmless old woman searching for love... or a murderer waiting to strike?

Determined to enjoy some peace and quiet in her tranquil home in the Sandhills, no-nonsense sheriff Kate Fox vows to keep herself out of trouble and steer clear of love. But try as she might, fate has a funny way of dragging her back into the fray.

After a mysterious woman from the town's past appears out of the blue – and then moves in with a pair of aging bachelor brothers – Kate fears the woman is up to no good. With the town buzzing over rumors of a hidden fortune, Kate jumps into a puzzling investigation to unearth the woman's secretive past and save the brothers from heartbreak.

But as she digs deeper, she begins to piece together a disturbing story that she never could have anticipated.

With innocent lives on the line, Kate must act fast to prevent disaster... and uncover the shocking truth behind a woman who isn't what she seems to be.

ACKNOWLEDGMENTS

First, I want to say a huge thank you to Kate's readers. It's such a blast for me to discover what Kate is up to and to write about her adventures and I'd never be able to keep doing that if you weren't along for the ride. You've allowed me to keep living the dream.

Much like Kate Fox, I hadn't been to Chicago before. So, I am especially grateful to Mason Rothwell and Chrissy Seiders for having a wedding and inviting us along. The event was beautiful, the jaunt around Chicago was enlightening and fun, and I'm so happy for Mason and Chrissy. Congratulations!

On the Chicago front I also thank Lori Rader-Day for providing details. As long as we're on the subject of Lori, I need to thank the rest of the crew: Jess Lourey, Susanna Calkins, and Erica Ruth Neubauer for laughs, commiseration, and support. You make this crazy ride fun.

To Janet Fogg: there aren't enough or the right kind of words to say thank you. Not only have you been the fulcrum of every single book, you've listened, inspired, shored-up, and walked with me through real life, which is definitely the twistier and more harrowing journey.

Jessica Morrell is an editor extraordinaire. Your keen eye and exacting soul have made my books better in every way.

More thanks go to Shawn Hebbert. Not only for answering my endless questions about how sheriffing works in the Nebraska Sandhills, but for all the fun anecdotes and for always returning my calls. You're the best kind of friend for a crime fiction writer.

Severn River Publishing is a writer's dream. Smart, savvy, compassionate, and fun. Thank you for believing in me and Kate Fox and making it all happen. A big shout out to Amber, who makes it all seem easy. Thanks to

Cate for attending to the tedious details. To Mo, who warms my heart even as she cracks the whip. Thanks to Holly for the artistic touch. To Keris, the numbers guy, and to Andrew, who got the wheels turning.

A special thank you to Megan Tusing, who narrates Kate's audio side with a giant talent and understanding.

Thank you to Jill Marsal for guidance, expertise, and a scary ability to return emails faster than a speeding bullet.

As always, to my daughters because you are so awesome.

Mostly, thank you to Dave because your crazy matches so well with mine.

ABOUT THE AUTHOR

Shannon Baker is the award-winning author of *The Desert Behind Me* and the Kate Fox series, along with the Nora Abbott mysteries and the Michaela Sanchez Southwest Crime Thrillers. She is the proud recipient of the Rocky Mountain Fiction Writers 2014 and 2017-18 Writer of the Year Award.

Baker spent 20 years in the Nebraska Sandhills, where cattle outnumber people by more than 50:1. She now lives on the edge of the desert in Tucson with her crazy Weimaraner and her favorite human. A lover of the great outdoors, she can be found backpacking, traipsing to the bottom of the Grand Canyon, skiing mountains and plains, kayaking lakes, river running, hiking, cycling, and scuba diving whenever she gets a chance. Arizona sunsets notwithstanding, Baker is, and always will be a Nebraska Husker. Go Big Red.

Sign up for Shannon Baker's reader list at
severnriverbooks.com

Printed in the United States
by Baker & Taylor Publisher Services